The Modern Novel Series

THE SHRIMP AND THE ANEMONE

THE MODERN NOVEL SERIES

L. P. HARTLEY

The Shrimp and the Anemone

COMMENTARY AND NOTES BY
PATRICIA D'ARCY, M.A.

HEINEMANN EDUCATIONAL BOOKS
LONDON

Heinemann Educational Books Ltd

LONDON EDINBURGH MELBOURNE AUCKLAND TORONTO
HONG KONG SINGAPORE KUALA LUMPUR NEW DELHI
NAIROBI JOHANNESBURG LUSAKA IBADAN
KINGSTON

ISBN 0 435 17386 3

Commentary and Notes © The Bodley Head Ltd 1967
First published 1944 by Putnam & Company Ltd
This edition first published by The Bodley Head Ltd 1967
First published in the Modern Novel Series 1973
Reprinted 1976

Published by
Heinemann Educational Books Ltd
48 Charles Street, London W1X 8AH
Printed in Great Britain by
Morrison & Gibb Ltd, London and Edinburgh

CHAPTER I

The Shrimp and the Anemone

'Eustace! Eustace!' Hilda's tones were always urgent; it might not be anything very serious. Eustace bent over the pool. His feet sank in its soggy edge, so he drew back, for he must not get them wet. But he could still see the anemone. Its base was fastened to a boulder, just above the water-line. From the middle of the other end, which was below, something stuck out, quivering. It was a shrimp, Eustace decided, and the anemone was eating it, sucking it in. A tumult arose in Eustace's breast. His heart bled for the shrimp, he longed to rescue it; but, on the other hand, how could he bear to rob the anemone of its dinner? The anemone was more beautiful than the shrimp, more interesting and much rarer. It was a 'plumose' anemone; he recognised it from the picture in his Natural History, and the lovely feathery epithet stroked the fringes of his mind like a caress. If he took the shrimp away, the anemone might never catch another, and die of hunger. But while he debated the unswallowed part of the shrimp grew perceptibly smaller.

Once more, mingled with the cries of the seamews and pitched even higher than theirs, came Hilda's voice.

'Eustace! Eustace! Come here! The bank's breaking! It's your fault! You never mended your side!'

Here was another complication. Ought he not perhaps to go to Hilda and help her build up the bank? It was true he had scamped his side, partly because he was piqued with her for always taking more than her fair share. But then she was a girl and older than he and she did it for his good, as she had often told him, and in order that he might not overstrain himself. He leaned on his wooden spade and, looking doubtfully round, saw Hilda signalling with her iron one. An ancient jealousy invaded his heart. Why should *she* have an iron spade? He tried to fix his mind on the anemone. The shrimp's tail was still visible but wriggling more feebly. Horror at its plight began to swamp all other considerations. He made up his mind to release it. But how? If he waded into the water he would get his socks wet, which would be bad enough; if he climbed on to the rock he might fall in and get wet all over, which would be worse. There was only one thing to do.

'Hilda,' he cried, 'come here.'

His low soft voice was whirled away by the wind; it could not compete with the elements, as Hilda's could.

He called again. It was an effort for him to call: he screwed his face up: the cry was unmelodious now that he forced it, more like a squeak than a summons.

But directly she heard him Hilda came, as he knew she would. Eustace put the situation before her, weighing the pros and cons. Which was to be sacrificed, the anemone or the shrimp? Eustace stated the case for each with unflinching impartiality and began to enlarge on the felicity that would attend their after-lives, once this situation was straightened out—forgetting, in his enthusiasm, that the well-being of the one depended on the misfortune of the other. But Hilda cut him short.

'Here, catch hold of my feet,' she said.

She climbed on to the boulder, and flung herself face down on the sea-weedy slope. Eustace followed more slowly, showing respect for the inequalities of the rock. Then he lowered himself, sprawling uncertainly and rather timidly, and grasped his sister's thin ankles with hands that in spite of his nine years still retained some of the chubbiness of infancy. Once assumed, the position was not uncomfortable. Eustace's thoughts wandered, while his body automatically accommodated itself to the movements of Hilda, who was wriggling ever nearer to the edge.

'I've got it,' said Hilda at last in a stifled voice. There was no elation, only satisfaction in her tone, and Eustace knew that something had gone wrong.

'Let me look!' he cried, and they struggled up from the rock.

6

The shrimp lay in the palm of Hilda's hand, a sad, disappointing sight. Its reprieve had come too late; its head was mangled and there was no vibration in its tail. The horrible appearance fascinated Eustace for a moment, then upset him so much that he turned away with trembling lips. But there was worse to come. As a result of Hilda's forcible interference with its meal the anemone had been partially disembowelled; it could not give up its prey without letting its digestive apparatus go too. Part of its base had come unstuck and was seeking feebly to attach itself to the rock again. Eustace took Hilda's other hand and together they surveyed the unfortunate issue of their kind offices.

'Hadn't we better kill them both?' asked Eustace with a quaver in his voice, 'since they're both wounded?'

He spoke euphemistically, for the shrimp was already dead.

But Hilda did not despair so easily.

'Let's put it in the water,' she suggested. 'Perhaps that'll make it come to.'

A passing ripple lent the shrimp a delusive appearance of life; when the ripple subsided it floated to the surface, sideways up, and lay still.

'Never mind,' said Hilda, 'we'll see if the anemone will eat it now.'

Again they disposed themselves on the rock, and Hilda, with her head downwards and her face growing redder every minute, tried her hardest to induce the anemone to resume its meal. For the sake of achieving this end she did not shrink from the distasteful task of replacing the anemone's insides where they belonged, but her amateur surgery failed to restore its appetite and it took no interest in the proffered shrimp.

'I wish we'd let them alone,' sobbed Eustace.

'What would have been the good of that?' demanded Hilda, wiping her brother's eyes. He stood quiescent, his hands hanging down and his face turned upwards, showing no shame at being comforted and offering no resistance, as though he was familiar with the performance and expected it. 'We had to do something,' Hilda continued. 'We couldn't let them go on like that.'

'Why couldn't we?' asked Eustace. All at once, as the thought struck him, he ceased crying. It seemed to cost him as little effort to stop as it costs a dog to wake out of sleep. 'They didn't mean to hurt each other.'

The disaster that had overtaken their remedial measures was so present to him that he forgot the almost equally painful situation those measures had been meant to relieve, and thought of the previous relationship of the shrimp and the anemone as satisfactory to both.

'But they *were* hurting each other,' remarked Hilda. 'Anyhow the anemone was eating the shrimp, if you call that hurting.'

Eustace could see no way out of this. His mind had no power to consider an unmixed evil, it was set upon happiness. With Hilda's ruthless recognition of an evil principle at the back of the anemone affair his tears started afresh.

'Now don't be a cry-baby,' Hilda not at all unkindly admonished him. 'There's Gerald and Nancy Steptoe coming, nasty things! If you stand still a minute,' she went on, preparing with the hem of her blue frock to renew the assault upon his face, 'they'll think it's only the wind.'

The appeal to Eustace's pride was one Hilda tried only for form's sake; she thought it ought to weigh with him, but generally, as she knew, it made him irritable.

'I want to go and talk to Nancy,' he announced. His attitude to other children was tinged with a fearful joy, altogether unlike his sister's intolerant and hostile demeanour. 'Gerald's left her by herself again: he's climbing up the cliffs, look, and she daren't go.'

'What do you want to talk to her for?' asked Hilda, a trifle crossly. 'It's her fault, she shouldn't have let him.'

'She can't stop him,' said Eustace. His voice had a triumphant ring, due partly to his knowledge of the Steptoes' private concerns and partly, as Hilda realised, to a feeling of elation at the spectacle of Gerald's independence. This spirit of rebellion she resolved to quench.

8

'Come along,' she said authoritatively, snatching his hand and whirling him away. 'You know,' she continued, with an exaggeration of her grown-up manner, 'you don't really want to talk to Nancy. She's stuck-up, like they all are. Now we'll see what's happened to the pond. Perhaps we shall be in time to save it.'

They scampered across the sands, Eustace hanging back a little and trying to wave to the lonely Nancy, who, deserted by her daring and lawless brother, had begun to dig herself a castle. Now that they seemed to be out of harm's way Hilda stopped and looked back. They could just see the ground plan of Nancy's fortress, which she had marked out on the sand with a spade and which was of an extravagant extent.

'She'll never get that done,' Hilda remarked. 'They're always the same. They try to make everything bigger than anybody else, and then they leave it half done and look silly.'

'Should we go and help her?' suggested Eustace. Nancy looked very forlorn, labouring away at the outer moat of her castle.

'No,' Hilda replied. 'She can do it quite well herself, or she could if Gerald would have come away from those cliffs where he's no business to be and may very likely cause an avalanche.'

'I want to go,' cried Eustace, suddenly obstinate.

'I say you can't,' said Hilda half teasingly.

'I will, I want to!' Eustace almost screamed, struggling to get free. Bent like a bow with the effort, his feet slipping from under him, his hat off, and his straight fair hair unpicturesquely rumpled, he looked very childish and angry. Hilda kept him prisoner without much difficulty.

Some three and a half years older than Eustace, she was a good deal taller and the passion and tenacity of her character had already left its mark on her heart-shaped, beautiful face. Her immobility made a folly of Eustace's struggles; her dark eyes looked scornfully down.

'Diddums-wazzums,' she at last permitted herself to remark. The phrase, as she knew it would, drove her brother into a frenzy. The blood left his face; he stiffened and stopped struggling, while he searched his mind for the most wounding thing to say.

'I want to play with Nancy,' he said at last, averting his eyes from his sister and looking small and spiteful. 'I don't want to play with you. I don't ever want to play with you again. I don't love you. You killed the shrimp and you killed the anemone' (he brought this out with a rush; it had occurred to him earlier to taunt Hilda with her failure, but a generous scruple had restrained him), 'and you're a murderer.'

Hilda listened to the beginning of the speech with equanimity; her features continued to reflect disdain. Then she saw that Nancy Steptoe had stopped digging and could both see and hear what was passing. This unnerved her; and the violence and venom of Eustace's attack touched her to the quick. The words were awful to her. An overwhelming conviction came to her that he did not love her, and that she was a murderer. She turned away, with great ugly sobs that sounded like whooping-cough.

'Then *go*,' she said.

Eustace did not go at once. Hilda always stooped when she was in trouble; he watched the bent figure making its way back to the scene of their pond-making. She lurched, walking uncertainly with long uneven strides, and she did not seem to notice where she was putting her feet, for twice she stumbled over a projecting stone. The outburst over, Eustace's anger had melted away; he wanted to follow Hilda and make it up. In such matters he had no pride; apology came easily to him, and he regretted intensely everything that he had said. But he didn't go. Hilda wouldn't have forgiven him; he would have to undergo her silence and her disapproval and the spectacle of her suffering which she would try to control but would not try to hide. He could not bear being disapproved of, and though he had a weakness for comforting people it withered away in the presence of Hilda's implacable and formidable grief. He had lost his wish to play with Nancy; the desire to have his own way rarely survived the struggle it cost him to get it. But he obscurely felt that he was committed to a line of action and must go through with it.

Trailing his spade he walked awkwardly across the sands to Nancy, and, arriving at a respectful distance, put up his disengaged hand to take off his hat. This polite gesture missed completion, however, for the hat was still lying where it had fallen in the course of his altercation with Hilda. A look of surprise crossed his face and, with hand still upraised, he gazed aloft, as though he expected to see the hat suspended above his head.

Nancy laughed. 'Good morning, Eustace,' she said.

Eustace advanced and shook hands formally with her. Dainty, his nurse, Miss Minney, had called her, and the word suited her well. Eustace often wanted smoothing down, but never more than at this moment. His blue jersey had worked up and was hanging about him in ungainly folds, one sock was on the point of coming down, his face was flushed and tearful and his whole appearance presented a sharp contrast to Nancy's. He was the more aware of this because Nancy, her pink-and-white complexion, her neatness and coolness and the superior way she wore her clothes, had often been held up as a model to himself and his sister.

'Good-morning, Nancy,' he said. His voice, in addressing strangers, had a peculiar and flattering intimacy; he seemed to find a secret pleasure in pronouncing the name of the person to whom he was speaking, as though it was a privilege to utter it. 'Would you like me to help you with your castle? I'll go on digging and you can just pat it down,' he added heroically.

Nancy accepted this chivalrous offer, thanking him briefly. One reason why Eustace liked her was that she never made a fuss. If she was crossed or disappointed she took it silently, like a grown-up person; she did not turn herself inside out and call up all the resources of her personality. And if pleased she still kept a kind of reserve, as though the present moment's gratification was slight compared to those she had had and would have. Four years older than Eustace, she already possessed an experience, additions to which were classified and examined instead of treated on their own merits as isolated prodigies and visitations of Heaven. She was not at all informal or domestic: she had standards.

'What made Hilda so batey just now?' she presently inquired.

'Batey' was a word from the outside world, the world of day-schools and organised games with which Nancy was familiar. Batey: Eustace's father, who disliked slang, had protested against it, and his aunt had forbidden him to use it. Whatever Hilda might be she was not that.

'She wasn't batey,' he said slowly.

'Well, what was she then?' demanded Nancy. 'I saw her pulling you about, and she went away kicking up no end of a din.'

Eustace pondered. If he should say that he had been unkind to Hilda, Nancy would laugh at him, in her polite, incredulous way. He was always acutely conscious of having to live up to her; that was one reason, among others, why he liked being with her. He wanted to make a good impression. But how could he do that without sacrificing his sister's dignity, which was dear to him and necessary to his sense of their relationship?

'She was very much upset,' he said at last.

Nancy nodded sagely, as though she understood what Eustace had left unexpressed and respected his reticence. Sunning himself in the warmth of her hardly won approval, and feeling he had done his best for Hilda, Eustace let his sister and her troubles slip out of his mind. He redoubled his exertions and soon, to the accompaniment of a little desultory conversation, a large mound, unmistakably castellated, began to rear itself in the midst of Nancy's plot.

Eustace took a pride in seeing it grow, but Nancy— beyond seconding his efforts with a few negligent taps— seemed content to resign the task to him. He is only an infant, she thought, in spite of his engaging manners.

CHAPTER II

Patching it Up

LEFT to himself, Eustace fell into a day-dream. He thought of his toys and tried to decide which of them he should give to his sister Barbara; he had been told he must part with some of them, and indeed it would not make much difference if they were hers by right, since she already treated them as such. When he went to take them from her she resisted with loud screams. Eustace realised that she wanted them but he did not think she ought to have them. She could not use them intelligently, and besides, they belonged to him. He might be too old to play with them but they brought back the past in a way that nothing else did. Certain moments in the past were like buried treasure to Eustace, living relics of a golden age which it was an ecstacy to contemplate. His toys put him in touch with these secret jewels of experience; they could not perform the miracle if they belonged to someone else. But on the single occasion when he had asserted his ownership and removed the rabbit from Barbara who was sucking its ears, nearly everyone had been against him and there was a terrible scene. Minney said he never took the slightest interest in the rabbit until Barbara wanted it, his aunt said he must try not to be mean in future, and Hilda urged that he should be sent to bed on the spot. 'It will be good for him in the end,' she said.

Eustace's resistance was violent and, since Hilda hardly obtained a hearing, really unnecessary; but in his heart he agreed with her. Expiation already played a part in his life; it reinstated him in happiness continually. Hilda was the organiser of expiation: she did not let him off: she kept him up to the scratch, she was extreme to mark what was done amiss. But as the agent of retribution she was impersonal: she only adjudicated between him and a third party. It was understood that from their private disputes there was no appeal to a disinterested tribunal; the bitterness had to be swallowed and digested by each side. If Hilda exposed her wounded feelings she did not declare that Heaven was outraged by the spectacle: she demanded no forfeit, no acknowledgment even. She did not constitute herself a law court but met Eustace on his own ground.

The thought of her, intruding upon his reverie, broke it up. There she sat, on the large rock in their pond which they had christened Gibraltar, her back bent, her legs spread out, her head drooping. It was an ugly attitude and she would grow like that, thought Eustace uncomfortably. Moreover, she was sitting recklessly on the wet seaweed which would leave a green mark and give her a cold, if salt water could give one a cold. Minney was superstitious, and any irrational belief that tended to make life easier was, Eustace instinctively felt, wrong. Still Hilda did not move. Her distress conveyed itself to him across the intervening sand. He glanced uneasily at Nancy who was constructing a garden out of seaweed and white pebbles at the gateway of the castle—an incongruous adjunct, Eustace thought, for it was precisely there that the foemen would attack. He had almost asked her to put it at the back, for the besieged to retire into in their unoccupied moments; where it was it spoilt his vision of the completed work and even sapped his energy. But he did not like the responsibility of interfering and making people do things his way. He worked on, trying to put Hilda out of his mind, but she recurred and at last he said:

'I think I'll go back now, if it's all the same to you.'

He hoped by this rather magnificent phrase to make his departure seem as casual as possible, but Nancy saw through him.

'Can't leave your big sister?' she inquired, an edge of irony in her voice. 'She'll get over it quicker if you let her alone.'

Eustace declined this challenge. It pained him to think that his disagreement with Hilda was public property.

'Oh, she's all right now,' he told Nancy airily. 'She's having a rest.'

'Well, give her my love,' said Nancy.

Eustace felt a sudden doubt, from her tone, whether she really meant him to deliver the message.

'Shall I?' he asked diffidently. 'I should like to.'

Something in the question annoyed Nancy. She turned from him with a whirl of her accordion-pleated skirt, a garment considered by Eustace miraculous and probably unprocurable in England.

'You can say I hate her, if you'd rather,' she remarked. She looked round: her blue eyes sparkled frostily in her milk-white face.

Eustace stood aghast. He didn't think it possible that strangers—people definitely outside the family circle— could ever be angry.

'I'll stay if you can't get on so well without me,' he said at length, feeling his way.

She laughed at him when he said this—at his concerned face and his earnestness, his anxiety to please. So it was nothing, really: he was right, you couldn't take much harm with strangers. If they seemed cross it was only in fun: they wouldn't dare to show their feelings or make you show yours: it was against the rules. They existed to be agreeable, to be a diversion . . . Nancy was saying:

'It's very kind of you to have stayed so long, Eustace. Look what a lot you've done!' A kind of comic wonder, mixed with mockery, crept into her voice: Eustace was fascinated. 'Gerald will never believe me when I tell him I built it all myself!'

'Will you tell him that?' Eustace was shocked by her audacity, but tried to keep his voice from showing disapproval.

'Well, I'll say you did all the work while I looked on.'

Gerald will think me a muff, decided Eustace. 'Couldn't you say we did it together?'

Nancy's face fell at the notion of this veracious account. Then it brightened. 'I know,' she said. 'I'll tell him a stranger came in a boat from the yacht over there, and *he* helped me. A naval officer. Yes, that's what I'll tell him,' she added teasingly, seeing Eustace still uneasy at the imminent falsehood. 'Good-bye, Mr Officer, you mustn't stay any longer.' With a gentle push to start him on his way she dismissed him.

It was too bad of Hilda to leave his hat lying in a pool. However cross she might be she rarely failed to retrieve his personal belongings over which, even when not flustered and put out, he had little control. Now the ribbon was wet and the 'table' of *Indomitable*, a ship which he obscurely felt he might be called upon at any moment to join, stood out more boldly than the rest. Never mind, it was salt-water, and in future the hat could be used for a barometer, like seaweed, to tell whether bad weather was coming. Meanwhile there was Hilda. It was no good putting off the evil moment: she must be faced.

But he did not go to her at once. He dallied among the knee-high rounded rocks for which the beach of Anchorstone (Anxton, the Steptoes called it in their fashionable way) was famous. He even built a small, almost vertical castle, resembling, as nearly as he could make it, the cone of Cotopaxi, for which he had a romantic affection, as he had for all volcanoes, earthquakes and violent manifestations of Nature. He calculated the range of the lava flow, marking it out with a spade and contentedly naming for destruction the various capital cities, represented by greater and lesser stones, that fell within its generous circumference. In his progress he conceived himself to be the Angel of Death, a delicious pretence, for it involved flying and the exercise of supernatural powers. On he flew. Could Lisbon be destroyed a second time? It would be a pity to waste the energy of the eruption on what was already a ruin; but no doubt they had rebuilt it by now. Over it went and, in addition, an enormous tidal wave swept up the Tagus, ravaging the interior. The inundation of Portugal stopped at Hilda's feet.

For some days afterwards Eustace was haunted at odd

times by the thought that he had accidentally included Hilda in the area of doom. He clearly hadn't got her all in but perhaps her foot or her spade (which, for the purpose of disaster, might be reckoned her) had somehow overhung the circle, or the place where the circle would have been if he had finished it. The rocks couldn't take any harm from the spell, if it really was one, and he hadn't meant to hurt her, but it was just this sort of misunderstanding that gave Fate the opportunity to take you at your word. But Eustace had no idea that he was laying up trouble for himself when, with arrested spade, he stopped in front of Hilda.

'It only just missed you,' he remarked cryptically.

Silence.

'You only just escaped; it was a narrow shave,' Eustace persisted, still hoping to interest his sister in her deliverance.

'What fool's trick is this?' demanded Hilda in a far-away voice.

Discouraging as her words were, Eustace took heart; she was putting on her tragedy airs, and the worst was probably over.

'It was an eruption,' he explained, 'and you were the city of Athens and you were going to be destroyed. But they sacrificed ten Vestal Virgins for you and so you were saved.'

'What a silly game!' commented Hilda, her pose on the rock relenting somewhat. 'Did you learn it from Nancy?'

'Oh no,' said Eustace, 'we hardly talked at all—except just at the end, to say good-bye.'

Hilda seemed relieved to hear this.

'I don't know why you go and play with people if you don't talk to them,' she said. 'You wouldn't if you weren't a goose.'

'Oh, and Nancy sent you her love,' said Eustace.

'She can keep it,' said Hilda, rising from the rock, some of which, as Eustace had feared, came away with her. 'You've been very cruel to me, Eustace,' she went on. 'I don't think you really love me.'

Hilda never made a statement of this kind until the

17

urgency of her wrath was past. Eustace also used it, but in the heat of his.

'I do love you,' he asserted.

'You don't love me.'

'I do.'

'You don't—and don't argue,' added Hilda crushingly. 'How can you say you love me when you leave me to play with Nancy?'

'I went on loving you all the time I was with Nancy,' declared Eustace, almost in tears.

'Prove it!' cried Hilda.

To be nailed down to a question he couldn't answer gave Eustace a feeling of suffocation. The elapsing seconds seemed to draw the very life out of him.

'There!' exclaimed Hilda triumphantly. 'You can't!'

For a moment it seemed to Eustace that Hilda was right: since he couldn't prove that he loved her, it was plain he didn't love her. He became very despondent. But Hilda's spirits rose with her victory, and his own, more readily acted upon by example than by logic, caught the infections of hers. Side by side they walked round the pond and examined the damage. It was an artificial pond—a lake almost—lying between rocks. The intervals between the rocks were dammed up with stout banks of sand. To fill the pond they had to use borrowed water, and for this purpose they dug channels to the natural pools left by the tide at the base of the sea-wall. A network of conduits criss-crossed over the beach, all bringing their quota to the pond which grew deeper and deeper and needed ceaselessly watching. It was a morning's work to get the pond going properly, and rarely a day passed without the retaining wall, in spite of their utmost vigilance, giving way in one place or other. If the disaster occurred in Eustaces's section, he came in for much recrimination, if in Hilda's, she blamed herself no less vigorously, while he, as a rule, put in excuses for her which were ruthlessly and furiously set aside.

But there was no doubt that it was Hilda who kept the spirit of pond-making alive. Her fiery nature informed the whole business and made it exciting and dangerous. When anything went wrong there was a row—no clasping of hands, no appealing to Fate, no making the best of a bad job. Desultory, amateurish pond-making was practised by many of the Anchorstone children: their puny, half-hearted, untidy attempts were, in Hilda's eyes, a disgrace to the beach. Often, so little did they understand the pond-making spirit, they would wantonly break down their own wall for the pleasure of watching the water go cascading out. And if a passer-by mischievously trod on the bank they saw their work go to ruin without a sigh. But woe betide the stranger who, by accident or design, tampered with Hilda's rampart! Large or small, she gave him a piece of her mind; and Eustace, standing some way behind, balanced uncertainly on the edge of the conflict, would echo some of his sister's less provocative phrases, by way of underlining. When *their* wall gave way it was the signal for an outburst of frenzied activity. On one never forgotten day Hilda had waded knee-deep in the water and ordered Eustace to follow. To him this voluntary immersion seemed cataclys-mic, the reversal of a lifetime's effort to keep dry. They were both punished for it when they got home.

The situation had been critical when Eustace, prospecting for further sources of supply, came upon the anemone on the rock; while he delayed, the pond burst, making a rent a yard wide and leaving a most imposing delta sketched with great ruinous curves in low relief upon the sand. The pond was empty and all the imprisoned water had made its way to the sea. Eustace secretly admired the out-rush of sand and was mentally transforming it into the Nile estuary at the moment when Hilda stuck her spade into it. Together they repaired the damage and with it the lesion in their affections; a glow of reconciliation pervaded them, increas-ing with each spadeful. Soon the bank was as strong as before. But you could not help seeing there had been a catastrophe, for the spick-and-span insertion proclaimed its freshness, like a patch in an old suit. And for all their assiduous dredging of the channels the new supplies came down from the pools above in the thinnest trickle, hardly covering the bottom and leaving bare a number of small stones which at high water were decently submerged. They had no function except by the order of their disappearance to measure the depth of the pond; now they stood out, emblems of failure, noticeable for the first time, like a handful of conventional remarks exchanged between old friends when the life has gone out of their relationship.

Presently Hilda, who possessed a watch, announced that it was dinner time. Collecting their spades and buckets they made their way across the sand and shingle to the concrete flight of steps which zigzagged majestically up the red sandstone cliffs for which Anchorstone was famous. Their ascent was slow because Eustace had formed a habit of counting the steps. Their number appealed to his sense of grandeur, and though they usually came to the same total, a hundred and nineteen, he tried to think he had made a mistake and that one day they would reach a hundred and twenty, an altogether more desirable figure. He had grounds for this hope because, at the foot of the stairs, six inches deep in sand, there undoubtedly existed another step. Eustace could feel it with his spade. A conscientious scruple forbade him to count it with the rest, but—who could tell? —some day a tidal wave might come and lay it bare. Hilda waited patiently while he reassured himself of its existence and—a rare concession—consented to check his figures during the climb. She even let him go back and count one of the stages a second time, and when they reached the top she forbore to comment on the fact that the ritual had had its usual outcome. Standing together by the 'Try-Your-Grip' machine they surveyed the sands below. There lay the pond, occupying an area of which anyone might be proud, but—horrors!—it was completely dry. It could not have overflowed of itself, for they had left it only a quarter full. The gaping hole in the retaining wall must be the work of an enemy. A small figure was walking away from the scene of demolition with an air of elaborate unconcern. 'That's Gerald Steptoe,' said Hilda. 'I should like to kill him!'

'He's a very naughty boy, he doesn't pay any attention to Nancy,' remarked Eustace, hoping to mollify his sister.

'She's as bad as he is! I should like to——' Hilda looked around her, at the sky above and the sea beneath.

'What would you do?' asked Eustace fearfully.

'I should tie them together and throw them off the cliff!' Eustace tried to conceal the pain he felt.

'Oh, but Nancy sent you her love!'

'She didn't mean it. Anyhow I don't want to be loved by her.'

'Who would you like to be loved by?' asked Eustace.

Hilda considered. 'I should like to be loved by somebody great and good.'

'Well, I love you,' said Eustace.

'Oh, that doesn't count. You're only a little boy. And Daddy doesn't count, because he's my father so he has to love me. And Minney doesn't count, because she . . . she hasn't anyone else to love!'

'Barbara loves you,' said Eustace, trying to defend Hilda from her own gloomy conclusions. 'Look how you make her go to sleep when nobody else can.'

'That shows how silly you are,' said Hilda. 'You don't love people because they send you to sleep. Besides, Barbara is dreadfully selfish. She's more selfish than you were at her age.'

'Can you remember that?' asked Eustace timidly.

'Of course I can, but Minney says so too.'

'Well, Aunt Sarah?' suggested Eustace doubtfully. 'She's so good she must love us all—and specially you, because you're like a second mother to us.'

Hilda gave one of her loud laughs.

'She won't love you if you're late for dinner,' she said, and started at a great pace up the chalky footpath. Eustace followed more slowly, still searching his mind for a lover who should fulfil his sister's requirements. But he could think of no one but God or Jesus, and he didn't like to mention their names except in church or at his prayers or during Scripture lessons. Baffled, he hurried after Hilda along the row of weather-beaten tamarisks, but he had small hope of catching up with her, and the start she had already gained would be enough to make her in time for dinner and him late. What was his surprise, then, when she stopped at the corner of Palmerston Parade (that majestic line of lodging-houses whose beetling height and stately pinnacles always moved Eustace to awe) and called him.

He came up panting. 'What is it, Hilda?'

'Sh!' said Hilda loudly, and pointed to the left, along the cliffs.

But Eustace knew what he was to see before his eyes, following the inexorable line of Hilda's arm, had taken in the group. Fortunately they had their backs to him. He could only see the long black skirt and bent head of Miss Fothergill's companion as she pushed the bath-chair. That was something to be thankful for, anyhow.

'It'll only take you a minute if you go now!' said Hilda.

Eustace began to wriggle.

'Oh please, Hilda, not now. Look, they're going the other way.'

But Hilda was not to be moved. 'Remember what Aunt Sarah said. She said, "Eustace, next time you see Miss Fothergill I want you to speak to her".'

'But next time was last time!' cried Eustace, clutching at any straw, 'and I didn't then so I needn't now. Anyhow I can't now or we shall be late for dinner!'

'Aunt Sarah won't mind when she knows why,' said Hilda, her determination stiffening under Eustace's contumacy. 'If she saw us (perhaps she can from the dining-room window) she'd say, "Go at once, Eustace".'

'I can't. I can't,' Eustace wailed, beginning to throw himself about. 'She frightens me, she's so ugly! If you make me go, I shall be sick at dinner!'

His voice rose to a scream, and at that moment, as luck would have it, the bath-chair turned round and began to bear down on them.

'Well, you certainly can't speak to her in that state,' said Hilda, 'I should be ashamed of you. I am ashamed of you anyhow. You're growing up a spoilt little boy. Come along, I wouldn't let you go now even if you wanted to.'

Eustace had won his point. He moved to the other side of Hilda, so as to put her between him and the slowly advancing bath-chair, and they walked without speaking across the green. Houses surrounded it on three sides; on the fourth it was open to the sea. They opened a low wooden gate marked 'Cambo', crossed a tiny square of garden and, with elaborate precautions against noise, deposited their spades and buckets in the porch. The smell of food, so strong that it must already have left the kitchen, smote them as they opened the door. 'I won't say anything about Miss Fothergill this time,' whispered Hilda.

CHAPTER III

The Geography Lesson

THE days passed quickly: August would soon be here. Hilda and Eustace were sitting one on each side of the dining-room table, their lessons in front of them. Hilda stared at her sketch map of England, Eustace stared at her; then they both glanced interrogatively and rather nervously at Aunt Sarah, enthroned between them at the head of the able.

'Rutland,' said Aunt Sarah impressively.

Eustace liked geography; he knew the answer to Rutland, and he was also aware that Hilda didn't know. When they played 'Counties of England' Rutland invariably stumped her. Eustace pondered. His map was already thickly studded with county towns while Hilda's presented a much barer appearance. She wouldn't mind if he beat her, for she always liked him to excel, indeed she insisted on it; she minded more if he failed over his lessons than if she did. Often when she reproved him for poor work he had protested 'Anyhow I did better than you!' and she, not at all abashed, would reply, 'That's got nothing to do with it. You know you can do better than that if you try.' The effort to qualify for his sister's approval was the ruling force in Eustace's interior life: he had to live up to her idea of him, to fulfil the ambitions she entertained on his behalf. And though he chafed against her domination it was necessary for him; whenever, after one of their quarrels, she temporarily withdrew her jealous supervision saying she didn't care now, he could get his feet wet and be as silly and lazy and naughty as he liked, she would never bother about him again, he felt as though the bottom had dropped out of his life, as though the magnetic north had suddenly repudiated the needle. Hilda believed that her dominion was founded upon grace: she shouldered her moral responsibilities towards Eustace without misgiving: she did not think it necessary to prove or demonstrate her ascendency by personal achievements outside the moral sphere. Nor did Eustace think so; but all the same his comfortable sense of her superiority was troubled whenever she betrayed, as she was certainly doing now, distinct signs of intellectual fallibility. It was painful to him, in cold blood, to expose her to humiliation even in his thoughts, so with a sigh he checked his pen in mid-career and refrained from writing Oakham.

'That's all,' said Aunt Sarah a few minutes later. 'Let's count up. And then I've got something to tell you.'

'Is it something nice?' asked Eustace.

'You always want to know that, Eustace,' said Aunt Sarah not unkindly. 'I notice that Hilda never does. It is a great mistake, as you will find in after life, always to be wondering whether things are going to be nice or nasty. Usually, you will find, they are neither.'

'Eustace is better now at doing things he doesn't like,' observed Hilda.

'Yes, I think he is. Now, how many towns have you got, Hilda?'

'Twenty-five.'

'That's not at all bad, especially as I sent you out shopping all yesterday morning. And you, Eustace?'

'Thirty-two—no, thirty-one.'

'That's not very many. I expected you to do better than that.'

'But I helped Hilda shopping,' objected Eustace. 'I carried the bread all the way home.'

'He wouldn't go into Lawsons' because he's afraid of the dog.'

'Isn't that rather silly of you, Eustace? If it doesn't hurt Hilda, why should it hurt you?'

'It doesn't like little boys,' said Eustace. 'It growled at Gerald Steptoe when he went in to buy his other pocket-knife.'

'Who wouldn't?' asked Hilda rudely.

'Hilda, I don't think that's very kind. And talking of the Steptoes—but first, what did you leave out, Eustace?'

With many pauses Eustace noted the names of the missing towns.

'And Oakham, too! But you know Oakham perfectly well: or had you forgotten it?'

'Of course he hadn't,' said Hilda with feeling. 'He always remembers it—just because it's not important.'

'No,' said Eustace slowly. 'I hadn't forgotten it.'

'Then why didn't you put it down?'

Eustace considered. He was painfully, scrupulously truthful.

'I didn't want to.'

'Didn't want to! Why, what a funny boy! Why didn't you want to?'

Again Eustace paused. An agony of deliberation furrowed his forehead.

'I thought it was best to leave it out,' he said.

'But, what nonsense! I don't know what's come over you. Well, you must write out twice over the names of the towns you missed, and Oakham five times. Hilda, you have been busy, so it will do if you mark them on your map in red ink. Then you can go and play. But first I want to tell you about Thursday.'

'Oh, is it to be Thursday?' asked Eustace.

'Wait a minute. You must learn not to be impatient, Eustace. Thursday may never come. But I was going to say, your father doesn't go to Ousemouth on Thursday afternoon so we're all going for a drive.'

'Hurray!' cried both children at once.

'And Mrs Steptoe has very kindly invited us to join them on the Downs for a picnic.'

Hilda looked utterly dismayed at this.

'Do you think we ought to go?' she asked anxiously. 'Last year when we went Eustace was sick after we got home.'

'I wasn't!' Eustace exclaimed. 'I only felt sick.'

'Eustace must try very hard not to get excited,' Aunt Sarah said in a tone that was at once mild and menacing. 'Otherwise he won't be allowed to go again.'

'But he always gets excited,' Hilda persisted, ignoring the

26

faces that Eustace, who had jumped up at the news, was making at her from behind his aunt's back. 'Nancy excites him; he can't really help it.'

Aunt Sarah smiled, and as her features lost their habitual severity of cast they revealed one of the sources from which Hilda got her beauty.

'It's Eustace's fault if he lets Nancy make him behave foolishly,' she said with rather chilly indulgence. 'He must remember she is only a little girl.'

'But she's older than me,' said Eustace. 'She's quite old; she's older than Hilda.'

'In years, perhaps. But not in other ways. Hilda has an old head on young shoulders, haven't you, Hilda?'

At the compliment Hilda smiled through her portentous frowns.

'I'm sure I know better than she does what's good for Eustace,' she announced decidedly.

'Then you must see that he doesn't run about like a little mad thing and over-eat himself,' said Aunt Sarah. 'If you do that everything will be all right.'

'Oh yes,' cried Eustace ecstatically, 'I'm sure it will. Hilda always tells me to stop playing when I begin to look tired.'

'Yes, I do,' said Hilda a trifle grimly, 'but you don't always stop.'

Aunt Sarah was moving to the door when Eustace called after her. 'May I do my corrections in the nursery?'

'Do you think Minney will want you when she's busy with Baby?'

'Oh, she won't mind if I keep very still.'

'I think I'd better come too,' said Hilda.

'Yes, do come,' said Eustace. 'But mightn't two be more in the way than one?'

'Very well, I'll stay here since you don't want me.'

'I do want you, I do want you!' cried Eustace. 'Only I didn't think there was any red ink in the nursery.'

'That shows all the more you don't want me!' said Hilda. 'When you come down I shall have gone out.'

'Don't go far!'

'I shall go a long way. You won't be able to find me.'

'Where shall you go?'

'Oh, nowhere in particular.' And then as Eustace was closing the door she called out, 'Perhaps towards the light-house.'

Eustace knocked at the nursery door. 'It's me, Minney.'

'Come in, Eustace.... Goodness gracious! what have you got there?'

She bustled up, a small, active woman with a kind round face and soft tidy hair. 'Whatever's that?'

'It's what I've done wrong,' said Eustace gloomily.

'Is it? Let me look. I don't call that much. I should be very proud if I made no more mistakes than that.'

'Would you?' asked Eustace almost incredulously.

'Yes, I should. I'll be bound Hilda didn't get as many right as you did.'

Eustace considered. 'Of course she's very good at sums. . . . But you mustn't let me interrupt you, Minney.'

'Interrupt! Listen to the boy. I've got nothing to do. Baby's outside in the pram, asleep, I hope.'

'Oughtn't one of us to go and look at her, perhaps?'

'Certainly not. Now, what do you want? A table? Here it is. A chair? I'll put it there, and you on it.' Suiting the action to the word, she lifted Eustace, passive and acquiescent, on to the white chair. 'And now what? Ink? I'll go and fetch it.' Poor lamb, she murmured to herself outside the door, how tired he looks!

Left alone, Eustace fell into a reverie. Though he could not have formulated the reason for it, he felt an exquisite sense of relief; the tongues of criticism, that wagged around him all day, at last were stilled.

'Here's the ink,' said Minney, appearing with a great impression of rapid movement, 'and the blotting-paper and a pen. My word, you want a lot of waiting on, don't you?'

'I'm afraid I do,' said Eustace humbly. 'Hilda says you spoil me.'

'What nonsense! But mind you, don't make a mess, or else you'll hear about it.'

'Do you think I'm messy?' asked Eustace anxiously.

'No, you're always a good boy.' This favourable judgement surprised Eustace into a shocked denial.

'Oh no,' he said, as though the idea were blasphemous.

'Yes, you are. You're just like your mother.'

'I wish I could remember her better.'

'Well, you were very young then.'

'Why did she die, Minney?'

'I've told you ever so many times, she died when your sister Barbara was born.'

'But mothers don't always die then.'

'No . . .' said Minney, turning away, 'but she did . . . Now get on, Eustace, or you'll have the whole morning gone.'

Eustace began to write. Presently his tongue came out and followed his pen with sympathetic movements.

'Good gracious, child, don't do that—if the wind changed——'

'I'm sorry, Minney.'

'And don't for heaven's sake sit all hunched up. You'll grow into a question mark.'

Obediently Eustace straightened himself, but the effort of sitting upright and keeping his tongue in was so great that the work proceeded twice as slowly as before.

'That's better,' said Minney, coming and standing behind him, her sewing in her hand. 'But what do you call that letter, a C? It looks more like an L.'

'It's a capital C,' explained Eustace. Oh dear! Here was the voice of criticism again, and coming, most disappointingly, from Minney's mouth. 'Don't you make them like that?'

'No, I don't, but I dare say I'm old-fashioned.'

'Then I like people to be old-fashioned,' said Eustace placatingly.

'I always tell them you'll get on in the world, Eustace. You say such nice things to people.'

'Dear Minney!'

It was delicious to be praised. A sense of luxury invaded Eustace's heart. Get on in the world . . . say nice things to people . . . he would remember that. He was copying 'Oakham' for the fourth time when he heard a shout at the window, repeated a second later still more imperiously, 'Eustace! EUSTACE!'

'Gracious!' said Minney. 'She'll wake the baby. When she wants a thing she never thinks of anyone else.'

Eustace was already at the window. 'Coming, Hilda!' he cried in a raucous whisper. 'I was afraid you'd gone to the lighthouse.'

CHAPTER IV

The Picnic on the Downs

CAMBO was the last house in its row; nothing intervened between it and the sea except the Rev A. J. Johnson's preparatory school, a large square brown building which, partly from its size, partly from the boys it housed and at stated hours disgorged in crocodile form, exerted a strong influence over Eustace's imagination. He had been told that when he grew older and his father richer he might be sent there. The thought appalled him—he devoted certain private prayers to the effect that he might never become any older than he was, and he continually asked Minney, 'Daddy isn't any richer now, is he?'—simply for the sake of hearing her say, 'You ought to be glad if your father makes more money,' an answer he rightly interpreted to mean that he was not doing so yet.

But this morning, as for the fifth time he opened the garden gate, he did not even notice the menacing shape on his right. His eyes were turned away from the sea to the houses at the top of the square and the road where surely, by this time, he would see something to reward his vigil. Yes, there was the landau, with Brown Bess between the shafts, and the driver in his bowler hat sitting enthroned above. He never would drive down to Cambo, the road was so full of ruts and there was no room, he said, to turn the horses.

Eustace lingered to make sure there could be no mistake and then dashed into the house, colliding with his father in the doorway.

'Oh, Daddy, it's there!'

'Well, you needn't knock me over if it is,' said Alfred Cherrington, recoiling a little at the impact.

'Oh, Daddy, have I hurt you?'

'Not seriously, but I should like to know what you're in such a hurry about?'

'Oh, Daddy, you do know.'

His father's pale blue eyes under their straw-coloured lashes narrowed in pretended ignorance.

'Were you being chased by a bull?'

'Oh, Daddy, there aren't any bulls on the green.'

'There might be if they saw your red jersey.'

'You're teasing me.'

'Well, what was it?'

'Why, the carriage, of course.'

'What carriage? I don't know anything about a carriage. Has it come to take you to school?'

'No, it's going to take us to the Downs,' cried Eustace. 'You must hurry. Mustn't he hurry, Aunt Sarah?' He appealed to his aunt who had appeared in the porch, a grey veil drawn over her hat and tied tightly under her chin.

'I don't think you ought to tell your father to hurry,' Aunt Sarah said.

Eustace became anxious and crestfallen at once.

'Oh, I didn't really mean he was to hurry . . . Only just not . . . not to waste time. You knew what I meant, didn't you, Daddy?'

He looked up at his father, and Aunt Sarah looked at him too. Mr Cherrington was silent. At last he said:

'Well, I suppose you ought to be careful how you talk to me.'

'Has Eustace been rude to Daddy again?' inquired Hilda, who had joined the group.

'Oh, nothing much,' said Mr Cherrington awkwardly. 'Come along now, or we shall never get started.' He spoke with irritation but without authority. Eustace looked back into the hall.

'Isn't Minney coming?'

'No,' said Aunt Sarah. 'I told you before, she has to look after Barbara.'

They started up the hill towards the carriage.

Hilda and Eustace took turns to sit on the box. Eustace's turn came last. This meant missing a bird's-eye view of the streets of Anchorstone, but certain interesting and venerated landmarks such as the soaring water-tower, a magnificent structure of red brick which he never passed under without a thrill, thinking it might burst with the weight of water imprisoned in it, could be seen almost as well from inside. He loved the moment when they turned off the main road on the brink of Frontisham Hill, that frightful declivity with its rusty warning to cyclists, and began to go inland. Every beat of the horses' hoofs brought the Downs nearer. Hilda would talk to the driver with an almost professional knowledge of horses. He let her use the whip and even, when they got clear of the town, hold the reins herself. Eustace had once been offered this privilege. At first he enjoyed the sensation of power, and the touch of the driver's large gloved hand over his gave him a feeling of security. But suddenly the horse stumbled, then broke into a gallop, and the driver, snatching the reins, swore with a vehemence that terrified Eustace. He had never seen anyone so angry before, and though the man, when he calmed down, assured him he was not to blame, he felt he was, and refused to repeat the experiment. A conviction of failure clung to him, reasserting itself when Hilda, erect and unruffled, displayed her proficiency and fearlessness; in fact whenever he saw a horse. And everyone assured him that he would never be a man until he learned how to drive. Indeed, the future was already dull and menacing with the ambitions other people entertained on his behalf. It seldom occurred to him to question their right to cherish these expectations. Not only must he learn to drive a horse, he must master so many difficult matters: ride a bicycle, play hockey, play the piano, talk French and, hardest of all, earn his living and provide for his sisters and his Aunt Sarah and his father when he got too old to work . . . The future was to be a laborious business. And if he did not fulfil these obligations, everyone would be angry, or at least grieved and disappointed.

In self-defence Eustace had formed the mental habit of postponing starting to make a man of himself to an un-specified date that never came nearer, remaining miraculously just far enough away not to arouse feelings of nervous dread, but not so far away as to give his conscience cause to reproach him with neglect of his duties. The charm did not always work, but it worked today: his enjoyment of the drive was undisturbed by any sense of private failure. Presently Hilda announced that it was time for him to take her place on the box. The carriage stopped while he climbed up.

Searching for a subject of conversation that might interest his neighbour, he said, 'Have you ever ridden a racehorse?'

The driver smiled.

'No, you want to be a jockey to do that.'

A jockey: no one had ever proposed that Eustace should be a jockey. It always gave him pleasure to contemplate a profession with which his future was not involved.

'Do jockeys get rich?' he presently inquired.

'Some of 'em do,' the man replied.

'Richer than you?' Eustace was afraid the question might be too personal so he made his voice sound as incredulous as possible.

'I should think they did,' said the driver warmly.

'I'm sorry,' said Eustace. Then, voicing an ancient fear, he asked, 'It's very hard to make money, isn't it?'

'You're right,' said the driver. 'It jolly well is.'

Eustace sighed, and for a moment the Future loomed up, black and threatening and charged with responsibility. But the appearance of a ruined roofless church made of flints, grey and jagged and very wild-looking, distracted him. Its loneliness challenged his imagination. Moreover, it was a sign that the Downs were at hand.

'Soon we shall see the farm-house,' he remarked.

The driver pointed with his whip. 'There it is!'

A cluster of buildings, shabby and uncared for, came into view.

'And there's the iron spring,' cried Eustace. 'Look, it's running.'

A trickle of brownish water came out of a pipe under the farm-house wall. The ground around it was dyed bright orange; but disappointingly it failed to colour the pond which received it a yard or two below.

'If you was to drink that every day,' observed the driver, 'you'd soon be a big chap.'

'You don't think I'm very big now?'

'You'll grow a lot bigger yet,' said the driver diplomatically.

Eustace was relieved. He had been told that he was undersized. One of the tasks enjoined on him was to increase his stature. Some association of ideas led him to say:

'Do you know a girl called Nancy Steptoe?'

'I should think I did,' said the driver. 'If I wasn't driving you today I should be driving them.'

'I'm glad we asked you first,' said Eustace politely. The man seemed pleased. 'She's a nice girl, isn't she?'

No answer came for a moment. Then the driver said:

'I'd rather be taking you and Miss Hilda.'

'Oh!' cried Eustace, emotions of delight and disappointment struggling in him, 'but don't you like Nancy?'

'It's not for me to say whether I like her or whether I don't.'

'But you must know which you do,' exclaimed Eustace.

The driver grunted.

'But she's so pretty.'

'Not so pretty as Miss Hilda by a long sight.'

Eustace was amazed. He had heard Hilda called pretty, but that she should be prettier than Nancy—the gay and the daring, the care-free, the well-dressed, the belle of Anchorstone—he could not believe it. Hilda was wonderful; everything she did was right; Eustace could not exist without her, could not long be happy without her good opinion, but he had never imagined that her supremacy held good outside the moral sphere and the realm of the affections.

'She doesn't think she's pretty herself,' he said at last.

'She will some day,' said the driver.

'But, Mr Craddock,' exclaimed Eustace (he always called Craddock Mr having received a hint from Minney: the others never did), 'she's too good to be pretty.'

Mr Craddock laughed.

'You say some old-fashioned things, Master Eustace,' he said.

Eustace pondered. He still wanted to know why the driver preferred taking them, the humble Cherringtons, to the glorious, exciting Steptoes.

'Do you think Nancy is proud?' he asked at last.

'She's got no call to be,' Mr Craddock said.

Eustace thought she had, but did not say so. He determined to make a frontal attack.

'Do you often take the Steptoes in your carriage, Mr Craddock?'

'Yes, often.'

Naturally he would. To the Steptoes, a picnic was nothing unusual: they probably had one every day. Eustace was still surprised at being asked to join them. He thought Gerald must want to swap something, and had put in his pocket all his available treasures, though ashamed of their commonplace quality.

'When you drive them,' he proceeded, 'what do they do different from us?'

Mr Craddock laughed shortly. 'They don't pay for my tea.'

'But aren't they very rich?'

'They're near, if you ask me.'

Eustace had scarcely time to digest this disagreeable information when he heard his father's voice: 'Eustace, look! There are the Steptoes—they've got here first.'

By now the Downs were upon them, green slopes, low but steep, enclosing a miniature valley. The valley swung away to the left, giving an effect of mystery and distance. The four Steptoes were sitting by the stream—hardly perceptible but for its fringe of reeds and tall grasses—that divided the valley. Nancy had taken her hat off and was shaking back her golden hair. Eustace knew the gesture well; he felt it to be the perfection of sophistication and *savoir-faire*. He raised his hat and waved. Nancy responded with elegant negligence. Major and Mrs Steptoe rose to their feet. Something made Eustace look back into the

36

landau at Hilda. She could see the Steptoes quite well, but she didn't appear to notice them. A small bush to the left was engaging her attention: she peered at it from under her drawn brows as though it was something quite extraordinary and an eagle might fly out of it. Turning away, Eustace sighed.

'I hope you will have a nice time, Mr Craddock,' he said.

'Don't you worry about that, Master Eustace.'

'Will you have some more cake, Nancy?'

'No, thank you, Eustace.'

'Will you have some of the sandwiches we brought, though I'm afraid they're not as nice as your cake?'

'They're delicious, but I don't think I'll have any more.'

'I could easily make you some fresh tea, couldn't I, Aunt Sarah?'

'Yes, but you must take care not to scald yourself.'

'Well, if it's absolutely no trouble, Eustace. You made it so beautifully before.'

Eustace glowed.

'Look here, Gerald,' said Major Steptoe, turning on his massive tweed-clad elbow, 'you're neglecting Hilda.'

'She said she didn't want any more,' remarked Gerald a trifle curtly.

'If you pressed her she might change her mind.'

'Thanks, I never change it.'

Hilda was sitting on the Steptoes' beautiful blue carriage rug, her heels drawn up, her arms clasping her knees, her head averted, her eyes fixed on some distant object down the valley.

'What a determined daughter you've got, Cherrington.'

'Well, she is a bit obstinate at times.'

'Aunt Sarah said if you keep on changing your mind no one will respect you,' said Hilda in lofty accents and without looking round.

'She's hardly eaten anything,' said Gerald, who was Eustace's senior by a year. 'Just one or two of their sandwiches and none of our cakes.'

There was an awkward pause. Eustace came to the rescue. 'She hardly ever eats cakes, do you, Hilda?'

'What an unusual little girl!' said Mrs Steptoe with her high laugh.

'You needn't be afraid of getting fat, you know,' said Major Steptoe, gently pinching Hilda's thin calf with his large strong hand. Hilda rounded on him with the movement of a horse shaking off a fly.

'It doesn't do to be greedy at my time of life.'

'Why ever not?'

Eustace whispered nervously to Nancy, 'She doesn't like being touched. Isn't it funny? She doesn't mind so much if you hit her.'

'Why, have you tried?'

Eustace looked shocked. 'Only when we play together.'

Major Steptoe rose and stretched himself. 'Well, Cherrington, what about these toboggans? We've given our tea time to settle.'

Miss Cherrington stopped folding up some paper bags and said:

'Alfred and I both think it would be too much for Eustace.'

'Oh come, Miss Cherrington, the boy'll only be young once.'

'Oh, do let me, Aunt Sarah,' Eustace pleaded.

'It's for your father to decide, not me,' said Miss Cherrington. 'We remember what happened last time Eustace tobogganed, don't we?'

'What did happen, Eustace?' asked Nancy with her flattering intimacy.

'Oh, I couldn't tell you here.'

'Why not?'

'I was much younger then, of course.'

'Well,' said Major Steptoe, looming large over the little party, 'we can't let the boy grow up into a mollycoddle.'

'I was thinking of his health, Major Steptoe.'

'What do you say, Bet?'

'I think it would do him all the good in the world,' said Mrs Steptoe.

'Well, Cherrington,' said Major Steptoe, 'the decision rests with you and your sister.'

Mr Cherrington also rose to his feet, a slight figure beside Major Steptoe's bulk.

'All things considered, I think——'

'Remember, you agreed with me before we started, Alfred.'

Mr Cherrington, unhappily placed between his sister and Major Steptoe, looked indecisively from one to the other and said:

'The boy's not so delicate as you think, Sarah. You fuss over him too much in my opinion. One or two turns on the toboggan will do him no harm. Only remember' (he turned irritably to Eustace) 'you must let it stop at that.'

Eustace jumped up, jubilant. Miss Cherrington pursed her lips and Hilda whispered, 'Isn't that like Daddy? We can't depend on him, can we? Now Eustace will be sick.'

The males of the party started off towards the farm and presently reappeared each laden with a toboggan. Eustace could not manage his; his arm was too short to go round it; when he tried pulling it over the rough roadway it kept getting stuck behind stones. Major Steptoe, who was carrying the big toboggan with places for three on it, relieved Eustace of his.

'How strong you must be, Major Steptoe!'

'So will you be at my age, won't he, Cherrington?'

And Eustace's father, feeling as if Major Steptoe had somehow acquired his parental prerogative, agreed.

Then arose the question of who was to make the first descent.

'The thing is,' said Gerald, 'to see who can go furthest on the flat. Now if Mother and Miss Cherrington sit here, on that stone, they'll mark the furthest point anyone's ever got to.'

'I don't want to sit on a stone, thank you,' said Mrs Steptoe, 'and I don't suppose Miss Cherrington does either.'

'Well then, sit in this cart-rut, it's the same thing. Now you must keep a very careful watch, and mark each place with a stick—I'll give you some.'

'Thank you.'

'And you mustn't take your eyes off us for a second, and only where the last part of the body touches the ground counts: it might be the head, you know.'

'I suppose it might.'

'Now we'll begin. Should I go first, just to show you what it's like?'

'I think you might ask Hilda to go with you.'

Gerald's face fell. 'Will you come, Hilda?'

'No, thank you. I shall have plenty to do looking after Eustace.'

'Then I'll start.' Gerald took one of the single toboggans and climbed the slope with great alacrity and an unnecessary amount of knee movement. 'Coming,' he cried. The toboggan travelled swiftly down the grassy slope. The gradient was the same all the way until twenty feet or so before the bottom when, after a tiny rise, it suddenly steepened. It was this that gave the run its thrill. Gerald's toboggan took the bump only a shade out of the straight: only a shade but enough to turn it sideways. He clung on for a moment. Then over he went, and sliding and rolling arrived at the bottom of the slope. The toboggan, deprived of his weight, slithered uncertainly after him and then stopped. It was an ignominious exhibition, and it was received in silence. Suddenly the silence was broken by a loud burst of laughter.

'He said he was going to show us what it was like,' Hilda brought out at last, between the convulsions of her mirth. 'Didn't he look funny?'

'Perhaps he meant to show us it doesn't really hurt falling,' suggested Eustace charitably.

Gerald ignored them. 'I'm glad I fell, in a way,' he explained, 'because now you can all see the dangerous point. Of course, I should really have done it better if I'd come down head first. That's the way I usually do it, only

40

of course it wouldn't have been any good showing you that way, because that way needs a great deal of practice.' He looked at his father for confirmation.

'Not one of your best efforts, my boy,' said Major Steptoe. 'Let's see what Eustace can do.'

As Eustace climbed the slippery hillside tugging at the rope of the toboggan with determined jerks, he suddenly thought of the Crucifixion and identified himself with its principal figure. The image seemed blasphemous so he tried to put it out of his mind. No, he was a well-known mountaineer scaling the Andes. On the other side of the valley lay the Himalayas, and that large bird was a condor vulture, which would pick his bones if he were killed . . . No, it wouldn't, for it would have to reckon with Hilda; she would be sure to defend his body with her life. There she was, quite small now, and not looking up at him, as the others were. Eustace sighed. He wished she was enjoying herself more. Mentally he projected himself into Hilda. Immediately she began to talk and smile; the others all gathered round her; even Mrs Steptoe, aloof and mocking, hung on her lips. What a delightful girl! Not only a second mother to Eustace, but pretty and charming as well. Then he caught sight of Hilda's face, sullen and set, and the vision faded . . . It was high time, for they must be wondering why he was so long coming down. Perhaps they thought he was frightened. Eustace's heart began to beat uncomfortably. They were all looking at him now, even Hilda, and he heard a voice—Gerald's—call out 'Hurry up!' It was 'hurry up', wasn't it, not 'funk', a horrible word Gerald had got hold of and applied to everyone he didn't like and many that he did. Eustace tentatively paid out a few inches of the rope. The toboggan gave a sickening plunge. Again the voice floated up: 'Come on!' It was 'come on', wasn't it, not that other word? Gerald would hardly dare use it in the presence of his parents. The difficulty with the toboggan, he remembered, was to sit on it properly before it started off. The other times his father had always held it for him, and he would have done so now, Eustace thought with rising panic, only Major Steptoe hadn't wanted him to. Should he just walk down and say he didn't feel very well? It was quite true: his heart was jumping about in the most extraordinary way and he could hardly breathe. He would be ill, just as they said he would be. He need never see the Steptoes again: Hilda would be delighted if he didn't. As for Nancy——

At that moment Eustace saw his father turn to Major Steptoe and say something, at the same time pointing at Eustace. Major Steptoe nodded, his father rose to his feet, the tension in the little group relaxed, they began to look about them and talk. It was clear what had happened: his father was coming up to help him.

This decided Eustace. Holding the dirty rope in one hand, while with the other he supported his weight, he lowered himself on to the toboggan. Before he had time fairly to fix his heels against the cross-bar it was off.

The first second of the run cleared Eustace's mind marvellously. He was able to arrange himself more firmly in his seat and even, so sharpened were his senses by the exhilaration of the movement, to guide the toboggan a little with his body. And when the pace slackened at the fatal bump he felt excited, not frightened. For a moment his feet seemed to hang over space; the toboggan pitched forward like a see-saw as the ground fell away under it. The pace was now so breath-taking that Eustace forgot where he was, forgot himself, forgot everything. Then, very tamely and undramatically, the toboggan stopped and he looked up to see the party scattering right and left, laughing and clapping their hands. He had finished up right in the middle of them.

'Bravo!'

'Well done, Eustace!'

'He didn't need any help, you see.'

'He looks rather white, I'm afraid, Alfred.'

'I believe you've broken the record, Eustace,' said Nancy.

'Oh no, he's not done that, because you see at the last moment he put his elbow on the ground, and that's two feet, at least it's two of my feet' (explained Gerald, measuring) 'short of the Record Stone. You were just coming off, really, weren't you, Eustace?'

'Well, perhaps I was.' Being a hero Eustace felt he could afford to be generous.

'What do you think of your brother now, Miss Hilda?' asked Major Steptoe playfully.

Hilda, who had resumed her seat on the rug, let her glance rest on the feet of her interlocutor.

'I'm glad in a way,' she admitted.

'You ought to be very proud of him.'

'I should certainly have been ashamed of him if he hadn't.'

'Hadn't what?'

'Broken the record, or whatever Nancy said he did.'

An astonished pause greeted this remark. It was broken by Mrs Steptoe's light, ironical voice.

'Your sister expects a lot of you, doesn't she, Eustace?'

'Doesn't Nancy expect a lot of Gerald?' Eustace asked.

'Oh, I've given Gerald up, he's hopeless,' said Nancy. 'I won't trust myself on the toboggan with him. You're so good, Eustace, may I come with you?'

Eustace, in the seventh heaven of delight, got up and looked round awkwardly at the company.

'You've got a great responsibility now, Eustace!'

'I feel quite safe,' said Nancy airily.

'Will you have a turn with Gerald, Hilda?' asked Major Steptoe, 'or will you watch?'

'I might as well watch.'

'Then, Cherrington, what about you and me and Gerald trying our luck together?'

'Rather.'

The five of them trooped up the hill, leaving Mrs Steptoe and Miss Cherrington and Hilda to rather desultory conversation.

'You sit in front, Nancy!'

'Oh, Eustace, I should feel much safer if you did.'

'Should we take turns?'

'They may separate us.'

'Oh, would they do that?'

'Well, you know how they do at dances.'

'I've never been to a dance,' said Eustace.

'But you go to the dancing class.'

'Sometimes, if I'm well enough.'

'You've never danced with me.'

'No, because you're too good, you're in A set.'

'We must dance together, some time.'

'Oh, that would be lovely!'

'Well, I'll go in front this time . . . Ooo, Eustace, how brave you are not to scream.'

'That's the third time Nancy and Eustace have come down together,' observed Miss Cherrington.

'Yes. Don't they look charming? And not one spill. Eustace is an expert, I must say. Here they all come. Don't you feel tempted, Hilda?'

No reply.

'We think you ought to try a new formation now, don't we, Miss Cherrington?' Mrs Steptoe persisted. 'What about a boys' double, Gerald and Eustace? And perhaps Mr Cherrington would take Nancy, and Hilda would go with Jack.'

Major Steptoe looked interrogatively at Hilda.

Hilda said nothing, and Eustace, who knew the signs, saw that she was on the brink of tears.

'Won't you come with me, Hilda?' he asked reluctantly.

'Go on as you are, I don't care,' Hilda replied, her words coming with difficulty and between irregular pauses. Mrs Steptoe raised her eyebrows.

'Well, I think you'd better break up a bit. Decide among yourselves. Toss for it. I beg you pardon, Miss Cherrington?'

'I'd rather they didn't do that, if you don't mind.'

Nancy took advantage of this debate between the elders to whisper to Eustace, 'Come on, let's have one more together.' Laughing and excited they trudged up the hill again.

'You know,' Nancy said as confidentially as her loud panting permitted, 'I arranged all this, really.'

'You arranged it?'

'Yes, the picnic.'

'Why?' asked Eustace breathlessly.

'Can't you guess?'

'So that you and I might——?'

'Of course.'

'Oh, Nancy!'

Once more the glorious rush through the darkening air. This time Nancy was riding in front. The wind of the descent caught her long golden hair and it streamed out so that when Eustace bent forward it touched his face. When they came to the bump his customary skill deserted him; the toboggan turned sideways and they rolled and slithered to the bottom. Eustace was first on his feet. He gave his hand to Nancy and spluttered, gasping:

'Your hair got in my eyes.'

'I'm sorry.'

'I didn't mind.'

Mrs Steptoe received them with a little smile. 'Well, children, it's getting late. I think the next ought to be the last. What do you say, Miss Cherrington?'

'I think Eustace has had quite enough.'

'Cherrington and I have broken every bone in our bodies,' remarked Major Steptoe amiably.

Both the fathers had withdrawn from the fray some time ago and were smoking their pipes. The sun was hanging over the hill behind them, a large red ball which had lost its fierceness. The grass on the opposite slope was flecked with gold; the shadows lengthened; the air turned faintly blue.

'Last round,' called Major Steptoe. 'Seconds out of the ring. We're nearly all seconds now, what, Cherrington? How is it to be this time?'

Eustace and Nancy gave each other a covert glance.

Suddenly Hilda said in a strident, croaking voice:

'I should like to go with Eustace.'

This announcement was followed by a general murmur of surprise, which soon turned into a chorus of approval.

'That's right, Hilda! Don't let Nancy monopolise him! Let's have a race between the two families—the Cherringtons versus the Steptoes.'

So it was arranged that Gerald and Nancy should have one of the double toboggans, Hilda and Eustace the other. Mr Cherrington was to act as starter, Major Steptoe as judge. Hilda waited till her father and the two Steptoes were half-way up the slope and then said:

'You've been very unkind to me, Eustace.'

Eustace was feeling tired: he wished Hilda had offered to help him pull up the toboggan. Her accusation, acting on his nerves, seemed to redouble his weariness.

'Oh why, Hilda? I asked you to come and you wouldn't.'

'Because I saw you wanted to be with Nancy,' said Hilda sombrely. 'You never left her alone for a moment. You don't know how silly you looked—both of you,' she added as an afterthought.

'You didn't see us,' Eustace argued feebly, 'you were always looking the other way.'

'I did try not to see you,' said Hilda, remorselessly striding up the slope, her superior stature, unimpaired freshness and natural vigour giving her a great advantage over Eustace. 'But when I couldn't see you I could hear you. I was ashamed of you and so was Aunt Sarah and so was Daddy.'

'Daddy said he was proud of me.'

'Oh, he said that to please Major Steptoe.'

Eustace felt profoundly depressed and, as the tide of reaction rolled over him, a little sick. But the excitement of the start, of getting into line, of holding the toboggan with Hilda on it and then jumping into his place at the word 'Go!' banished his malaise. Off shot the two toboggans. When they reached the dreaded rise they were abreast of each other; then Gerald's exaggerated technique (learned, as he had explained, from a tobogganist of world-wide renown) involved him, as so often, in disaster. The Cherringtons won, though their finish was not spectacular: the grass, now growing damp, held them back. Hilda and Eustace stumbled to their feet. They looked at each other without speaking but there was a gleam in Hilda's eye. Major Steptoe joined the group.

'A decisive victory for your side, I'm afraid, Cherrington,' he said. 'Now what about packing up?'

Gerald was heard muttering something about 'our revenge'.

'What does he say?' asked Hilda.

'He wants to challenge us again,' said Eustace importantly.

'Now, children, it's too late for any more. Look, the moon's rising!' But Mrs Steptoe's clear, decided tones had no effect whatever on Hilda.

'The sun's still there,' she said. 'Come on, Eustace. I want to beat them again.'

'But we mightn't win another time,' said Eustace cautiously.

However, Hilda had her way. The second race resulted in a win for the Steptoes. Again the parents and Miss Cherrington decreed the revels should end. But Hilda would not hear of it. They must have a third race to decide who were the real winners.

'I feel a little sick, Hilda,' whispered Eustace as he toiled after her up the slope.

'What nonsense! You didn't feel sick with Nancy.'

'I do now.'

'You don't—you only think you do.'

'Perhaps you know best.'

The third race was a near thing because both parties finished without mishap. The Cherringtons, however, were definitely in front. But apart from Major Steptoe, the judge, there was no one to hail their triumph; the others had gone on towards the carriages which could be seen a couple of hundred yards away drawn up on the turf, facing each other.

'We've won! We've won!' cried Hilda, her voice echoing down the valley. Her eyes were sparkling, her face, glowing against her dark hair, was amazingly animated. Eustace, who had seldom seen her like this, was excited and afraid. 'We've won, we've won!' she repeated.

'All right then, come along!' Aunt Sarah's voice, with a note of impatience in it, reached them thinly across the grassy expanse.

'Wait a minute!' screamed Hilda, 'I'm going to make Eustace take me again.'

Major Steptoe's deep, conversational tones sounded strangely composed after her wild accents.

'What about giving up now? The horses'll be getting restive.'

'I don't care about the horses. Come on, Eustace.'

For the first time she took the toboggan herself, and began running up the hill. It was so wet now that she slipped and stumbled with every step, and Eustace, quite tired out, could hardly get along at all.

'Oh, do hurry, Eustace: you're so slow.'

'I'm trying to keep up with you, Hilda!'

Suddenly she took his hand. 'Here, hang on to me.'

'Won't they be angry if I'm sick?'

'Not if you're with me. There, you sit at the back. Isn't it glorious us being together like this?'

'It's getting so dark, Hilda.'

From the wood where the valley curved an owl called.

'What was that, Hilda?'

'Only an owl, you silly!'

The toboggan rushed down the slope. It was too dark to see the irregularities in the ground. They felt a bump; Hilda stuck out her foot; the toboggan pitched right over and brother and sister rolled pell-mell to the bottom.

Hilda pulled Eustace to his feet. 'Wasn't it lovely, Eustace?'

'Yes, but oh, Hilda, I do feel sick!'

Suddenly he was sick.

'I'm all right now, Hilda.'

'That's a good thing. Let me take the toboggan—Coming, Major Steptoe.'

'He looks a bit white,' said Aunt Sarah, as they settled themselves into the landau. 'Whatever made you take him up again, Hilda?'

'I knew he really wanted to,' said Hilda. 'Didn't you, Eustace?'

'Yes,' said Eustace faintly. 'But I think I won't go on the box tonight.'

'I won't either,' announced Hilda.

'Can we go back by Anchorstone Hall?' asked Eustace. 'Then Mr Craddock needn't turn round.'

They waved farewells to the Steptoes, who were going the other way. The road led through woods and open clearings.

'I keep feeling better,' Eustace whispered to Hilda. 'Wasn't it lovely, our last ride?'

'Better than the ones you had with Nancy?' muttered Hilda, affectionate menace in her tone.

'Oh, much, much better,' whispered Eustace.

'And do you love me more than her?'

'Oh, much, much more.'

So they conversed, with mutual protestations of endearment, until suddenly a great sheet of water opened out before them, and beyond it rose the chimneys and turrets and battlements of Anchorstone Hall. The moon made a faint pathway on the water, but the house was still gilded by the setting sun. Eustace was enchanted. 'Oh, isn't it lovely? If I ever make enough money to buy it, will you come and live there with me, Hilda?'

'Cambo's good enough for me.'

'Oh, but this is so grand!'

'Silly, Eustace, you always like things grand.'

'That's why I like you.'

'I'm not grand.'

'Yes, you are.'

'No, I'm not.'

49

'Oh, children, shut up!' said Mr Cherrington, turning round from the box.

'Yes, for goodness' sake be quiet,' said Aunt Sarah.

There was silence for a space. Then Eustace whispered: 'I think I feel quite well now, Hilda.'

CHAPTER V

A Lion in the Path

NEXT morning Eustace was not allowed to get up to breakfast: he was considered to be too tired. So he spent the first part of the morning, not unwillingly, in bed. Cambo boasted few bedrooms, and the one he shared with Hilda did not contain and could not have contained more furniture than their two narrow beds, set side by side, a washing-stand, a combined chest-of-drawers and dressing-table, two chairs with seats made of stout fibre, and some rings behind a curtain in lieu of wardrobe. The furniture and the wood-work were stained brown, the wallpaper was dark blue with a design of conventional flowers, and the curtains of the window, which looked out on the brown flank of the house next door, were of dark blue linen. Eustace greatly admired the curtain rings of oxidised copper, and also the door handle which was made of the same metal and oval in shape instead of round. It was set rather high in the door, recalling the way that some people, Eustace had noticed, shook hands.

Eustace loved the room, especially on mornings like this, when he was allowed to go into the bed Hilda had vacated and enjoy the less restricted view commanded by it. She would be shopping now; she was probably at Love's the butcher's, whose name they both thought so funny. He did not envy her that item in her list. He wondered if Nancy ever shopped. He could imagine her buying shoes and stockings and dresses of silk, satin and velvet, but he did not think she brought home the groceries, for instance, as he and Hilda often did. How she occupied herself most of the time was a mystery—a delightful mystery that it gave him increasing pleasure to try to solve. Only on rare occasions did she go down to the beach, as Eustace knew, for he always looked for her, and still more seldom was she to be seen on the cliffs. It was most unlikely that he would find her there this morning when he joined Hilda at the First Shelter, at twelve o'clock.

Just as he remembered this appointment Minney came in to tell him to get up. It was half-past eleven; how would he have time to wash his neck, clean his teeth and say his prayers?

Eustace was inwardly sure he would find time, unless he were held up by his prayers. During the last week or two they had presented a difficult problem. He wanted to include Nancy, if not in a special prayer, at any rate in the general comprehensive blessing at the end. This already included many people whom he did not like so much; he even had to mention Mr Craddock's dog, simply because Hilda was fond of it. There could be no harm, surely, in adding Nancy's name. But when the moment arrived he always flinched. He had to say his prayers aloud, usually to Hilda, but always to somebody, and he knew instinctively that the mention of Nancy's name would give rise to inquiry and probably to protest. To offer a silent prayer on her behalf seemed underhand and shabby. God would not approve and Nancy, if she knew, would feel ill used. So he made a compromise; he said Nancy's prayers out loud, but he waited till he was alone to say it. Minney was helping him to dress and she clearly meant to stay on to make the bed after he was gone. An inspiration seized him.

'Minney, would you fetch my sand-shoes? I left them in the hall to dry.'

'What a good, thoughtful boy! Of course I will.'

Rather guiltily Eustace sank on his knees and repeated very fast in a most audible voice: 'Please God bless Nancy and make her a good girl for ever and ever. Amen.'

Hilda was duly waiting for him at the First Shelter. There were three shelters on the cliff between the steps down to the sea and the lighthouse, more than a mile away: not only did they mark distances to Eustace and Hilda with an authority no milestone could ever compass, but they also, similar though they were in all respects to the casual eye, possessed highly developed personalities which could never for a moment be confused.

'Do you think we shall get as far as the Third Shelter?' asked Eustace as they set out.

'We've got an hour; we might even get to the lighthouse if you don't dawdle,' said Hilda.

They walked along the path at a respectful distance from the edge of the cliff. Some sixty feet deep, it was very treacherous. Anchorstone was full of legends of unwary or foolhardy persons who had ventured too near the brink, felt the earth give way under them, and been dashed to pieces on the rocks below.

'Gerald got as far as that once,' said Eustace, indicating a peculiarly dangerous-looking tuft of grass, between which and the true face of the cliff the weather had worked a deep trench, plain for all to see.

It was a thoughtless remark and Hilda pounced on it. 'The more fool he,' she said.

That subject was closed. They continued their walk till they came to a storm-bent hedge which clung giddily to the uttermost verge of the cliff. Every year it surrendered something to the elements. But buffeted and curtailed as it was, it presented a magnificent picture of tenacity, and Eustace never saw it without a thrill. This morning, however, it lacked the splendid isolation in which he liked to imagine it. Someone was walking alongside it, perhaps two people. But Hilda had better eyes than he and cried at once, 'There's Miss Fothergill and her companion.'

'Oh!' cried Eustace; 'let's turn back.'

But the light of battle was in Hilda's eye.

'Why should we turn back? It's just the opportunity we've been looking for.'

'Perhaps you have,' said Eustace. 'I haven't.'

He had already turned away from the approaching bath-chair and was tugging at Hilda's hand.

'The Bible says, "Sick and in prison and I visited you",' Hilda quoted with considerable effect. 'You've always been naughty about this, Eustace: it's the chief failing I've never been able to cure you of.'

'But she's so ugly,' protested Eustace.

'What difference does that make?'

'And she frightens me.'

'A big boy like you!'

'Her face is all crooked.'

'You haven't seen it—you always run away.'

'And her hands are all black.'

'Silly, that's only her gloves.'

'Yes, but they aren't proper hands, that's why she wears gloves. Annie told me.'

Annie was the Cherringtons' daily 'help'.

'She ought to have known better.'

'Anyhow we've been told ever so often not to speak to strangers.'

'She isn't a stranger, she's always been here. And it doesn't matter as long as they're old and . . . and ugly, and ill, like she is.'

'Perhaps she'll say, "Go away, you cheeky little boy. I don't want to talk to you. You want to beg, I suppose?" What shall I do then?'

'Of course she wouldn't. Ill people are never rude. Besides, she'll see me behind you.'

'But what shall I say to her?'

Hilda considered. 'You always find plenty to say to Nancy.'

'Oh, but I couldn't say those sort of things to her.'

'Well, say "How do you do, Miss Fothergill? It's a nice day, isn't it? I thought perhaps you would like me to help to push your bath-chair".'

'But I might upset her,' objected Eustace. 'You know how I once upset baby in the pram.'

'Oh, there wouldn't be any risk of that. Miss Fothergill's grown up—you'd only just be able to move her. Then you could say, "Aren't I lucky to be able to walk?" '

'Oh no,' said Eustace decisively. 'She wouldn't like that.'

'Then think of something yourself.'

'But why don't you speak to her, Hilda? Wouldn't that do as well? It would really be better, because if I speak to her she'll think you don't want to.'

'It doesn't matter about me,' said Hilda. 'I want her to see what good manners you've got.'

Eustace wriggled with obstinacy and irritation.

'But won't it be deceitful if I say how-do-you-do without meaning it? She won't know I'm doing it to please you and she'll think I'm politer than I really am. And Jesus will say I'm a whited-sepulchre like in that sermon we heard last Sunday. Besides, we are told to do good by stealth, not out in the open air.'

Hilda considered this. 'I don't think Jesus would mind,' she said at last. 'He always said we were to visit the sick, and that meant whether we wanted to or not. Those ministering children Minney read to us about were good because they visited the poor, the book didn't say they wanted to.'

'You don't know that Miss Fothergill is poor,' Eustace countered. 'I don't think she can be, because she lives in that big house, you know, all by itself, with lovely dark green bushes all round it. Jesus never said we were to visit the rich.'

'Now you're only arguing,' said Hilda. 'You said that about Jesus and not being polite on purpose because you don't want to do your duty. It isn't as if you were doing it for gain—that would be wrong, of course.'

'Of course,' said Eustace, horrified.

'She might give you a chocolate, though,' said Hilda, hoping to appeal to Eustace's charity through his appetite. 'Old ladies like that often have some.'

'I don't want her nasty chocolates.'

'There, I knew you'd say something naughty soon. Here she comes; if you speak to her now she'll know you don't really want to, you look so cross; so you won't be deceiving her.'

Eustace's face began to wrinkle up. 'Oh, Hilda, I can't!'

There was no time to be lost. Realising that argument and injunction had alike proved vain, Hilda adopted a new form of tactics—tactics, it may be said, she used but rarely.

'Oh, Eustace, please do it for my sake. Remember how I helped you with the toboggan yesterday, and how I always let you pat down the castles, though I am a girl, and I never mind playing horses with you, though Minney says I ought not to, at my age' (Hilda was much fonder of playing horses than Eustace), 'and how Aunt Sarah said you wouldn't be anywhere without me. And if you don't mind how I feel just think of poor Miss Fothergill going home and saying to the housemaid, "I met such a dear little boy on the cliff this morning; he spoke to me so nicely, it's quite made me forget"—well, you know, her face and her hands and everything. "I think I shall ask him to tea and give him a lot of lovely cakes".'

'Oh, that would be dreadful!' cried Eustace, much moved by Hilda's eloquence but appalled by the prospect evoked by her final sentence. 'You wouldn't let me go, would you? Promise, and I'll speak to her now.'

'I won't promise, but I'll see.'

Hilda fell back a pace or two, rather with the gesture of an impresario introducing a prima-donna. Standing unnaturally straight and holding his arm out as though to lose no time in shaking hands, Eustace advanced to meet the oncoming bath-chair. Then he changed his mind, jerkily withdrew the hand and took off his hat. The bath-chair halted.

'Well, my little man,' said Miss Fothergill, 'what can I do for you?' Her voice bubbled a little.

Eustace lost his head completely: the words died on his lips. Miss Fothergill's face was swathed in a thick veil, made yet more opaque by a plentiful sprinkling of large black spots. But even through this protection one could not but see her mouth—that dreadful wine-coloured mouth that went up sideways and, meeting a wrinkle half-way up her cheek, seemed to reach to her right eye. The eye was half closed, so she seemed to be winking at Eustace. His face registering everything he felt he hastily dropped his glance. Why was Miss Fothergill carrying a muff on this warm

56

summer day? Suddenly he remembered why and his discomfiture increased. Feeling that there was no part of Miss Fothergill he could safely look at, he made his gaze describe a half-circle. Now it rested on her companion, who returned the look with a disconcerting, unrecognising stare. Eustace felt acutely embarrassed.

'Well?' said Miss Fothergill again. 'Haven't you anything to say for yourself? Or did you just stop out of curiosity?'

Eustace was between two fires: he could feel Hilda's eyes boring into his back. 'Please,' he began, 'I wanted to say "How do you do, Miss Fothergill, isn't it a nice day?" '

'Very nice, but I don't think we know each other, do we?'

'Well, not yet,' said Eustace, 'only I thought perhaps you would let me push your—your' (he didn't like to say 'bath-chair') 'invalid's carriage for you.'

Miss Fothergill tried to screw her head round to look at her companion, then seemed to remember she couldn't, and said, 'You're very young to be starting work. Oughtn't you to be at school?'

Eustace took a nervous look at his darned blue jersey, and glancing over his shoulder at Hilda, pulled it down so hard that a small hole appeared at the shoulder.

'Oh, I have lessons at home,' he said, 'with Hilda.' Again he glanced over his shoulder: if only she would come to his rescue! She thought you might like——'

'This is very mysterious, Helen,' said Miss Fothergill, the words coming like little explosions from her wounded cheek. 'Can you make it out? Does he want to earn sixpence by pushing me, or what is it?'

Eustace saw that she was under a misapprehension.

'Of course I should do it for nothing,' he said earnestly. 'I have quite a lot of money in the Savings Bank, twenty-five pounds, and sixpence a week pocket money. You wouldn't have to do anything more than let me push you. If I was going to be paid, you would have had to ask me first, wouldn't you, instead of me asking you?'

Miss Fothergill's face made a movement which might have been interpreted as a smile.

'Have you tried before?'

'Well yes, with a pram, but you needn't be afraid because I only upset it on the kerbstone and there isn't one here.'

'I'm very heavy, you know.'

Eustace looked at her doubtfully.

'Not going downhill. It would be like a toboggan.'

'That would be too fast and my tobogganing days are over. Well, you can try if you like.'

'Oh, thank you,' said Eustace fervently. He turned to the companion. 'Will you show me how?'

'I think you'd better keep a hand on it, Helen,' said Miss Fothergill. 'I don't quite like to trust myself to a strange young man.'

With some slight hesitating reluctance the companion made way for Eustace, who braced himself valiantly to the task. The bath-chair moved forward jerkily. To his humiliation Eustace found himself clinging to the handle, instead of controlling it. They passed Hilda: she was gazing with feigned interest at the lighthouse.

'The path's a bit bumpy here,' he gasped.

'Well, St Christopher, you mustn't complain.'

'I beg your pardon,' said Eustace, 'but my name isn't Christopher, it's Eustace—Eustace Cherrington. And that girl we passed is my sister Hilda.'

'My name is Janet,' said Miss Fothergill, 'and Helen's name is Miss Grimshaw. Are you going to leave your sister behind?'

'Oh, she knows the way home,' said Eustace.

'Where is your home?'

'It's a house called Cambo, in Norwich Square. We used to live in Ousemouth where Daddy's office is. He's a chartered accountant.' Eustace brought this out with pride.

'Are you going to be a chartered accountant, too?'

'Yes, if we can afford it, but Baby makes such a difference . . . I may go into a shop . . .'

'Should you like that?'

'Not much, but of course I may have to earn a living for everybody in the end.'

'Helen,' said Miss Fothergill, 'run back, would you mind, and ask the little girl to come with us? I shall be safe, I think, for a moment.'

Miss Grimshaw departed.

'I should like to know your sister,' said Miss Fothergill.

'Yes, you would,' cried Eustace enthusiastically. Since he was in no danger of seeing any more of Miss Fothergill than the back of her hat, his self-confidence had returned to him. He remembered how Mrs Steptoe had described Hilda. 'She's a most unusual girl.'

'In what way? I saw she was very pretty, quite lovely, in fact.'

'Oh, do you think so? I didn't mean that. She doesn't care how she looks. She's so very good—she does everything—she does all the shopping—she's not selfish at all, you know, like me—she doesn't care if people don't like her—she wants to do what she thinks right, and she wants me to do it—she quite prevents me from being spoilt, that's another thing.'

'Does anyone try to spoil you?'

'Well, Minney does and Daddy would, I think, only Aunt Sarah doesn't let him and Hilda helps.'

'Does your mother——?' Miss Fothergill began, and stopped.

'Mother died when Barbara was born. It was a great pity, because only Hilda can really remember her. But we don't speak of her to Hilda because it makes her cry. Oh, here she is!'

Striding along beside Miss Grimshaw, Hilda drew level with the bath-chair.

'Stop a moment, Eustace,' said Miss Fothergill, 'and introduce me to your sister.'

'Oh, I thought you understood, it's Hilda!'

'Good morning, Hilda,' said Miss Fothergill. 'Your brother has been kind enough to take me for a ride.'

Eustace looked at Hilda a little guiltily.

'Good morning,' said Hilda. 'I hope you feel a little better?'

'I'm quite well, thank you.'

Hilda looked faintly disappointed.

'We didn't think you could be very well, that's why I said to Eustace——'

'What did you say to him?'

Hilda reflected. 'I can't remember it all,' she said. 'He didn't want to do something I wanted him to do, so I said he ought to do it.'

There was a rather painful pause. Eustace let go the handle and gazed at Hilda with an expression of agony.

'I see,' said Miss Fothergill. 'And now he's doing what you told him.'

'He was a moment ago,' replied Hilda, strictly truthful.

'I'm enjoying it very much,' said Eustace suddenly. 'Of course, when Hilda told me to, I didn't know you would be so nice.'

'Eustace is always like that,' said Hilda. 'When I tell him to do something, well, like taking the jelly to old Mrs Crabtree, he always makes a fuss but afterwards he enjoys it.'

Eustace, who had a precocious insight into other people's feelings, realised that Hilda was mishandling the situation. 'Oh, but this is quite different,' he cried. 'Mrs Crabtree is very poor and she has a tumour and she's very old and there's a nasty smell in the house and she always says, 'Bless you, if you knew what it was to suffer as I do——" ' Eustace paused.

'Well?' said Miss Fothergill.

'I mean, it's so different here, on the cliffs with the birds and the lighthouse and that hedge which I like very much, and—and you, Miss Fothergill—you don't seem at all ill from where I am, besides you say you're not, and I . . . I like pushing, really I do; I can pretend I am a donkey—and I can't think of anything I'd rather do except perhaps make a pond, or paddle, or go on the pier, or ride on a toboggan —and, of course, those are just pleasures. If you don't mind, let's go on as we were before Hilda interrupted.'

'All right,' said Miss Fothergill, 'only don't go too fast or you'll make me nervous.'

'Of course I won't, Miss Fothergill. I can go slowly just as easily as fast.'

The cavalcade proceeded in silence for a time, at a slow march. Eustace's face betrayed an almost painful concentration. 'Is that the right pace?' he said at last.

'Exactly.'

They passed the Second Shelter, and immediately Eustace felt the atmosphere of the town closing round him. Suddenly Hilda burst out laughing.

'What's the matter?' Eustace asked.

'I was laughing at what you said about pretending to be a donkey,' Hilda remarked. 'He doesn't have to pretend, does he, Miss Fothergill?'

'I'm very fond of donkeys,' said Miss Fothergill. 'They are so patient and hard-working and reliable and independent.'

'I've taught Eustace not to be independent,' said Hilda. 'But he's very fond of carrots. You ought to have some carrots in your hat, Miss Fothergill.' She laughed again.

'Oh no,' said Eustace. 'That would spoil it. I'm so glad I'm at the back here, because I can see the lovely violets. The violets are so pretty in your hat, Miss Fothergill, I like looking at them.'

'Why do all donkeys have a cross on their backs?' asked Hilda.

'Because a donkey carried Jesus,' Miss Fothergill said.

'Wouldn't it be funny if Eustace got one?'

'Minney says my skin is very thin,' said Eustace seriously.

'He oughtn't to say that, ought he, Miss Fothergill? It's tempting Providence,' said Hilda.

'I'm afraid his back may be rather stiff tomorrow after all this hard work.'

'Hard work is good for donkeys,' said Hilda.

Eustace felt hurt and didn't answer. They were approaching the flight of steps that led to the beach. On the downward gradient the bath-chair began to gather way. Eustace checked it in alarm.

'There,' said Miss Fothergill, 'thank you very much for

the ride. But you mustn't let me spoil your morning for you. Isn't it time you went to play on the beach?'

'Eustace doesn't expect to play this morning,' remarked Hilda. 'He played a great deal yesterday on the Downs.'

'Yes, but I count this play,' said Eustace stoutly.

Miss Fothergill smiled. 'I'm not sure that Helen would agree with you.'

'Of course,' Hilda began, 'when you've done a thing a great many times . . . Eustace doesn't like taking Barbara out in the pram.'

'It's because of the responsibility,' said Eustace.

'And don't you feel me a responsibility?'

'Not with Miss Grimshaw there.'

'But supposing Miss Grimshaw didn't happen to be here. Supposing you took me out alone?'

A little frown collected between Miss Grimshaw's thick eyebrows, which Eustace did not fail to notice.

'Oh, I should ask her to join us in about . . . about a quarter of an hour.'

'He's a tactful little boy,' said Miss Grimshaw coldly.

'Yes, I'm afraid so. Now, Eustace, you've been very kind but you mustn't waste your time any longer with an old woman like me. He wants to go and play on the sands, doesn't he, Hilda?'

Hilda looked doubtfully at Eustace.

'Very likely he does want to,' she said, 'but I'm afraid it's too late now.'

'Oh dear, I *have* spoilt your morning,' cried Miss Fothergill in distress.

'Oh no,' said Eustace. 'You hardly made any difference at all. You see, we didn't have time to do anything really, because I got up so late. So this was the best thing we could do. I . . . I'm very glad we met you.'

'So am I. Now let's make a plan. Perhaps you and your sister could come and have tea with me one day?'

The two children stared at each other. Consternation was written large on Eustace's face. Hilda's recorded in turn a number of emotions.

'Perhaps you'd like to talk it over,' suggested Miss Fothergill.

'Oh yes, we should,' said Hilda, gratefully acting upon the proposal at once. 'Do you mind if we go a little way away?' Seizing Eustace's hand she pulled him after her. At a point a few yards distant from the bath-chair they halted.

'I knew she was going to say that,' moaned Eustace.

'You'll enjoy it all right when you get there.'

'I shan't, and you'll hate it, you know you will.'

'I shan't go,' said Hilda. 'I shall be too busy. Besides it's you she wants.'

'But I daren't go alone,' cried Eustace, beginning to tremble. 'I daren't look at her, you know I daren't, only from behind.'

'Don't make a fuss. She'll hear you. You won't have to look at her very much. She'll be pouring out the tea.'

'She can't. Her arm's all stiff and she has hands like a lion.' Eustace's voice rose and tremors started through his body.

'Very well then, I'll tell her you're afraid to go.'

Eustace stiffened. 'Of course I'm not afraid. It's because she's so ugly.'

'If Nancy Steptoe had asked you instead you'd have said, "Thank you very much, I will".'

'Yes, I should,' said Eustace defiantly.

'Then I shall tell Miss Fothergill that.' Hilda was moving away, apparently to execute her threat, when Eustace caught at her arm. 'All right, I'll go. But if I'm sick it'll be your fault. I shall try to be, too.'

'You wicked little boy!' said Hilda, but tolerantly and without conviction. The battle won, she led him back to the bath-chair. 'We've talked it over,' she announced briefly.

'I hope the decision was favourable,' said Miss Fothergill.

'Favourable?' echoed Eustace.

'She means she hopes you'll go,' Hilda explained patiently. 'It was him you wanted, Miss Fothergill, wasn't it? Not me?'

'No, I asked you both to come.'

63

'I expect you felt you had to, but I'm always busy at tea-time and Eustace is sometimes better without me, he's not so shy when he thinks he can do what he likes.'

Miss Fothergill exchanged a glance with her companion. 'Very well, we'll take the responsibility of him. Now what day would suit you, Eustace?'

'Would it have to be this week?' asked Eustace, but Hilda hastily added, 'He can come any day except Tuesday, when he goes to the dancing class.'

'Let's say Wednesday then. That will give me time to have a nice tea ready for you.'

'Thank you very much, Miss Fothergill,' said Eustace wanly.

'No, thank *you* very much for helping me to pass the morning so pleasantly. Now'—for Eustace had sidled up to the bath-chair and was bracing himself to push—'you must run away and have luncheon. I'm sure you must be hungry after all that hard work.'

Flattered in his masculine pride Eustace answered, 'Oh, that was nothing.'

'Yes it was, and we shan't forget it, shall we, Helen?'

Miss Grimshaw nodded a little doubtfully.

'Remember Wednesday. I shall count on you, and if you can persuade Hilda to come too I shall be delighted.'

Miss Fothergill began to withdraw her hand from her muff, perhaps in a gesture of dismissal, perhaps—who knows?—to wave good-bye. Suddenly she changed her mind and the hand returned to its shelter.

'Good-bye,' said the children. They walked a few paces in a sedate and dignified fashion, then broke into a run.

'Wasn't she nice after all?' said Eustace, panting a little.

'I knew you'd say that,' Hilda replied.

CHAPTER VI

The Dancing Class

ALL the same as the week wore on Eustace felt less and less able to face Wednesday's ordeal. The reassurance conveyed by Miss Fothergill's presence ebbed away and only her more alarming characteristics remained. With these Eustace's fertile fancy occupied itself ceaselessly. About her hands the worst was already known, and he could add nothing to it; but the worst was so bad that the thought of it was enough to keep him awake till Hilda came up to bed. In virtue of her years she was given an hour's grace and did not retire till half-past eight. On Monday night, three days after the encounter on the cliff, Eustace prevailed on her to sacrifice her prerogative, and she appeared soon after he had said his prayers. She was not at all angry with him and her presence brought immediate relief. Without too much mental suffering, Eustace was able to make a visual image of himself shaking hands (only the phrase wouldn't fit) with Miss Fothergill. He almost brought himself to believe— what his aunt and Minney with varying degrees of patience continually told him—that Miss Fothergill's hands were not really the hands of a lion, they were just very much swollen by rheumatism—'as yours may be one day', Minney added briskly. But neither of his comforters could say she had ever seen the hands in question, and lacking this confirmation Eustace's mind was never quite at rest.

But it was sufficiently swept and garnished to let in (as is the way of minds) other devils worse than the first. With his fears concentrated on Miss Fothergill's hands, Eustace had not thought of speculating on her face. On Monday night this new bogy appeared, and even Hilda's presence was at first powerless to banish it. Eustace was usually nervous on Monday nights because on the morrow another ordeal lay before him—the dancing class. Now with the frantic ingenuity of the neurasthenic he tried to play off his old fear of the dancing class against the new horror of Miss Fothergill's face. In vain. He pictured himself in the most humiliating and terrifying situations. He saw himself sent by Miss Wauchope, the chief of the three dancing mistresses, alone into the middle of the room and made to go through the steps of the waltz. 'You're the slowest little boy I've ever tried to teach,' she said to him after the third attempt. 'Do it again, please. You know you're keeping the whole class back.' Never a Monday night passed but Eustace was haunted by this imaginary and (since Miss Wauchope was not really an unkind woman) most improbable incident, and nothing pleasant he could think of—ponds, rocks, volcanoes, eagles, Nancy Steptoe herself—would keep it at bay.

Yet this particular Monday he deliberately evoked it, in the hope that its formidable but manageable horror might overcome and drive away the rising terror he was feeling at the thought of Miss Fothergill's face. Perhaps she hadn't even got a face! Perhaps the black veil concealed not the whiskers and snub nose and large but conceivably kindly eyes of a lion, but just emptiness, darkness, shapeless and appalling.

'Hilda,' he whispered, 'are you awake?'

No answer.

I mustn't wake her, Eustace thought. Now supposing Miss Wauchope said, 'Eustace, you've been so very stupid all these months, I'm going to ask your aunt to make you a dunce's cap, and you'll wear it every time you come here, and I shall tell the rest of the class to laugh at you.'

For a moment Eustace's obsession, distracted by this new rival, lifted a little; he felt physically lighter. Then back it came, aggravated by yet another terror.

'Hilda! Hilda!'

She stirred. 'Yes, Eustace?'

'Oh, it wasn't anything very much.'

'Then go to sleep again.'

'I haven't been to sleep. Hilda, supposing Miss Fothergill hasn't got a face she wouldn't have a head, would she?'

'Silly boy, of course she's got a face, you saw it.'

'I thought I saw her eyes. But supposing she hadn't got a head even, how could her neck end?'

Hilda saw what was in Eustace's mind but it did not horrify, it only amused her. She gave one of her loud laughs.

Closing his eyes and summoning up all his will power, Eustace asked the question which had been tormenting him:

'Would it be all bloody?'

Still struggling with her laughter, Hilda managed to say:

'No, you donkey, of course it wouldn't, or she'd be dead.'

Eustace was struck and momentarily convinced by the logic of this. Moreover, Hilda's laughter had shone like a sun in the Chamber of Horrors that was his mind, lighting its darkest corners and showing up its inmates for a sorry array of pasteboard spectres. He turned over and was nearly asleep when the outline of a new phantom darkened the window of his imagination. Restlessly he turned his head this way and that: it would not go. He tried in vain to remember the sound of Hilda's laugh. The spectre drew nearer; soon it would envelop his consciousness.

'Hilda!' he whispered.

A grunt.

'Hilda, please wake up just once more.'

'Well, what is it now?'

'Hilda, do you think Miss Fothergill really is alive? Because if she hadn't got a head, and she wasn't bloody, she'd have to be——' Eustace paused.

'Well?'

'A ghost.'

Hilda sat up in bed. Her patience was at an end.

'Really, Eustace, you are too silly. How could she be a ghost? You can't see ghosts by daylight, for one thing, they always come at night. Anyhow there aren't any. Now if you don't be quiet I won't sleep with you again. I'll make Minney let me sleep with her—so there.'

The threat, uttered with more than Hilda's usual vehemence and decision, succeeded where her reasoning had failed. It restored Eustace to a sense of reality. At once lulled and invigorated by her anger he was soon asleep.

He slept, but the night's experience left its mark on the day that followed, changing the key of his moods, so that familiar objects looked strange. He was uncomfortably aware of a break in the flow of his personality; even the pond, to which (in view of the afternoon at the dancing class) they repaired earlier than usual, did not restore him to himself.

He was most conscious of the dislocation as he stood, among a number of other little boys, in the changing-room at the Town Hall. The act of taking his dancing shoes out of their bag usually let loose in him a set of impressions as invariable as they were acute. His habitual mood was one of fearful joy contending with a ragged cloud of nervous apprehensions, and accompanying this was a train of extremely intense sensations proceeding from well-known sounds and sights and smells. These were all present today: the pungent, somehow nostalgic smell of the scrubbed wooden floor of the changing-room; the uncomforting aspect of the walls panelled with deal boards stained yellow, each with an ugly untidy knot defacing it (Eustace had discovered one that was knotless, and he never failed to look at it with affectionate approval); and through the door, which led into the arena and was always left the same amount ajar, he could hear the shuffling of feet, the hum of voices, and now and then a few bars of a dance tune being tried over on the loud clanging piano.

All these phenomena were present this Tuesday, but somehow they had ceased to operate. Eustace felt his usual self in spite of them. He even started a conversation with another little boy who was changing, a thing that in ordinary circumstances he was far too strung-up to do. It was only when he approached the door and prepared to make his début on the stage that he began to experience the first *frisson* of the Tuesday afternoon transformation. Before him lay the immitigable expanse of polished floor, as hard as the hearts of the dancing mistresses. Beyond stood the wooden chairs, pressed back in serried ranks, apparently only awaiting the word to come back and occupy the space filched from them by the dancing class. And all round, the pupils lining up for their preliminary march past. There was a hot, dry, dusty smell and the tingle of excitement in the air. Avoiding every eye, Eustace crept along the wall to take his place at the tail of the procession. Then he timidly looked round. Yes, there was Hilda, in an attitude at once relaxed and awkward, as though defying her teachers to make a ballroom product of her. Twisted in its plait her dark lovely hair swung out at an ungainly angle; her face expressed boredom and disgust; she looked at her partner (they marched past in twos) as though she hated him. Eustace trembled for her, as he always did when she was engaged in an enterprise where her natural sense of leadership was no help to her. His gaze travelled on, then back. No sign of Nancy Steptoe. She was late! She wasn't coming! The pianist's hands were poised for the first chord when the door opened and Nancy appeared. What a vision in her bright blue dress! She came straight across the room, and late though she was, found time to flash a smile at the assembled youth of polite Anchorstone. How those thirty hearts should have trembled! Certainly Eustace's did.

The afternoon took its usual course. Hilda did her part perfunctorily, the arrogant, if partly assumed, self-sufficiency of her bearing shielding her from rebuke. Eustace, assiduous and anxious to give satisfaction, got the steps fairly correct but missed, and felt he missed, their spirit. He was too intent on getting the details right. His air of nervous and conciliatory concentration would have awakened the bully in the most good-natured of women; little did Eustace realise the bridle Miss Wauchope put on her tongue as she watched his conscientious, clumsy movements. Sometimes, with propitiatory look he caught her eye and she would say, 'That's better, Eustace, but you must listen for the beat,' which pleased his conscience but hurt his pride. He would never be any good at it! Yet as the hand of the plain

municipal clock wormed its way to half-past three, pro-
claiming that there was only half an hour more, Eustace
missed the feeling of elation that should have come at that
significant moment. Where would he be, tomorrow at this
time? On his way to Laburnum Lodge, perhaps standing
on the doorstep, saying good-bye to Minney who had
promised to escort him, though she would not fetch him
back because, she said, 'I don't know how long you'll be.'
How long! All the phantoms of the night before began to
swarm in Eustace's mind. Oblivious of his surroundings he
heard his name called and realized the exercise had stopped.
Ashamed he stepped back into his place.

'Now we're going to have a real waltz,' Miss Wauchope
was saying, 'so that you'll know what you have to do when
you go to a real dance. You, boys, can ask any girl you like
to dance (mind you do it properly) and when the music
stops you must clap to show you want the waltz to go on.'
(All loth, Eustace reminded himself to do this.) 'And the
second time the music stops you must lead your partner to
a chair and talk to her as politely as you can for five minutes.
That's what they do at real balls.'

Eustace looked round him doubtfully. Already some of
the bigger boys had found partners; Eustace watched each
bow and acceptance, and the sheepish look of triumph
which accompanied them filled him with envy and heart-
burning. In a moment the music would begin. Unhappy,
Eustace drifted to where the throng was thickest. A little
swarm of boys were eddying round a central figure. It was
Nancy. With the sensations of some indifferent tennis-
player who in nightmare finds himself on the centre court
at Wimbledon Eustace prepared to steal away; perhaps
Hilda would dance with him, though they never made a
good job of it, and brother and sister were discouraged from
dancing with each other. He could not help turning to see
to whom Nancy would finally accord her favours when,
incredibly, he heard her clear voice saying 'I'm afraid I can't
today, you see I promised this dance to Eustace Cherrington.' Eustace could scarcely believe his ears, but he saw

70

the foiled candidates falling back with glances of envy in his direction, and the next thing he knew he had taken Nancy's hand. They moved into an empty space. 'You never bowed to me, you know,' Nancy said. 'I'm not sure I ought to dance with you.'

'But I was so surprised,' said Eustace. 'I don't remember you saying you'd dance with me. I'm sure I should if you had.'

'Sh!' said Nancy. 'Of course I didn't, only I had to tell them so.'

Eustace gasped. 'But wasn't that——?'

Nancy smiled. 'Well, you see, I wanted to dance with you.'

Eustace had been told that lying was one of the most deadly sins, and he himself was morbidly truthful. Recognition of Nancy's fib struck him like a smack in the face. A halo of darkness surrounded her. His mind, flying to fairy stories, classed her with the bad, with Cinderella's horrible sisters, even with witches. Then as suddenly his mood changed. She had committed this sin, violated her conscience, on his behalf. For him she had made a sacrifice of her peace of mind. It was an heroic act, comparable in its way to Grace Darling's. He could never be worthy of it. The inky halo turned to gold.

The challenge to his moral standards deflected his mind from the business in hand, and to his intense surprise he found he had been dancing for several minutes unconsciously, without thinking of his steps. This had never happened before, it was like a miracle, and, like other miracles, of but brief duration. Directly he remembered his awful responsibility, that he was actually the partner of the belle of the ball, and chosen by her too, his feet began to falter. 'What's the matter?' Nancy asked. 'You were dancing so well a moment ago.'

'I can't really dance as well as that,' Eustace muttered.

'You could if you didn't try so hard,' said Nancy with an insight beyond her years. 'Just keep thinking about the music.'

71

'But I keep thinking about you,' said Eustace.

His intonation was so despairing that Nancy laughed. Delicious wrinkles appeared in the corners of her eyes. 'Oh, Eustace, you say such funny things. But you're dancing much better now. I knew you could.'

To have so signally pleased Nancy had indeed robbed Eustace of his nervousness, and his feet now seemed the most creditable part of him. They had advanced him to glory. Never, even in the most ecstatic moments of the toboggan run, had he felt so completely at harmony with himself, or with the rest of the world: he found himself smiling self-confidently at the other couples as he steered, or fancied he was steering, Nancy through them. But he did not recognise them; he did not even notice Hilda passing by on the arm of a tall youth in spectacles. Only when the music stopped did he realise how giddy he was. 'Turn round the other way,' advised Nancy, with her laugh that made light of things.

'But I want to clap,' cried Eustace, afraid the dance might not continue for lack of his plaudits. But it did; and the sweetness of those last five minutes, made more poignant by his consciousness of their approaching end, left an impression Eustace never forgot.

'Now you've got to talk to me,' said Nancy, when they were seated in two wooden chairs (her choice) somewhat apart from the rest. 'What shall we talk about?'

Eustace felt completely at sea. 'They didn't tell us, did they?' he said at length.

'Oh, Eustace, you're always waiting to be told. I believe you'd like to go and ask Hilda.'

'No, I shouldn't,' said Eustace. 'It wouldn't be one of the things she knows. Would it do if I thanked you very much for that beautiful dance?'

'Well, now you've said that.'

'Oh, but I could say a lot more,' said Eustace. 'For instance you make me dance so well. I didn't think anybody could.' He paused and went on uncertainly: 'That's polite, isn't it?'

72

'Very.'

'I mean it, though. But perhaps that isn't the same as being polite? I could talk easier without being.'

'Eustace, you're always very polite.'

Eustace glowed.

'I thought it meant saying how pretty you were, though I should like to, but you can't talk much about that, can you?'

'It depends if you want to.'

'Yes . . . well . . . should we talk about the beach? You weren't there yesterday.'

'No, I find it gets stale. Yesterday I went out riding.'

'Oh, I hope you didn't fall off?'

'Of course not; I've been told I ride as well as I dance.'

'You must be clever. Can you hunt?'

'There's no hunting round about here. It's such a pity.'

'Yes, it is,' said Eustace fervently. He felt he was being taken into deep waters. 'Though I feel sorry for the fox.'

'You needn't, the fox enjoys it too.'

'Yes, of course, only it would be nice if they could have a hunt without a fox, like hare and hounds.'

'Have you ever been for a paper-chase?' asked Nancy.

'No, I should like to. But what do the hounds do to the hare if they catch him? Do they hurt him?'

Nancy smiled. 'Oh no. Somebody touches him and then he gives himself up and they all go home together . . . Eustace!'

'Yes, Nancy.'

'Would you like to try?'

'What, hare and hounds? Oh, I should.'

'Well, come with us tomorrow. I was going to ask you, only it's not much fun being one of the hounds. But Gerald's got a cold and he can't go.'

'Should I be a hare, then?'

'Yes, one of them.'

'Who's the other?'

'I am.'

'And it's tomorrow afternoon?'

Nancy nodded.

Eustace was silent. His mind was suddenly possessed by a vision of tomorrow afternoon, in all its horror. Tomorrow afternoon meant Miss Fothergill, her gloves, her veil, her . . . His imagination tried not to contemplate it; but like a photographic plate exposed to the sun, it grew every moment darker.

He turned to Nancy, golden, milk-white and rose beside him. 'I'm sorry, Nancy, I can't,' he said at length.

'You mean Hilda wouldn't let you?'

Eustace winced. 'It's not altogether her. You see I said I would go to tea with Miss Fothergill and I don't want to, but I must because I promised.'

'What, that funny old hag who goes about in a bath-chair?'

'Yes,' said Eustace miserably, though his chivalrous instincts perversely rebelled against this slighting description of Miss Fothergill.

'But she's old and ugly, and I suppose you know she's a witch?'

Eustace's face stiffened. He had never thought of this. 'Are you sure?'

'Everyone says so, and it must be true. You know about her hands?' Eustace nodded. 'Well, they're not really hands at all but steel claws and they curve inwards like this, see!' Not without complacency Nancy clenched her pretty little fingers till the blood had almost left them. 'And once they get hold of anything they can't leave go, because you see they're made like that. You'd have to have an operation to get loose.'

Eustace turned pale, but Nancy went on without noticing.

'And she's mad as well. Mummy called on her and she never returned it. That shows, doesn't it? And you've seen that woman who goes about with her—well, she's been put there by the Government, and if she went away (I can't imagine how she sticks it) Miss Fothergill would be shut up in an asylum, and a good thing too. She isn't safe . . .

Oh, Eustace, you can't think how worried you look. I know I wouldn't go if I were you!'

As a result of the waltz and four minutes' polite conversation Eustace had begin to feel quite sick.

'They'll make me go,' he said, trying to control the churning of his stomach by staring hard at the floor in front of him, 'because I promised.'

His tone was pathetic but Nancy preferred to interpret it as priggish.

'If you'd rather be with her than me,' she said tartly, 'you'd better go. She's very rich—I suppose that's why you want to make friends with her.'

'I don't care how rich she is,' Eustace wailed. 'If she was as rich as . . . as the Pope, it wouldn't make any difference.'

'Don't go then.'

'But how can I help it?'

'I've told you. Come with me on the paper-chase.'

Miss Wauchope had risen and was walking into the middle of the room. There was a general scraping of chairs and shuffling of feet. The voices changed their tone, diminished, died away. Nancy got up. Eustace's thoughts began to whirl. 'Don't go,' he whispered.

'Well?'

'But how can I do it?'

'Meet me at the water-tower at half-past two,' Nancy said swiftly. 'We're going to drive to the place.'

'Oh, Nancy, I'll try.'

'Promise?'

'Yes.'

'You must cross your heart and swear.'

'I daren't do that.'

'Well, I shall expect you. If you don't come the whole thing will be spoilt and I'll never speak to you again!'

Quite dazed by the turmoil within him Eustace heard Miss Wauchope's voice: 'Hurry up, you two. You've talked quite long enough.'

CHAPTER VII

Hare and Hounds

EUSTACE was faced with nothing more dreadful than the obligation to choose between a paper-chase and a tea-party, but none the less he went to bed feeling that the morrow would be worse than a crisis; it would be a kind of death. To his imagination, now sickened and inflamed with apprehension, either alternative seemed equally desperate. For the first time in his life he was unable to think of himself as existing the next day. There would be a Eustace, he supposed, but it would be someone else, someone to whom things happened that he, the Eustace of tonight, knew nothing about. Already he felt he had taken leave of the present. For a while he thought it strange that they should all talk to him about ordinary things in their ordinary voices; and once when Minney referred to a new pair of sandshoes he was to have next week he felt a shock of unreality, as though she had suggested taking a train that had long since gone. The sensation was inexpressibly painful, but it passed, leaving him in a numbed state, unable to feel pain or pleasure.

'You're very silent, Eustace,' said his father, who had come back for a late tea. 'What's up with the boy?'

Eustace gave an automatic smile. His quandary had eaten so far into him that it seemed to have passed out of reach of his conscious mind: and the notion of telling anyone about it no longer occurred to him. As well might a person with cancer hope to obtain relief by discussing it with his friends.

This paralysis of the emotions had one beneficial result —it gave Eustace an excellent night, but next day, the dreaded Wednesday, it relaxed its frozen hold, and all the nerves and tentacles of his mind began to stir again, causing him the most exquisite discomfort. Lessons were some help; he could not give his mind to them, but they exacted from him a certain amount of mechanical concentration. At midday he was free. He walked down to the beach without speaking to Hilda; he felt that she was someone else's sister. Meanwhile a dialogue began to take place within him. There was a prosecutor and an apologist, and the subject of their argument was Eustace's case. He listened. The apologist spoke first—indeed, he spoke most of the time.

'Eustace has always been a very good boy. He doesn't steal or tell lies, and he nearly always does what he is told. He is helpful and unselfish. For instance, he took Miss Fothergill for a ride though he didn't want to, and she asked him to tea, so of course he said he would go, though he was rather frightened.' 'He must be a bit of a funk,' said the prosecutor, 'to be afraid of a poor old lady.' 'Oh no, not really. You see she was nearly half a lion, and a witch as well, and mad too, so really it was very brave of him to say he would go. But it kept him awake at night and he didn't complain and bore it like a hero . . .' 'What about his sister?' said the prosecutor. 'Didn't he ask her to come to bed early, because he was frightened? That wasn't very brave.' 'Oh, but she always thinks of what's good for him, so naturally she didn't want him to be frightened. Then he went to the dancing class and danced with a girl called Nancy Steptoe because she asked him to, though she is very pretty and all the boys wanted her to dance with them. And he danced very well and then they talked and she said Miss Fothergill was a witch and not quite all there, and tried to frighten him. And at last she asked him to go with her for a paper-chase instead of having tea with Miss Fothergill. But he said, "No, I have given my promise." He was an extremely brave boy to resist temptation like that. And Nancy said, "Then I shan't speak to you again," and he said "I don't care".'

At this point the prosecutor intervened violently, but Eustace contrived not to hear what he said. He was conscious of a kind of mental scuffle, in the course of which the prosecution seemed to be worsted and beaten off the field, for the apologist took up his tale uninterrupted.

'Of course Eustace could never have broken a promise because it is wrong to, besides Hilda wouldn't like it. Naturally he was sorry to disappoint Nancy, especially as she said she was relying on him and the paper-chase couldn't happen without him. But if he had gone he would have had to deceive Hilda and Minney and everyone, and that would have been very wicked. Eustace may have made mistakes but he has never done anything wrong and doesn't mean to. And now he's not afraid of going to see Miss Fothergill: as he walks to her house with Minney he'll feel very glad he isn't being a hare with Nancy. For one thing he is delicate and it would have been a strain on his heart.

'When he got to Miss Fothergill he told her about Nancy and she said "I'm so glad you came here instead. I like little boys who keep their word and don't tell lies and don't deceive those who love them. If you come a little nearer, Eustace, I'll let you see my hand—no one has ever seen it before—I'm going to show it to you because I like you so much. Don't be frightened . . ." '

The reverie ceased abruptly. Eustace looked round, they had reached the site of the pond. It was a glorious day, though there was a bank of cloud hanging over the Lincolnshire coast.

'A penny for your thoughts,' said Hilda.

'They're too expensive now. Perhaps I'll tell you this afternoon.'

'What time ?'

'When I get back from Miss Fothergill's.'

They began to dig, and the pond slowly filled with water.

'Hilda,' said Eustace, pausing with a spadeful of sand in his hand, 'should you go on loving me if I'd done anything wrong ?'

'It depends what.'

'Supposing I broke a promise ?'

'Perhaps I should, if it was only one.'

Eustace sighed. 'And if I was disobedient ?'

'Oh, you've often been that.'

'Suppose I deceived you?'

'I'm not afraid of that. You couldn't,' said Hilda.

'Supposing I told a lie?'

'After you'd been punished, I suppose I might. It wouldn't be quite the same, of course, afterwards.'

'Supposing I ran away from home,' said Eustace, looking round at the blue sky, 'and came back all in rags and starving, like the Prodigal Son?'

'I should be very angry, of course,' said Hilda, 'and I should feel it was my fault for not watching you. But I should have to forgive you, because it says so in the Bible.'

Eustace drew a long breath.

'But supposing I did all those things at once, would that make you hate me?'

'Oh yes,' Hilda answered without hesitation. 'I should just hand you over to the police.'

Eustace was silent for a time. Some weak places in the bank needed attention. When he had repaired them with more than usual care he said:

'I suppose you couldn't come with me this afternoon to Miss Fothergill?'

Hilda looked surprised. 'Good gracious, no,' she said. 'I thought that was all settled. Minney's going to take you and I'm to stay and look after Baby till she comes back. She won't be long, because Miss Fothergill didn't ask her to stay to tea.'

Almost for the first time in the history of their relationship Eustace felt that Hilda was treating him badly. Angry with her he had often been. But that was mere rebelliousness and irritation, and he had never denied her right of domination. Lacking it he was as helpless as the ivy without its wall. Hilda's ascendency was the keystone in the arch that supported his existence. And the submissiveness that he felt before her he extended, in a lesser degree, to almost everyone he knew; even Nancy and the shadowy Miss Fothergill had a claim on it. At Hilda's peremptory and callous-seeming refusal to accompany him into the lion's den, to which, after all, she had led him, he suddenly felt aggrieved. It did not occur to him that he was being unfair. After her first refusal he hadn't urged her to go; and she might be excused for not taking his night fears very seriously. To be sure he had complained and made a fuss in the family circle, at intervals, ever since the invitation had been given, but this was his habit when made to do something he did not want to do. He had cried 'Wolf !' so often that now, when the beast was really at the door, no one, least of all the unimaginative Hilda, was likely to believe him. Moreover, there was just enough pride and reserve in his nature to make an unconditional appeal to pity unpalatable. He did not hesitate to do so when his nerves alone were affected, as they were the evenings he could not sleep; but when it was a question of an action demanding will-power he tried to face the music. He made a trouble of going to the dentist, but he did not cry when the dentist hurt him.

For the first time, then, he obscurely felt that Hilda was treating him badly. She was a tyrant, and he was justified in resisting her. Nancy was right to taunt him with his dependence on her. His thoughts ran on. He was surrounded by tyrants who thought they had a right to order him about: it was a conspiracy. He could not call his soul his own. In all his actions he was propitiating somebody. This must stop. His lot was not, he saw in a flash of illumination, the common lot of children. Like him they were obedient, perhaps, and punished for disobedience, but obedience had not got into their blood, it was not a habit of mind, it was detachable, like the clothes they put on and off. As far as they could, they did what they liked; they were not haunted, as he was, with the fear of not giving satisfaction to someone else.

It was along some such route as this, if not with the same stopping-places, that Eustace arrived at the conviction that his servitude must be ended and the independence of his personality proclaimed.

'Eustace had never been disobedient before,' ran the self-congratulatory monologue in his mind, 'except once or twice, and now he was only doing what Gerald and Nancy Steptoe have always done. Of course they would be angry with him at home, very angry, and say he had told a story but that wouldn't be true, because he had slipped out of the house without telling anyone. (Eustace's advocate unscrupulously mixed his tenses, choosing whichever seemed the more reassuring.) And it was not true that acting a lie was worse than telling one. Eustace would have liked to tell Minney but knew she would stop him if he did. He was a little frightened as he was running along in front of the houses in case they should see him, but directly he was out of sight in Lexton Road he felt so happy, thinking that Miss Fothergill would be there all alone, with no one to frighten. And Nancy came out from under the water-tower and said, "Eustace, you're a brick, we didn't think you'd dare, we're so grateful to you and it's going to be a lovely day." Then they drove off to the place, and the hounds went to another, and he and Nancy each had a bag full of paper and they ran and ran and ran. Nancy got rather tired and Eustace helped her along and even carried her some of the way. Then when the hounds were close Eustace laid a false trail, and the hounds went after that. But of course Eustace was soon back with Nancy, and after running another hour or two they got home. The hounds didn't come in till much later, they said it wasn't fair having to hunt the two best runners in Anchorstone. And Major Steptoe said, "Yes, they are". And when Eustace got back to Cambo they were all very glad to see him, even Hilda was, and said they didn't know he could have done it, and in future he could do anything he wanted to, as long as it wasn't wicked.'

Here the record, which had been wobbling and scratching for some time past, stopped with a scream of disgust. Nervously Eustace tried another.

'And when Eustace got home they were all very angry, especially Hilda. And they said he must go to bed at once, and Hilda said he oughtn't to be allowed to play on the sands ever again, as a punishment. And Eustace said he didn't care. And when Minney wouldn't come to hear him say his prayers he began to say them to himself. But God said, "I don't want to hear you, Eustace. You've been very wicked. I'm very angry with you. I think I shall strike you dead . . . " '

Hilda turned round to see Eustace leaning on his spade.

'Why, Eustace, you're looking so white. Do you feel sick?'

At the sound of her voice he began to feel better.

'You've been standing in the sun too much,' said Hilda.

'No, it was some thoughts I had.'

'You shouldn't think,' said Hilda, with one of her laughs. 'It's bad for you.'

Eustace tried to smile.

'Minney heard the doctor say my heart wasn't very strong.'

'She shouldn't have told you. But it'll be all right if you don't overtire yourself.'

Eustace relapsed into thought.

'Then the doctor said, "I wouldn't have believed it, Miss Cherrington, the way that boy's heart has improved since he took to going on those runs. He's quite a sturdy little fellow now." "Yes, isn't it wonderful, Doctor Speedwell? We were afraid he might have injured it . . . injured it . . . injured it . . ." (The monologue began to lose its sanguine tone.) "I'm afraid, Miss Cherrington, Eustace *has* injured his heart. It's broken in two places. I'm sorry to have to say it to his aunt, but I'm afraid he may fall down dead at any moment." '

With an effort he shut his thoughts off, for again he was aware of oncoming faintness. But Hilda, occupied at a danger spot in the wall, didn't notice the pallor returning to his face. In a moment he began to feel better; his ebbing consciousness returned to his control. Looking up, he could just see the rounded summit of the water-tower soaring above the roofs of Anchorstone.

Banishing fantasy from his mind he summoned all his will-power.

'I don't care what happens,' he thought, 'I *will* go, and they shan't stop me.'

It was past four o'clock when Hilda got back to Cambo. Miss Cherrington was standing on the door-step.

'Well?' she said anxiously.

'Oh, Aunt Sarah, I went all the way along the beach to Old Anchorstone, and I did what you said, I went as near the cliffs as was safe and I looked everywhere in case—you know—Eustace had fallen over, but there was nothing and I asked everyone I met if they'd seen a little boy in a blue jersey which was what Eustace was wearing at dinner-time. But they hadn't seen him, though some of them knew him quite well.'

'Come in,' said Miss Cherrington, 'it's no use standing out here. I've sent Minney to Miss Fothergill in case Eustace did go there after all. She ought to be back in a few minutes.'

'She won't find him there, Aunt Sarah,' said Hilda, dropping into a plush-covered armchair, a luxury she seldom allowed herself. 'He didn't want to go at all.'

'I know, but he's like that, he often says he won't do a thing and then does it.'

There was a baffled, anxious pause.

'Ah, there's Minney,' said Miss Cherrington, getting up.

Minney bustled in, her habitual cheerfulness of movement belied by the anxiety on her face.

'I see you haven't found him,' she said, 'and I didn't find him either. But that Miss Fothergill she was so kind. She'd got a lovely tea all ready, and water boiling in a silver kettle —you never saw so many silver things in your life as there were in that room. And servants, I don't know how many. I saw three different ones while I was there.'

Hilda remained unmoved by this, but Miss Cherrington raised her head.

'I shouldn't have stayed as long as I did, but she made me have a cup of tea—china tea like hay with no comfort in it —and all the while she kept asking me questions, where we thought Eustace could have gone and so on. She seemed every bit as concerned as we are. And she said, "Do you think he was shy and afraid to come by himself, because he seemed rather a nervous little boy?" and of course when I looked at her I knew what she meant, with those black gloves and that mouth going up at the corner. Eustace takes a lot of notice what people look like, I often tell him we're all the same underneath.'

'He would never have spoken to her if I hadn't made him,' observed Hilda. 'He was in one of his most obstinate moods.'

'I suppose she hadn't any other suggestions to offer?' asked Miss Cherrington.

'No, I told her we were afraid he might have been run over by one of those motor-car things. I saw another yesterday, that makes four in a fortnight. I said he was always walking about like Johnny Head-in-air. She seemed quite upset, as if she was really fond of him.'

'She'd only seen him once,' objected Hilda.

'He's a taking child to those that like him.' Minney took out her handkerchief; the excitement of the recital over, her anxiety was beginning to re-assert itself. 'Oh yes, and she said we were to let her know if she could do anything, like telling the police or the town-crier.'

At these words, with their ominous ring, suggesting that the disappearance of Eustace had passed outside the family circle and become an object of official concern, a silence fell on them all.

'We'd better wait till his father comes in,' said Miss Cherrington at length, 'before we do anything like that.' She looked at the black marble clock. 'He'll be here in half an hour.' She went to the window and drew aside one of the lace curtains. 'But I don't like the look of that cloud. I'll go and see after Baby, Minney. You sit down and have a rest. There's daylight for some hours yet, thank goodness!' The door closed after her.

'Minney,' said Hilda, 'if Eustace has stayed away on purpose, what punishment shall we give him?'

'Don't talk of punishments,' said Minney in a snuffly voice. 'If he was to come in at this moment, I should fall down on my knees in thankfulness.'

Meanwhile Nancy and Eustace were trotting down a green lane, fully four miles away from Cambo. Slung from her shoulder, Nancy carried a bag made of blue linen with a swallow, cut out of paper, appliqué on it. Eustace carried a more manly, and slightly larger, bag, made of canvas, and his emblem of speed was a racehorse. Both bags were three-quarters full of paper. Eustace was just going to pull out a handful when Nancy said, 'Wait a bit. We mustn't make it too easy for them.'

Eustace withdrew his hand at once. 'I thought they mightn't have noticed yours behind that tree.'

'That's their look-out,' said Nancy. 'Don't forget there are ten of them.'

Eustace looked worried. After a minute or two he said: 'Shall I drop some now?'

'Yes, but don't let it show too much.'

Making a slight detour to a gorse bush Eustace scattered a generous contribution to the trail. Nancy watched him. When he rejoined her she said:

'Be careful. We've got to make this last out till we get to Old Anchorstone Church.'

'How far is that now?'

'About two miles if we don't miss the way.'

'But you said you knew it.'

'I'm not sure after we get into the park.'

'Hadn't we better join the road, as you said at first?'

'Well, the road's so dull. It's a short cut through the park, and they wouldn't think of our going that way because it's closed to the public except on Thursdays.'

Eustace remembered it was a Thursday when they drove through on their way from the Downs.

'Shouldn't we be trespassers?' he said.

'I expect so.'

'But mightn't we be prosecuted?'

85

'Oh, come on, Eustace, you said you were going to be different now.'

'Of course. I'm glad you said that. I was brave about coming, wasn't I? I stole out right under their noses.'

'You told us that before.'

'Oh, I'm sorry. Do you think they've missed me by now?'

'I shouldn't wonder.'

'Do you think they'll be worried?'

'It doesn't matter if they are.'

This was a new idea to Eustace. He had always believed that for people to be worried on his account was, next to their being angry, the worst thing that could happen. Cautiously he introduced the new thought into his consciousness and found it took root.

'Perhaps they're looking for me everywhere,' he remarked in a devil-may-care voice which came strangely from his lips.

Nancy stooped down to pick a long grass, which she sucked.

'You bet they are.'

'Isn't it funny,' said Eustace bravely, 'if we got lost they mightn't ever find us. We should be like the Babes in the Wood.'

'Should you mind?'

'Not as long as you were with me.'

'I might run away and leave you.'

A shadow crossed Eustace's face. 'Yes, I should get tired first. You see I ran all the way to the water-tower to begin with.'

'You told us about that.'

'Oh, I'm sorry. Do you think I'm boastful?'

'Not for a boy.'

For some reason the answer pleased Eustace. He mended his pace and caught up with Nancy who had got a little ahead of him. At this point the lane widened out into a glade. Nancy and Eustace continued to follow the cart-tracks. On their left was a belt of trees the shadows of which touched them as they ran and sometimes mingled with their

86

own. On the right the ground fell away and rose again in a rough tangly tract of discoloured grass, planted with tiny fir trees. The contrast between the brilliant green foreground already aglow with evening gold and the incipient fir plantation, shaggy, grey and a little mysterious, delighted Eustace. He had forgotten Cambo and Miss Fothergill; the pleasure of the hour absorbed him. He watched the pattern made by the shadows of the trees, rounded shapes like clouds, that pressed on his path like an advancing army. He found himself thinking it would be unlucky if one of these shadows overtopped his. Twice, when a threatening dome of darkness soared into the green, he ran out towards the sunlight to avoid being engulfed. Nancy watched his manœuvres and laughed. But the third time he tried to outwit Fate he failed. The shadow not only overtook him, it galloped across the glade, swallowing light and colour as it went. The very air seemed darker.

They both stopped and looked at the sky.

Half-way across it stretched an immense cloud, rounded and white at the edges, purple in the middle. The edges were billowing and serene, but in the middle something seemed to be happening; grey smoke-like wisps hurried this way and that, giving the cloud a fearful effect of depth and nearness.

Eustace stared at Nancy without speaking.

'Come on,' she said, 'it may not mean anything. We're close to the entrance to the park. We mustn't wait or they'll catch us.'

'But——' began Eustace.

'Now, don't argue, because we only had twenty minutes' start. Let's give them a bit of trail here, so they can't say we've cheated.'

The 'entrance' to the park was a mere gap in the hedge that bounded the belt of trees. They squeezed through it into the undergrowth, which here was almost as thick as the hedge. Forcing their way through, they came out into a clearing.

'Now we're safe,' said Nancy.

87

A moment later, as though in denial of her words, there came a rumble of thunder, distant but purposeful. Eustace's heart began to beat uncomfortably.

'Shouldn't we be safer on the road than under all these trees ?'

'We can't go back now,' said Nancy, 'or we'd run right into them. Listen! Perhaps you can hear them going by.'

They strained their ears, but there was no sound save the thunder, still far away but almost continuous now.

'I suppose it isn't any use me laying the trail,' said Eustace mournfully, 'since they've lost us.'

'You talk as though you wished they'd caught us,' replied Nancy tartly, divining what was in Eustace's mind. 'Of course we mustn't come in with any paper left: they'd say we hadn't played fair. Look here, this is what I'm going to do.' She began to shake the bits of paper from her bag, while Eustace stared at her in amazement.

'Now,' she said, with her gay, mocking smile, 'you see it's all been used.'

Eustace transferred his gaze to the little heap.

'But how will they find us now ?'

'They won't be able to, you goose.'

A drop of rain fell on Eustace's neck. Unwillingly he began to empty his bag on to Nancy's heap. Reversed, the racehorse waved its limbs wildly. The rain pattered down on the untidy pile of paper, speckling the white with sodden splotches of greenish grey. It was a forlorn spectacle.

'There's almost enough to cover us,' said Eustace tragically. Then stooping down he picked up a handful of the now soppy paper and replaced it in his bag.

'What's that for ?' asked Nancy.

'Well, just in case we *wanted* them to find us.'

Nancy snorted.

'Eustace, you are a cake. When we have tea I'll eat you.'

'What sort of cake should I be ?'

'A Bath bun, I think. Now cheer up. It's only a mile or so to the church, where Mummy and Daddy are waiting for us.'

Eustace's spirits rose.

'It'll be this way,' Nancy added confidently.

There was no path. They set off in a diagonal direction across the clearing, the far side of which was just visible in the now teeming rain. Eustace was soon wet through: where his little toes stretched his sandshoes the water bubbled and oozed. He felt exhilarated; nothing like this had ever happened to him before.

Full of high hopes they reached the farther side. Alas, there was no opening, and the undergrowth was thickly fortified with brambles. 'It must be this way,' said Nancy, plunging forward. A thorn caught her arm, leaving a scarlet trail.

'Oh, Nancy!'

'That's nothing. Come on!' They fought their way through the dripping hostile stalks while overhead and all round lightning flashed and thunder rent the sky. 'It's no good,' said Nancy, 'we must go back and try another place. But that was easier said than done; they had lost their bearings and it took them twice as long to get out as it had to get in. As they stumbled into open space a flash of lightning lit up the whole extent of the clearing. 'I saw a way in there,' cried Nancy, pointing, 'I'm sure I did.' But her words were almost lost in the tearing crash that followed: it was as though the lightning had struck a powder magazine. Surreptitiously, and even in his extremity of alarm hoping that Nancy would not notice, Eustace pulled out a handful of almost liquid paper. Someone might see it. He notice that the racehorse was gone, torn off no doubt by the brambles. A small thing, but it increased his sense of defeat. Ahead of him in the gloom he could see Nancy's white blouse. He wanted to call to her, but the words didn't come. 'Of course I can't run and shout at the same time,' he thought, for his mind had not understood the message that his failing strength kept whispering to it. He stood still, and his tired heart recovered somewhat. 'Nancy,' he called, 'I can't go on.' He could not tell whether she had heard, or see whether she was coming back, for the darkness suddenly turned black, only this time it was not outside him, he felt it rushing up from within.

'It's nine o'clock,' said Miss Cherrington. 'Hilda, you'd better go to bed. You can't do any good by staying up.'

Hilda did not move. Her face, as much of it as was visible, was blotchy with tears, shed and unshed, her long thin hands were pressing her features out of place, piling the flesh up above the cheek bones. Her elbows resting on her knees she looked like a study for the Tragic Muse.

'Daddy said I needn't go till the police come,' she said, almost rudely. 'If I did go to bed I shouldn't sleep. I don't suppose I shall ever sleep again,' she added.

Silence followed this statement. 'All right, Hilda,' said her father at length. 'You mustn't take it to heart so. He'll turn up all right.' He tried to put conviction into his voice.

'He won't, he won't!' cried Hilda, raising her head and staring at the gas mantle, which was mirrored in the pools of her eyes. 'It was all my fault. I could have saved him. I ought not to have let him out of my sight. It was I who saw him last. He was washing his hands in the bathroom. He never does that unless he's told to. I might have known he was up to something.' Her tears started afresh.

'She never leaves the boy alone, does she, Miss Cherrington?' Minney broke out, unable to contain her resentment at Hilda's determination to claim the lion's share both of responsibility and grief. 'I don't say it, mind, but it wouldn't surprise me if that was partly why he slipped out—to be by himself for once, where she couldn't be always bossing him.'

Hilda said nothing, but she turned on Minney a look of hatred that was almost frightening in so young a face. Miss Cherrington took up the cudgels on her behalf.

'You shouldn't say that, Minney, it's cruel. Eustace will never know how much he owes to Hilda.' She paused, not liking the sound of the words. 'I mean he won't till he's older.'

'Oh, stop wrangling,' cried Mr Cherrington. 'Why do

90

you keep on discussing the boy? You've been at it all the evening.' Perhaps ashamed of his outburst, he walked to the window and looked out. 'It's stopped raining, that's one blessing,' he said. 'Hullo, there's someone getting off a bicycle. It's the policeman. I'll go.'

They awaited his return in silence. He came back with a set face.

'There's no news up to now. The bobby said'—his voice faltered—'there are so many little boys in blue jerseys in Anchorstone. But they're going on with the search ... You'd better go to bed now, Hilda.'

Hilda undressed slowly. The sight of Eustace's empty bed affected her so painfully it might have been his coffin. She saw that his nightgown had not been folded properly; it made an unsightly lump in his Eustace-embroidered nightdress case. Taking it out rather gingerly she folded it again; her tears fell on it; she carefully dabbed them up with a handkerchief. Then she changed her mind, took the nightgown once more from its case, and put it in her bed. 'I'll keep it warm for him,' she thought. Her mind, as she lay in bed, kept returning torturingly to the events of the day. She reproached herself for a score of lapses in supervision. She ought, she told herself, to have been more strict with Eustace; she ought to have brought him up in such a way that he simply could not have gone off on his own like that . . . Unless, as Minney had suggested, some gipsy . . . But that was absurd. Fate would have had no power to tamper with a trust that had been properly discharged. 'Perhaps I was careless,' thought Hilda, 'after I had made him promise to go to Miss Fothergill.'

A noise disturbed her meditation. It was like no sound she had ever heard at Cambo at this time of night—but it could be nothing else—a horse and cart stopping outside the house. Now there were voices, muffled at first, then quite loud for an instant, then muffled again. They had passed, whoever they were, through the hall into the drawing-room.

There was no light on the landing. Hilda leaned over the

banisters. They had forgotten to shut the drawing-room door, so she could hear quite well. She recognised Major Steptoe's booming tones. 'He's quite dry now, poor little chap. They lent him some clothes at the Hall. Bit big for him, what? Yes, he looks rather blue about the gills, but he hasn't had a return of that other thing. Nancy said she was properly frightened . . . alone with him over an hour, until young Dick Staveley came along. Wasn't that a bit of luck—or he'd be there now. Oh, we were at the church all the time, getting pretty anxious I can tell you. They sent a message from the Hall, fellow on a bicycle.'

The conversation became general again and Hilda could not follow it. Then she heard Mrs Steptoe say, as though excusing herself, 'You know we did wonder . . . but he said he could run all right. Of course if we'd known . . .' 'Plucky little chap,' from Major Steptoe . . .

Mrs Steptoe went on: 'Yes, he's shivering again. Bed, I quite agree, as soon as possible . . . Tonight? . . . Do you think it necessary? Then may we leave a message with Dr Speedwell on our way home? And, Miss Cherrington' (here she lowered her voice, but Hilda could hear every word), 'he rambled a bit, you know—children often do—and kept on saying you would all be very angry with him, especially his sister. I tried to tell him you wouldn't be—but he's evidently got it on his mind. Nancy?'—in a voice like the lifting of an eyebrow—'Oh, we left her at home, thank you. She went through a pretty bad time, but she'll be all right. Good-night . . . good-night. Don't mention it —we're only too sorry . . . only too glad . . .'

The front door closed on them. 'All very angry with him, especially his sister.'

Hilda crept back to bed. A minute later Minney came in.

'He's found, the lamb,' she said. Hilda was silent, remembering her grievance against Minney. 'Only he's not very well—I've got to sleep with him tonight. You're to sleep in my room.'

Hilda sat up.

'I want to see him,' she said.

'Miss Cherrington says not tonight,' said Minney. 'It might excite him. Tomorrow you shall.'

As she left the room Hilda called over her shoulder: 'You'll find his nightgown in my bed.'

CHAPTER VIII

A Visitor to Tea

AFTER a timeless interval Eustace woke up one morning feeling that something pleasant was going to happen. For a moment he savoured the sensation, too happy to inquire into its cause. Then he turned over in bed and saw through the gloom Nurse Hapgood's face asleep on the pillow. Today she was leaving. That was it.

Eustace could not remember her coming. He gradually became aware of her face hanging over him in a mist, unnaturally large. It was still the largest woman's face he had ever seen, but he had got used to it now as he had got used to his illness. He liked her. She was kind, she increased, she even fostered, his sense of self-importance, and above all she would not let him worry.

'I don't want to hear any more of that conscience-scraping,' she would say when Eustace, after debating with himself for several hours, propounded one of his besetting problems.

'Would his father be ruined by the expense of his illness?' 'No,' said Nurse Hapgood, 'Mr Cherrington was still a long way from ruin. He had told her so.' 'Were they all really very angry with him because of . . . because of everything he had done? They didn't seem so, but he felt they must be.' 'No, they were not angry at all. They were just as fond of him as ever.' 'Was God very angry?' 'Obviously not, or He wouldn't have made Eustace get well so quickly.' 'Why had there been that long time when Hilda didn't come to see him? Wasn't it because she was angry?' 'Of course not, it was because she didn't feel very well after sitting in his room with the bronchitis kettle. Some people were like that.' 'Was his illness a punishment for being selfish and wicked and disobedient?' Nurse Hapgood admitted that he had been very silly, but said that many people were ill through no fault of their own. Many of her patients had been saintly characters. 'Did she think he would die, and if he did, would he have only himself to blame?'

'You think altogether too much about blame,' said Nurse Hapgood. 'But if you die, I shall blame you, I can tell you that.'

Eustace was not aware, of course, that the doctor had enjoined on his relations the necessity of fomenting his self-esteem. 'If he goes on chattering in this strain,' he remarked bluntly in the early stages of Eustace's illness, 'I won't answer for the consequences.'

That was another, perhaps the strongest, reason for keeping Hilda out of the sick room. She had been very much upset, it is true, to see him lying there propped up on pillows breathing hard and speaking with difficulty: she was old enough to realise the meaning of the steaming kettle, the spittoon, the glass of barley water capped with a postcard for a lid, and the array of bottles, particularly that small one which, she knew, contained the drops Eustace might need at any moment.

'It's best to be on the safe side,' the doctor had told Miss Cherrington in Hilda's hearing. 'There's nothing organically wrong with his heart, but it's weak and he's managed to shift it a little.'

The paper-chase did that, thought Hilda, and when she came to see Eustace she couldn't for the life of her help telling him so.

Nurse Hapgood noticed the effect on his spirits which were nearly as low as Hilda's after the interview, and she strongly advised that thereafter brother and sister should for their own sakes be kept apart. This was the less difficult to arrange because since Nurse's advent Hilda had had, for reasons of space, to be boarded out; a room had been found for her above the Post Office and she only came home for meals.

Nurse Hapgood's departure meant Hilda's return; that was why he felt so light-hearted this sunny morning. He knew it was sunny because the strip of light on the ceiling was brilliant, nearly orange-coloured, and it was almost over

95

the door, which meant that he had had a good night, another cause for self-congratulation. The strip of sunlight acted as his clock during the early hours. It also provided him with an absorbing game, which consisted in checking his estimate of the time by the silver watch (a loan from his father, much treasured) under his pillow. It added to the excitement of the game if he could perform this manœuvre without coughing. On waking, the slightest movement started him off, and of course roused Nurse into the bargain. 'A quarter-past seven,' he said to himself, then cautiously felt for the watch. Good guess, it was five minutes past; but all the same he had lost half his bet; there came the familiar tickle stirring at the root of his throat and with a convulsive movement he sat up in bed and abandoned himself to the paroxysm.

Nurse Hapgood opened her eyes. 'Have we begun spring-cleaning already?' she asked in her cheerful voice.

Eustace could not answer till his throat had gone through all those reflex actions by which it rid itself of pain.

'Yes, but it's quite late, really, Nurse. It's past seven. I was only ten minutes out this morning.'

'What a clever boy! Soon you won't need that watch. I shall take it for another little boy I know.'

Eustace remembered, but with less satisfaction than before, that today she was going.

'I wish you hadn't to go,' he said. 'You wouldn't have to if only Daddy would sleep with Aunt Sarah, like I said.'

Nurse Hapgood smiled.

'Brothers and sisters don't sleep together when they get to that age.'

'Oh, why?' said Eustace. 'I shall always want to sleep with Hilda, if she'll let me.'

'Oh no, you won't, you'll see.'

'Do you mean I shan't love her so much?'

'I dare say you will, but things are different when you're grown up.'

'You said Hilda wasn't going to sleep with me when she came back.'

'No, you'll have Miss Minney for a night or two. But you're not going to get rid of me, you know; I shall come back now and then to see you're behaving yourself.'

'Oh, I shall always do that,' said Eustace fervently.

'I wonder . . . Now I'm going to get up, so you must shut your eyes and think about something pleasant.'

Eustace shut his eyes. 'But I've thought of everything I know that's pleasant,' he said, 'several times over.'

'Think about Miss Fothergill. You know she's taken quite a fancy to you. She sent down to ask after you ever so many times.'

'I know I ought to like her, but I don't. She isn't pleasant.'

'Think about the nice boy who helped you when you felt ill in the park.'

'Young Mr Staveley? I thought about him yesterday.'

There was a pause, then Eustace said in the tone of one who re-opens an old controversy: 'Can't I think about Nancy?'

'Oh, I shouldn't bother about her. I don't think she's really a nice girl.'

Eustace sighed. Nurse Hapgood always said that. He decided to think about the Harwich Boat Express—a somewhat threadbare subject of contemplation, but it would soon be time for him to open his eyes.

'You're so well today,' said Minney, bustling in one morning with his breakfast, 'that you're going to be allowed to see a visitor. Guess who it is.'

Eustace searched his mind, but to no purpose.

'Hilda?' he suggested at lenth, with exactly the same sensation he had at lessons when he gave an answer he knew to be wrong.

'Why, you silly boy, she comes every day, besides she's a relation. Relations and visitors are not the same.'

A wild idea struck Eustace.

'Not Nancy?'

Minney pursed her lips. 'No, not Nancy. You don't want

to see her, do you? Mrs Steptoe has been very kind in making inquiries—the least she can do, *I* say.'

By such straws as these Eustace was able to gauge the strength of the tide of family feeling flowing against Nancy.

'No, I don't want to see her,' he said, and regretted the words the moment they were out of his mouth. 'But, of course, if she came,' he added, 'I should have to see her.'

'I don't think she'll come.' Again that significant tone. 'But if Nancy had been different to what she is, it wouldn't have been a bad guess. Now are you any warmer?'

On the contrary Eustace was still more mystified.

'Who was very kind to you one day in the rain?'

Eustace opened his eyes wide.

'You don't mean young Mr Staveley?'

'Yes. But he's not Mr, he's only a boy about fifteen or sixteen, I should say. He was out riding and he called here on his way home. He let Hilda hold his horse.'

'Did he? She didn't tell me.'

'I expect she forgot. But he's a fine-looking young gentleman.'

'I can't remember what he looks like. It's all so muddled. But he must be very strong—he carried me all the way to the Hall, and his gun too—I remember how shiny and wet it looked.'

'Well, he's coming this afternoon to have tea with you.'

'Will Hilda have to hold his horse all the time?'

'Oh, I expect he'll have a groom or something.'

Dick Staveley didn't ride over, he explained to Eustace, he was driven in a dog-cart, and when the coachman had done some errands in the town it was coming back to fetch him.

'I expect he's waiting at the top of your road now,' he said.

The idea that anyone should be kept waiting for him had always distressed Eustace, and after the paper-chase it seemed doubly sinful.

'Perhaps you ought to go, then?' he said with anxious politeness.

'Oh,' said his visitor airily, 'it'll do him no harm to wait.'

Eustace heard this callous utterance with a kind of shocked amazement, not unmingled with admiration. He felt he ought to protest, but the door opened and in came Minney with the tea.

'Oh, let me,' said Dick Staveley, taking the tray from her with a gesture of infinite grace. 'Now I'll put it on this chair and sit on the bed, so that we shall have it between us.'

'I'm afraid there's not much room,' said Minney apologetically, thinking of Anchorstone Hall and its more spacious accommodation.

'I'm very comfortable like this. Now shall I pour out the tea, then you won't have to bother?'

'I never heard of a young gentleman pouring out tea,' said Minney. There was an accent in her voice Eustace had never heard before, nor did he ever hear it again.

'Oh, but we do it at school.' He returned to Minney who was lingering near the door. 'I beg your pardon,' he exclaimed, swung his long legs over the bed and opened the door for her.

'Thank you,' said Minney. She was going to add something, then hesitated and went out.

Dick Staveley resumed his place on the bed.

'Is she an old family retainer?' he asked.

'Retainer?' Eustace was puzzled.

'Here's your tea. I mean, has she been with you a long time?'

'Oh yes, since before I can remember. She was Hilda's nurse and then mine, and now she's Barbara's, the baby, you know.'

'Then Miss Cherrington's a good deal older than you are? Have some bread and butter?'

'Thank you ever so much. You are kind. Oh yes, she's my aunt, you know.'

'I meant your sister.'

'Oh, Hilda!' Eustace had never thought of her as Miss Cherrington: how nice it sounded, how important, somehow. 'Yes, she's nearly four years older than I am.'

'She looks more, if I may say so.'

'That's because she's always had to look after me, you see.'

'Yes. I know you take a lot of looking after.'

Eustace blushed.

'I shan't do that again . . . ever. Oh, and I forgot to say, when you asked me how I was, that we are all so grateful to you for rescuing me.'

'Oh, that was nothing. Your sister thanked me too, as a matter of fact.'

'Wasn't I very heavy?'

Dick Staveley stretched himself. The afternoon sun did not come directly into the room, but was reflected, all tawny, from the wall of the house next door, and it glowed on Dick's face, sparkled in his dark-blue eyes and lit up his crisp, brown hair. His arms fell to his sides as though glad to be re-united to him.

'I didn't mind carrying you,' he said. 'I didn't want to have to carry your friend as well.'

'But Nancy wasn't ill.'

'She made out she was, though.'

Eustace reflected on this. 'They never told me anything,' he said.

'She was yelling like mad,' said Dick Staveley. 'That's how I found you. She'd quite lost her head. I bet your sister wouldn't have done.'

'I'm glad you like Hilda,' said Eustace.

'I've only seen her once. She seemed to like my horse. Do you think she'd care to go for a ride some time?'

'She doesn't know how to,' said Eustace. 'Wouldn't that be rather dangerous?'

'She'd be quite safe with me.'

Eustace looked at him with admiration. 'Yes, I'm sure she would.'

'Here, your cup's empty. Have some more. Let's ask her, shall we?'

'She's out shopping now.'

'When she gets back, then. Are you allowed cake?'

'One little bit.'

The conversation returned, under Eustace's direction, from Hilda to the scene of his arrival at Anchorstone Hall. He learned how Lady Staveley, Dick's mother, had plied him with brandy, and how Sir John Staveley had sent a footman with a message to Major and Mrs Steptoe at the church. How they fitted him out with an old suit of Dick's and how funny he looked in it; how he kept saying that he had killed himself and everyone would be very angry with him. 'I couldn't help laughing, you looked so funny,' Dick concluded. 'But you were in a bad way, you know. You don't look up to much now, but you're a king to what you were then.' He smiled at Eustace a fascinating, disconcerting smile, that began by being intimate and suddenly cooled, as though it was a gift not to be bestowed lightly. Eustace was enchanted. His grip on external reality, never very strong, lost its hold and he felt himself transported into another world, a world in which strange shapes and stranger shadows served as a background for heroic deeds, performed in company with Dick Staveley. The throng of glorious phantoms still pressed around him as he said rather wistfully:

'I don't suppose you ever play on the beach?'

'No, I ride on it sometimes.'

It seemed right to Eustace that so magnificent a being should spurn the humble sands beneath his palfrey's hoofs. 'It belongs to you, doesn't it?' he said.

'The beach? Yes. We are lords of the foreshore.' Dick Staveley laughed. 'The legend says it belongs to us as far as a man can ride into the sea and shoot an arrow.'

Instantly Eustace's imagination pictured Dick Staveley performing this symbolic feat. 'Well,' he said, 'perhaps one day when you are riding by you'll stop and talk to me and Hilda. She could hold your horse and you could . . .' Eustace paused, obscurely conscious of the inadequacy of this invitation, the first he had issued in his life.

'Thanks. Perhaps some day I will but I usually go the other way, you know, to avoid those beastly rocks.'

With a pang that was half pain, half pleasure, Eustace had a vision of his beloved rocks reduced to the meagre rôle of providing obstacles for Dick's horse to stumble over.

'But you must come and see us, you know,' Dick Staveley was saying; 'you and your sister, too, before I go back to Harrow on the twentieth. It's the fifth today, isn't it?'

Eustace shook his head. He knew the hour of the day but not the day of the month.

'And you got ill on the second of August. I remember, because it was the day I took out my new gun for the first time. You've been in bed nearly five weeks. What hopes of your being well enough to come before the twentieth?'

'I'll try to be,' said Eustace fervently.

'I'd better ask your sister myself.' He looked at his watch. 'Hullo! It's just six. I must be off. Perhaps I can speak to Miss Cherrington as I go out?'

'She ought to be home any minute now, Mr Staveley, if you could wait.'

'Call me Dick if you like.'

'Oh, thank you!'

'Well, I'll put this bed straight. I've made it in an awful mess. What a lucky chap you are to have two beds to choose from.'

'The other one's Hilda's, really, Dick,' said Eustace.

'Oh, is it?' The sound of patting and smoothing stopped, and Dick Staveley stared intently at the bed.

'So you have company? Very pleasant, I should think.'

'Oh yes, Dick, I'd much rather have Hilda than Nurse or even Minney.'

'I bet you would. Getting a bit big, isn't she?'

'Oh, but the bed's quite big, Dick,' said Eustace, misunderstanding him. 'Her feet don't touch the bottom, nearly.'

'Where do they come to?' Dick asked.

'Just about where your hand is.'

Dick Staveley stared at the hand, and then at the end of the bed, as if he were making some sort of calculation. Keeping his thumb on the place he spread his fingers out, then moved his thumb to where his little finger had been and repeated the process. Now his little finger touched the wooden rail. Two handbreadths. At this moment the door opened.

'Oh,' cried Hilda, and paused on the threshold apparently about to retreat. 'I came straight in . . . I didn't know . . .'

'That your brother had a visitor? How do you do, Miss Cherrington?' In a flash Dick Staveley had slipped off the bed and was standing with his back to the fireplace, where the bronchitis kettle puffed a little cloud of steam round his well-creased trousers—its dying breath, for it was to be abolished tomorrow. 'Take my place, Miss Cherrington,' Dick was saying. 'Eustace has just told me that it really belongs to you.'

Still breathing fast, her bosom rising and falling, her pigtail hanging down over it, very bedraggled at the end, Hilda looked away from her interlocutor. Eustace was distressed by her manner and still more by her appearance. Then, confused by the heat of the room, the smell of tea and the commanding figure by the fireplace, Hilda sat down on the edge of her bed.

'I thought you would have gone,' she said, without looking at Dick.

Eustace blushed for her; but Dick, in no way put out, said:

'I should, but I waited to see you. Eustace says there is a chance you might come over to Anchorstone one day and go for a ride.'

'Oh, I didn't quite say that,' interpolated Eustace.

'We've got a very quiet horse,' pursued Dick Staveley, not seeming to notice the interruption. 'Just the thing for you.' He looked down at her, nibbling the end of a long forefinger.

'I don't know why Eustace said that,' Hilda observed, continuing to look at her feet. 'He knows I can't ride.'

'But wouldn't you like to try?'

'No, thank you, I shouldn't.'

'But you told me you were fond of horses.'

103

'Just to look at.' Unwillingly Hilda raised her eyes to Dick's face.

'Oh, Hilda,' said Eustace, 'you know you've always wanted to ride. And he said I could come too, didn't you, Dick?'

'By all means if you're well enough. We couldn't leave him at home, could we?' he said to Hilda.

Eustace looked at her imploringly.

'I don't know why you both want me to do something I don't want to do,' said Hilda as ungraciously, it seemed to Eustace, as she could.

'We only thought you might enjoy it, didn't we, Eustace?'

'Then you thought wrong,' said Hilda, but she spoke without conviction. Dick's determination to get his way was so strong that Eustace could almost feel it in the room. Suddenly Hilda's resistance seemed to crumble. For a moment she turned the lovely oval of her face towards Dick Staveley: it wore a puzzled, defenceless look that Eustace had never seen before. 'I'll ask Aunt Sarah,' she said, 'when you've gone.'

'Splendid!' said Dick. Leaving the fireplace he came out into the room like a victorious advancing army. 'Good-bye, Eustace. I'm so glad you're better. But no more paper-chases, mind. And thank you very much for my nice tea.' He turned to Hilda with his hand outstretched.

Looking frightened and hypnotised, she entrusted hers to it.

'So you'll let me know when to expect you, Miss Cherrington. We'll fetch you and bring you back. Don't let it be too long.'

He was gone and romance with him.

'Good riddance!' said Hilda.

'You mustn't say that, when he's been so kind.'

'Oh, I don't know,' said Hilda wearily. 'Look, there's a ladder in my stocking. I only hope he saw it.'

The excitement of the prospective visit to Anchorstone Hall carried Eustace gaily over the next few days. Besides the delicious sensations of convalescence, he now had something definitely to look forward to. The colour returned to his cheeks; he was allowed to get up in his bedroom, next he would be downstairs wrapped in his brown dressing-gown.

Eustace was accustomed to being ill, though not so ill as this: and he dwelt with exquisite, lingering satisfaction on the successive stages of his recovery. He savoured them in prospect even more keenly than in actuality, yet he was loth, too, to let them go, loth to put off the special privileges and immunities of illness and to assume the responsibilities and above all the liability to criticism that went with good health. But now something disturbed, though it by no means destroyed, his ecstatic visions of the immediate future. Always, in the past, they had worked up to one invariable climax: his first visit, with Hilda, to the pond. Dick Staveley's invitation had troubled this image of perfect felicity and constituted itself a substitute, a rival. Like a man in love with two people, Eustace tried to reconcile them, dwelling on each in turn. But it wouldn't do: they injured each other. Eustace could not help remembering how petty and trivial the pond—indeed all the aspects of life on the beach—had seemed when Dick Staveley spoke of riding the other way to avoid those beastly rocks. Eustace's old loyalty was being severely tested, and it did not emerge unscathed from the ordeal. Every time he asked Hilda—and he asked her in season and out of season—whether she had written to Dick to name a day for their visit, the pond, the rocks, the sand, the cliffs seemed to lose their magic. When he invoked them, he had to pretend to himself that Dick had never been to Cambo, trailing alien clouds of glory, otherwise they sulked and would not quicken his imagination.

But on the whole he rather enjoyed the war between the two futures. The announcement that Hilda did not mean to go to Anchorstone Hall came like a bombshell. It was presented to Eustace as a *fait accompli*. She did not tell him till the letter of refusal had been sent. It was in vain for

Eustace to weep and declare with customary exaggeration that now he had nothing to get well for. Hilda had apparently won over both her father and her aunt. She had produced arguments. What was the good of learning to ride when they would never be able to afford a horse of their own? Furthermore, she astonished Eustace by saying that she did not possess the right clothes, an objection that, so far as he remembered, she had never found occasion to put forward before. 'And anyhow I don't want to go,' she had added. Eustace was quite prepared to believe this. What was his surprise, then, to find her, shortly afterwards, in tears, a thing so unusual with her that his own dried at the sight. He besought her to tell him what was the matter, but she answered, between sobs, that she didn't know, but he wasn't to tell anyone.

Comforted himself by the effort to comfort Hilda, Eustace looked about for pleasant thoughts further to allay his disappointment, and soon found one. Why had it not occurred to him before? From being a mere hope it quickly grew into a certainty. Hilda had indeed refused Dick Staveley's invitation, but that was no reason why he, Eustace, shouldn't go to Anchorstone Hall. Dick had asked him first; he only asked Hilda (so Eustace reasoned) as a second thought, and because she happened to be there. When he found she couldn't go, he would naturally ask Eustace to go without her. There were still six days before the fatal twenty-first; Dick would probably not trouble to write, he would just send over a message, as being quicker. To-morrow Eustace was to be allowed out for half an hour in the sun, so there could be no objection to his going to Anchorstone Hall, say, the day after tomorrow. He had become vividly day-conscious . . . How splendid it would be to drive in the dog-cart, with a large and no doubt friendly dog. Eustace had never travelled in any but a hired conveyance, and the prospect of going in a private one intoxicated him. He would find it waiting for him at the top of the road, opposite Boa Vista, perhaps; they would all come to see him start, the groom would help him in, the dog would wag its tail, a flick of the whip and they would be off, Eustace waving his red silk handkerchief. They would drive smartly through the park, which would be quite empty, as the public, poor creatures, were not admitted that day. They would cross the moat, and there at the front door would be Dick and Sir John Staveley and Lady Staveley, and perhaps a lot of servants, and they would run out to welcome him and say how glad they were that he was well again. Then they would have tea and after that . . .

There were a great many versions of what was to happen after tea. Eustace's imagination had never been more fertile than in devising incidents with which to glorify his new friendship. Often Dick rescued him from a violent death, from a mad bull, perhaps, which had long haunted the park and terrorised its owners. Sometimes their respective rôles were reversed and Eustace saved Dick's life. But this would be a less sensational occurrence, and consisted, as often as not, in his nursing Dick through a long illness contracted in Central Africa. Or he would throw himself into the jaws of a lion, thus giving Dick time to free himself and shoot it. Eustace often perished in these encounters and had an affecting death-bed scene, in which Dick acknowledged all he owed him and sometimes asked forgiveness for some long-forgiven injury. But Dick never died; Eustace had not the heart to kill him.

Not all their adventures together, however, entailed death or danger of death. Often they would simply stroll about the park, and Dick would jump a wide chasm, which conveniently opened at their feet, instructing Eustace how to do the same, or shin up a perpendicular tree, supporting Eustace with his left hand. At nightfall they would return scratched and scarred. Lady Staveley (whom Eustace, in spite of dim memories to the contrary, had fashioned in the likeness of Queen Alexandra) would shake his hand affectionately and say, 'I'm very glad Dick has made such a nice friend.' Any version of the visit was incomplete without this parting scene.

The precious days passed but no message came from Anchorstone Hall. Eustace could no longer get his daydreams in focus: their golden glow faded in the grey light of reality. On the seventeenth he wrote a letter.

DEAR DICK,

Thank you very much for asking Hilda to ride. It was a great pity she could not go. It was not my fault as I told her how much she would enjoy it and I should as I am quite well now and alowed to go out. It is a great pitty you have to go to Harrough so soon.

Your sincer friend,

EUSTACE CHERRINGTON

Hope surged up in Eustace's breast after the dispatch of this letter and the daydreams became more frequent and more intoxicating than ever. But when the morning of the twentieth came he was still waiting for an answer.

CHAPTER IX

Laburnum Lodge

Mr Cherrington and his sister were sitting together in the drawing-room, he with his pipe, she with her knitting. Her brows were furrowed and she looked at her brother, who was making no effort to conceal the sense of relaxation he felt after a day's work, with a certain irritation. This care-free humour must not continue.

'I can't think what's come over Eustace,' she said, 'he's been so difficult this last day or two. The fact is, since he got ill, we've all combined to spoil him.'

'Well, we were only acting on the doctor's orders,' replied her brother, placidly puffing at his pipe.

'I know; I always wondered if they were wise. Anyhow we can't go on like this, or the boy will become perfectly impossible.'

'What's he been doing?' Mr Cherrington asked.

'Well, you know how fond he used to be of playing on the sands with Hilda? And it's the best thing in the world for him, especially after an attack like this. Well, today I said he might go down. It's the first time, mind you, since he's been out, and I expected he would be wild with delight.'

'And wasn't he?'

'Far from it. He actually told me he didn't want to go; he said, if you please, he was tired of the beach—tired, when he hasn't been near it for two months. So I took him at his word and made him go for a walk along the cliffs instead. I told him he'd be sorry afterwards, and when he came back to dinner I could see he was.'

'Well, that doesn't sound very serious,' said Eustace's father, smoking comfortably.

'Not to you, perhaps. But listen. On the cliffs they met Miss Fothergill, who was so distressed when Eustace ran away; and all the time he was ill, you remember, she sent to ask how he was getting on and gave him that lovely bunch of grapes.'

'The half-paralysed old lady who goes about in a bath-chair?'

'Yes. Hilda made Eustace stop and speak to her—he didn't even want to do that—and she was so pleased to see him and asked Eustace if he would push her bath-chair for her. He did that once before, perhaps you remember? And Eustace actually said he wouldn't because he wasn't supposed to exert himself since he'd been ill! And whose fault was it that he was ill, I should like to know?'

'His own, of course.'

'I should think so. And then she asked him to go to tea the day after tomorrow, and Hilda couldn't make him say yes, he said he must ask first, though he knew perfectly well we should be delighted for him to go.'

'I suppose he oughtn't to have said that.'

'Of course not, and it's unlike him too; usually he's so docile. He was quite nasty to Hilda about it, she told me afterwards, and she doesn't often complain of him.'

'He doesn't give her much to complain of, as a rule.'

'Oh, doesn't he? You don't know. Well, then he came to me, and said quite defiantly, why was it that Nancy Steptoe had never been to see him, he felt sure we'd kept her away, and it wasn't fair that we should expect him to have tea with Miss Fothergill who was old and ugly and dreadful and a lot more—stories he's picked up somewhere —when we wouldn't let him see Nancy who was all that was perfect—really, if he wasn't such a little boy you might have thought he was in love with her. Thereupon, doctor or no doctor, I told him a little of what we thought about Nancy and the dance she'd led him.'

'No, I don't think she's a good influence for him. But what do you want me to do?'

'I want you to talk to him seriously. There's no need to frighten the child, only it's quite time he realised that all the anxiety and expense we've had from his illness is entirely his fault. It's all owing to his stupid trick of running away that day. We never punished him for it, he was too ill, for one thing, and the doctor said not; but he's well enough to be told now what a trial he has been to us. Unless we do, he'll think he's done something rather fine and his whole character will be ruined, if it isn't already.'

'All right,' said Mr Cherrington. 'Don't get tragic about it. I'll have a word with the boy tomorrow.'

Like many amiable and easy-going people, Mr Cherrington made the business of administering discipline far more painful to the culprit than it need have been. He opened in such a mild and conciliatory manner that a much older boy than Eustace would have had no inkling of what was in his mind. Accordingly Eustace put forward his case, such as it was, quite expecting sympathy. He explained more fully than he had ever done except to Hilda, that he was frightened of Miss Fothergill, and that was partly why he had run away on the day of the paper-chase. But he was too reserved and perhaps too shy to tell his father the true measure of his terror. Again, when asked why he had not been nice to Hilda he tried to make him realise how disappointed he had been when she refused Dick's invitation; and his father listened so attentively that he even began to draw aside the veil from the less extravagant of the Staveley-Anchorstone Hall fantasies. The mistake he made was not to let his confessions go far enough. Mr Cherrington was not a stupid man and had a good deal of the child left in him still; he might have understood, had not Eustace's shyness checked his self-revelation half-way, that the boy lived in his imagination and that the fancied horror of Miss Fothergill's, like the untested delights of Dick Staveley's society, were more real to him than any actual experience, as yet, could be. Instead, he got the impression that Eustace was exaggerating his fancies and trying to substitute them for arguments. He found his son's eloquence unconvincing largely because Eustace was self-conscious and unsure of himself from the effort to make the ruling forces of his inner life plain to the limited capacities of the adult mind. Aware of this, Eustace grew more nervous and would gladly have resumed the natural reticence out of which his father's sympathetic attitude had surprised him.

'You see,' he said, fidgeting in his chair, 'the beach hasn't seemed the same after what Dick said about it, and whenever I remember how we should have been friends only Hilda didn't want to I feel angry with her and don't want to play with her.'

'Your sister can do what she pleases,' said Mr Cherrington. 'It's very sensible of her not to want to break her neck. It's a pity that you didn't feel the same way about the paper-chase.'

Eustace was silent, unhappily conscious of the change in his father's mood. Listening to Eustace's apologia he had adopted the rôle of father-confessor. This is a weakness, he thought. I promised Sarah to give the boy a good talking-to. So, venting on Eustace his irritation with his own inadequacy, he said, with an alarming transition into sternness: 'I don't want to hear any more of your being rude to Hilda, Eustace. She's backed you up through thick and thin. She's been like a mother to you.' He stopped. Resentment at having been betrayed into mentioning his wife in such a trivial connection as this surged up in him. 'You seem to have forgotten,' he said still more angrily, 'all the trouble and anxiety and expense you've given us this summer. Without telling anyone, you deliberately ran away and nearly frightened us all to death.' He paused to make certain that his indignation was still functioning. 'And then on top of it all you must needs fall ill. I don't say you actually meant to, but you were quite old enough to know what might happen if you overtaxed your strength in such a stupid way. You're not a baby now. How old are you?'

'Nearly half-past nine,' sobbed Eustace, in his agitation mistaking years for hours. He had often been asked his age, but never roughly, always in tones of solicitude and affectionate interest.

'At your age——' Mr Cherrington checked himself; he could not remember what he was doing at his son's age;

but Eustace's conscience filled in the blank. 'I was earning a living for my family.' 'Anyhow,' his father went on, 'it was a most stupid trick.' (Eustace couldn't bear the word stupid; he flinched every time it came.) 'I hoped you'd have the sense to see that this illness was in itself a punishment; but it seems you haven't. You need something extra. Well, you'll probably get it. What with the doctor and the nurse and having to take a room for Hilda outside, we've used up our money and may have to leave Cambo; you won't like that, will you?'

Eustace opened wide his tear-filled eyes in horrified surprise; already he saw the dingy side street in Ousemouth and smelt the confined musty smell of the house where they lived at such close quarters round and above his father's office. 'You didn't realise that, did you? You're so cock-a-hoop at getting well, you think nothing else matters; you don't bother about the sacrifices you've inflicted on us all, because you didn't suspect they were going to affect you.'

Mr Cherrington might well have finished here, for though Eustace had stopped crying out of fright, his distress was obvious enough. But he didn't want to leave the job half done and also (to do him justice) he didn't want ever to refer to the matter again. He loathed scenes, or he would no doubt have managed them better. He wanted to resume his old, genial, jocular relationship with Eustace, which he couldn't do, he felt, till he had thoroughly thrashed the matter out. So, like a surgeon performing an abdominal operation, he looked round for something else to straighten out before the wound closed for ever.

'And now I hear,' he said, 'that you actually have the cheek to want to see this Nancy Steptoe again.' (Eustace had been about to explain that he hadn't much wanted to see Nancy until the removal of Dick Staveley from the foreground of his imagination had necessitated the introduction of a substitute that he could feel romantic about.) 'I should have thought your commonsense would have told you better. She's a silly, vain, badly-brought-up little girl, who's done you nothing but harm, and your aunt has forbidden you ever to speak to her again.'

'But what am I to do,' said Eustace in a choking voice, 'if she speaks to me? I'm always seeing her, on the beach, in the street, everywhere. I can't help it.'

'You must raise your hat and walk away,' said Mr Cherrington firmly. 'But she won't speak to you; she knows quite well what we think about her.'

Even in his misery Eustace winced at the grim self-satisfaction in his father's voice.

'And another thing, Eustace—don't cry so, you only make matters worse by behaving like a baby. Sit up, Eustace, and don't look so helpless. Another thing I hear is that you're again making a fuss about going to tea with Miss Fothergill. Now don't let me hear another word of this. She's a very good, kind, nice woman, and she wants to be kind to you, and the least you can do is to go and see her when she asks you. We haven't told her more than we could help about your stupid behaviour over the paper-chase, though I'm surprised she still wants to see you after being let down once so badly. She knows you've been a silly little boy, that's all.'

This seemed such a moderate and generous estimate of his character that Eustace's tears started afresh.

'Now don't cry any more. Let's begin turning over a new leaf from today. Why, Eustace, what's the matter?'

'Oh, Daddy, I do feel so sick.'

Mr Cherrington gave his son a troubled, rueful look. 'Bless the boy! Hold on a second!' He went into the passage, shouting, 'Minney, Minney, I want you—here in the dining-room.'

About four o'clock the next day two figures emerged from the white, wood-slotted gate of Cambo and walked slowly up the hill. Both were obviously wearing their best clothes. Minney's dark-blue coat and skirt were not new for they shone where the light caught them, but they were scrupulously neat and free from creases. Eustace was wearing a fawn-coloured coat with a velvet collar of a darker shade of brown; his head looked small and his face pale under a bulging cloth cap with ribs that converged upon a crowning button. Round his neck, and carefully crossed over his chest, was a red silk scarf. He walked listlessly, lagging half a pace behind his companion, and occasionally running forward to take the arm she generously offered him.

'That's all right,' said Minney. 'But you aren't tired yet, you know.'

'I feel rather tired,' said Eustace, availing himself shamelessly of the support. 'You forget I was sick four times.'

'But that was yesterday,' said Minney, 'you're a different boy today.'

Eustace sighed.

'Yes, I am different. I don't think I shall ever be the same again.'

'What nonsense! There, mind you don't put your new shoes in that puddle. What makes you think you've changed? I don't see any difference. You're the same ugly little boy I've always known.'

'Oh, I dare say I look the same,' said Eustace. 'But I don't feel it. I don't think I love anyone any more.'

'Don't you love me?'

'Yes, but you don't count. I mean,' Eustace added hastily and obscurely, 'it wouldn't matter so much if I didn't love you.'

'Who don't you love, then?'

'Daddy and Aunt Sarah and Hilda.'

'Oh, you soon will.'

'No, I shan't. I didn't ask God to bless them last night.'

'You did, because I heard you.'

'I know, but afterwards, secretly, I asked Him not to.'

'Perhaps He didn't listen when you said that, but it wasn't very kind.'

'Well, they haven't been kind to me. Of course I shall go on being obedient and doing what they tell me. I shan't speak to Nancy. I shan't ever again do anything I really want to do. That's partly why I'm going to Miss Fothergill's now.'

'You told me you weren't really frightened.'

'I was till yesterday. After that it didn't seem to matter.'

'What didn't seem to matter?'

'Whether I was frightened or whether I wasn't. I mean it was so much worse when Daddy said all those things to me.'

'He only said them for your good. You'll thank him one day when everyone tells you how much nicer you are than one or two spoilt little boys I could mention.'

'I shan't thank him,' said Eustace mournfully, 'and if I do it'll only be because he expects me to. I shall always do what other people expect me to. Then they can't be angry.'

'I shall be angry with you if you're not more cheerful,' said Minney briskly. 'Look, here's the water-tower. How many gallons did you say it holds?'

'Two hundred and fifty-six thousand five hundred,' said Eustace in a dull voice.

'Good gracious, what a memory you've got. And how long would it take you to drink it?'

'One million and twenty-six thousand days, if I drank a pint a day,' said Eustace, a shade more interest in his tone.

'You *are* good at mental arithmetic,' said Minney admiringly.

Eustace saw through her efforts to cheer him and the genuine unhappiness he felt beneath his attempts to dramatise it returned and increased.

'I didn't do that in my head,' he confessed. 'Daddy told me. He used to tell me interesting things like that.'

'Well, he will again.'

'No, he won't, he'll be too busy trying to make money because it's cost such a lot me being ill.' Eustace began to weep.

'There, there, it's no use crying over spilt milk. You'll know better another time. Now we're nearly there. That's Miss Fothergill's gate, between those bushes.'

'Yes, I know.'

'Now dry your eyes, you mustn't let her see you've been crying. You'll find she's ever so kind. I expect you'll fall in love with her and forget about us all. Isn't it a beautiful gate?'

Miss Fothergill's gate boasted at least five bars and was made of fumed oak, with studs and other iron embellishments painted blue. Across the topmost bar the words 'Laburnum Lodge' were written in old English characters.

'Are these all laburnums?' asked Eustace, staring respectfully at the thick shrubs.

'No, they're laurels. I expect we shall see some laburnums but they won't be in flower now.'

They passed through the gate and walked on. The house was almost hidden by an immense oval clump of shrubs. 'Those are rhododendrons,' whispered Minney.

'Are they really? Which way do we go now?'

Here the carriage road, deep in yellow gravel, divided and flowed majestically round the soaring rhododendrons.

'The left is quickest. There's the house.'

Built of the tawny local stone, not very high but long and of incalculable depth, Miss Fothergill's mansion might have been designed to strike awe into the beholder. Eustace got an impression of a great many windows. They stopped in front of the porch. It framed a semi-circular arch of dark red brick, surmounted by a lamp of vaguely ecclesiastical design.

'It looks like a church,' whispered Eustace.

'Not when you get inside. There's the bell—isn't it funny, hanging down like that? Don't pull it too hard.'

Eustace was much too confused to have any clear memory of what followed. The interior which was to become so familiar to him left little impression that afternoon beyond the gleam of dark furniture, the shine of white paint, and the inexplicable to-and-fro movement of the maid, taking his cap and coat, and hiding them away. Then she opened a door and they entered a long low room flooded with afternoon sunlight and full of objects, high up and low down, which, from Eustace's angle of vision, looked like the indented skyline of some fabulous city.

Bewildered by the complexity of his sensations, Eustace came to a halt. There was a stirring at the far end of the room, between the window and the fireplace. Threading her way through chairs and stools and tables, Miss Grimshaw bore down upon them. She did not speak but from somewhere behind her came a voice that, like the singing tea-kettle, bubbled a little.

'Well,' it said, 'here comes the hero of the paper-chase. This *is* nice! I'm sorry I can't get up to greet you. Can you find me over here?'

'She said I was a hero,' Eustace found time to whisper to Minney before, joined now by Miss Grimshaw, they approached the tea-table. Miss Fothergill was still hidden behind the silver tea-kettle. What would he see? The hat, the veil, the gloves? Eustace faltered, then, rounding the table-leg, he found himself looking straight at the subject of so many waking nightmares.

It certainly was a shock. Neither the hat nor the veil was there. All the same in that moment Eustace lost his terror of Miss Fothergill, and only once did it return. Before tea was over he could look squarely and without shrinking at her brick-red face, her long nose which was not quite straight, her mouth that went up sideways and had a round hole left in it as though for ventilation, even when her lips were meant to be closed. Most surprising of all, he did not mind her hands, the fingers of which were now visible, peeping out of black mittens curiously humped. That afternoon marked more than one change in Eustace's attitude towards life. Physical ugliness ceased to repel him and conversely physical beauty lost some of its appeal.

'He'd better sit there,' said Miss Fothergill, 'so as to be near the cakes.'

Eustace was too young to notice that, as a result of this arrangement, Miss Fothergill had her back to the light.

'And you sit here, Miss Minney,' she continued. 'You'll stay and have a cup of tea, too?'

'Just one, thank you, but I really ought to be getting on.'

Minney glanced at Eustace, who had already helped himself to a cake. 'I think he can manage by himself.'

'I'm sure he can.'

Eustace's features suggested no denial of this. 'What time shall I come for him?' Minney asked a little wistfully. She noticed how Eustace's small figure was contentedly adapting itself to the lines of his chair. He looked up and said almost airily:

'Oh, Minney, I can find my way all right.'

Slightly wounded, Minney hit back. 'What about that black dog near the post-office?'

Eustace hesitated. 'Helen will see him home if it'll save you,' said Miss Fothergill, 'won't you, Helen?'

Miss Grimshaw indicated assent but no more. 'We'll get him back somehow,' said Miss Fothergill pacifically.

'Then I shan't have to start at any special time, shall I?' observed Eustace, evidently relieved.

'Tonight the hare can rest his weary bones,' said Miss Fothergill with a smile. But Minney looked grave.

'We don't want anything like that to happen again,' she said, as she rose to take her leave. Eustace gave her an abstracted smile, then his eyes slid from her face and wandered round the room, pleased with the bright soft colours, the glint of silver and china, the clusters of small objects.

'I shall be quite safe as long as I'm here,' he said.

CHAPTER X

When Shall I See You Again

IT was another September, but Eustace had not lost his taste for Miss Fothergill's company nor she for his. The room they sat in drew him now as surely as it had once repelled him. He went there not only to meet Miss Fothergill but the self that he liked best.

The curtains had not yet been drawn, but tea was over and instead of the tea-table they had between them a tall round stool, the canvas top of which was worked in a pattern of gay flowers in wool. It made a rather exiguous card-table, but then piquet does not take much space.

'Shall I deal for you?'

'If you don't mind.'

'Is this how Miss Grimshaw does it?' asked Eustace, dealing the cards in alternate twos and threes.

'No, she has another way, but the one I showed you is the right way.'

Eustace looked pleased, then a shadow crossed his face.

'You do still play with her sometimes, don't you?'

'Every now and then, but I think she's glad of a rest.'

'She didn't say so the other evening.'

'What did she say?'

Eustace hesitated. 'Oh, she said she wished those evenings could come back when you and she always played together.'

'Did she? Well, speak up. I expect you're ashamed to declare a point of seven.'

'I threw one away,' admitted Eustace.

'Foolish fellow! You must count the pips up now.'

A complacent smile upon his face Eustace did so.

'Fifty-six.'

'No good. Now you can see what comes of throwing away your opportunities.'

'Well, I had to keep my four kings.'

'Ah! I might have known you had a rod in pickle for me somewhere.'

'Yes, four kings, fourteen, three aces, seventeen, three knaves, twenty.' Eustace hurried over these small additions and tried not to let exultation at the impressive total show in his voice. Then he said diffidently, 'And I've got a carte major too.'

'Well, don't say it as if you were announcing a death. You know you're pleased really.'

'I suppose I am.'

'You certainly ought to be. It's a great mistake not to feel pleased when you have the chance. Remember that, Eustace.'

'Yes, Miss Fothergill.' He groped on the floor and came up with some cards. 'Here's your discard. I haven't looked at it,' he added virtuously.

'No, you're much too good a boy to do that, aren't you?'

Eustace scented criticism in these friendly words.

'Do you think I'm too good?'

'That would be impossible.'

The suggestion of irony in Miss Fothergill's last remark was a little disturbing. When they had reached the end of the partie, which resulted in a heavy victory for Eustace, Miss Fothergill asked for her bag. Eustace found it and undid the clasp. Clearly the action had become second nature to him, for he performed it automatically. But tonight there was a furrow between his brows.

'Is it a great deal?' asked Miss Fothergill. 'Have you ruined me? You look so distressed.'

'It isn't that,' said Eustace uncomfortably.

'You don't mind my being ruined?'

'Of course I should . . . Only they say I oughtn't to play cards for money.'

'Who says so?'

'At home they do.'

'I noticed you hadn't come so often lately. Was that why you didn't come last week and only once the week before?'

Eustace did not answer.

'But there's nothing to object to, surely,' said Miss Fothergill, 'in the arrangement we've made? I should have thought it was ideal. You don't mind having the money, do you?'

'No,' said Eustace, 'I like it very much. Only they say I ought to be too proud to take it.'

'Oh, I think that's a trifle unreasonable.' Miss Fothergill's voice bubbled, as it always did when she was nervous or excited, and the mittened, swollen hand lying in her lap described a fidgety little circle. 'What harm could a penny or two more a week possibly do you?'

'It's the principle of the thing,' said Eustace, evidently quoting something he had heard before on the lips of an indignant grown-up person. 'It might get me into bad ways.'

Miss Fothergill sighed. 'Well, well, let's play for love. But then I shan't be able to claim my side of the stakes. But perhaps they mind that too!'

'They don't, but——'

Eustace turned scarlet.

'But you do?'

Eustace jumped from his chair in an agony of denial. He had got used to the look of physical suffering that often crossed Miss Fothergill's face: it was present even in the photograph she had given him, taken many years ago. But he had never seen the expression of anger and mortification, like a disguise on a disguise, that transformed her features now.

'Of course not!' he cried. 'Of course not! . . . Why,' he said, thinking manlike that a reason would carry more weight than an asseveration, 'I always kissed you, Miss Fothergill, long before we started to play piquet, long before' (he had a happy thought) 'you asked me to, even! Don't you remember,' he said, innocently taking it for granted that of course she must, 'it was under the mistletoe, that day you had the Christmas tree?'

Miss Fothergill's expression relaxed somewhat. 'Yes,' she said, 'I remember perfectly.'

'You didn't think,' said Eustace, subsiding with relief

into his chair, 'that I only kissed you because . . . because . . . it was part of the game?'

'No, of course not,' said Miss Fothergill. She spoke with an exaggerated composure which Eustace slightly resented: it suggested, somehow, that he had been wanting in taste to take up so strongly her challenge about the kisses. 'I thought perhaps piquet was a rather grown-up game for you,' she went on, 'and it might make it more . . . more amusing if we each paid a forfeit when we lost—I sixpence a hundred and you—you——' Here Miss Fothergill's voice, which rarely failed her completely, dissolved into a bubbling.

'A kiss.' Eustace finished her sentence for her. 'It was a very good plan, for me, you know—and it's always worked beautifully.'

Miss Fothergill smiled.

'Till now. I wonder why Helen didn't like it!' she added carelessly. 'Perhaps she told you?'

Eustace stared at Miss Fothergill from under his lashes. He had not, he never would have, told her that it was Miss Grimshaw who had objected to the kisses. She had been helping him on with his coat but really she was only pretending to, for when it was half on she gave him a little shake that startled him very much and whispered so unkindly in his ear: 'They won't catch me kissing you—or giving you half-crowns either.' For days he had been afraid she might do it again. The scene was re-enacted before his eyes while he looked at Miss Fothergill. She seemed amused, not at all angry.

'I didn't *say* it was Miss Grimshaw,' he said at last.

'No, but it was.'

Now, as often in the past, Eustace felt that the effort of finding the right thing to say was more than he could bear. At length he said:

'When you used to play with Miss Grimshaw'—he corrected himself—'when you play with her, do you have the same arrangement?' As Miss Fothergill did not answer, he went on, 'I mean——'

But she interrupted him. 'Yes, I understand what you mean. No, I don't think we did have that arrangement.'

'Well,' said Eustace soothingly, 'I expect she wished you had, and that annoyed her.'

'Oh, she was annoyed?' asked Miss Fothergill, smiling.

'Well, not really,' said Eustace. 'Not like Hilda would have been.'

'It is Hilda I have to thank for your coming here,' said Miss Fothergill, who seemed pleased to change the subject. 'I wish she came oftener herself. She's only been twice.'

'She's not as fond of pleasure as I am,' said Eustace. 'And she doesn't really like beautiful things or being shown pictures or talking about books.'

'Or playing cards?'

'No, she thinks that's waste of time.'

'I hope she doesn't think I am a bad influence for you,' said Miss Fothergill lightly.

'Oh no, she doesn't really think that, nobody does.'

Miss Fothergill considered this remark and said: 'A year ago she seemed so anxious you should come and see me.'

'She was,' said Eustace eagerly, 'but that was because she thought I didn't want to—— No,' he took himself up, horrified even more by the explanations that must follow than by the indiscretion itself. Miss Fothergill's interruption saved him.

'But she is very fond of you, anyone can see that.'

'Oh yes, she is. They all are. But—I don't know how it is —if they see me really happy—for long together, I mean— they don't seem to like it.'

'And you're happy here?' said Miss Fothergill.

'Very,' said Eustace.

There was a long pause. Miss Fothergill stared into the fire, burning brightly in the steel grate that Eustace so much admired. Perhaps she saw a picture there. At last she turned to him.

'You mustn't come so often,' she said, 'if that's the way your father and your aunt feel about it. I shan't be hurt, you understand.'

Eustace's face fell.

'But I wish you had some . . . some other friends. What about the Staveley boy? Do you ever see him now?'

Eustace's face grew even longer.

'He wrote to Hilda at Christmas and asked her again to go riding with him but she wouldn't.'

'I wonder why. But couldn't you go without her?'

'He didn't ask me.'

'Well,' said Miss Fothergill, 'don't let's feel sad about it. Perhaps you'll go to school soon and make a whole lot of new friends.'

'Daddy can't afford to send me to a good school,' Eustace said sorrowfully, 'and Aunt Sarah won't let me go to a bad one.'

'She's quite right,' said Miss Fothergill. 'Perhaps you'll find yourself at a good one one of these days. How old are you?' she asked gently.

'Nearly ten and a half. I'm getting on.'

Since his father's outburst Eustace always felt that he was older than he had a right to be.

Miss Fothergill seemed to make a calculation. Suddenly her face grew extremely sad. A stranger might not have noticed it, so odd was her habitual expression. She began to fumble in her bag.

'You'll take the two shillings this time?' she said, and Eustace expected to see her get the money from her purse; but it was her handkershief she wanted. She blew her nose and then handed Eustace his winnings.

Immediately, though it was not in their contract, he got up and kissed her. There was a salt-tasting tear on her cheek. 'Are you crying?' he asked.

'As you would say, "Not really",' she replied. I ought to be glad, oughtn't I, that I'm going to save so many shillings in future?'

Young as he was Eustace already experienced the awkwardness that falls between people when discharging debts of honour.

'But you'll let me kiss you all the same?' he said. 'Once if I lose, twice if I win.'

Miss Fothergill did not answer for a moment. Then she said, 'When am I going to see you again?'

Eustace suggested the day after tomorrow.

'I'm afraid I've got some people coming then,' Miss Fothergill said. The answer chilled Eustace. She had often, he knew, put off her other friends on his account but she had never put him off on theirs. 'Let's look a little way ahead. What about Friday week?'

Eustace's face fell.

'Will you be busy all that time?'

'No, but I think perhaps you ought to be. You mustn't spend too long playing cards with an old woman.'

'It's what I like doing best,' said Eustace lugubriously.

'Let's say Wednesday then. Now ring the bell three times and someone will come and help you off the premises.'

This little ceremonial at his departure never failed to give Eustace exquisite pleasure. Even to press the electric bell—a luxury unknown at Cambo—was a delight.

'And say to your aunt,' said Miss Fothergill suddenly, 'that we do other things besides play cards. You read poetry to me and play the piano and take me for walks and have been known to write my letters and I—well, I enjoy it all,' she concluded rather lamely.

'You do much more than that,' cried Eustace warmly, 'you—you——' He saw Miss Fothergill looking at him expectantly. His heart was full of the benefits she had conferred on him, but his lips could not find words to name them. All about the room he was conscious of the influences —nourishing, refreshing, intoxicating—she had loosed in his direction. But he did not know in what currency of speech his debt could be acknowledged; and meantime the eager look on Miss Fothergill's face faded and changed to disappointment. 'You have a civilising effect on me,' at last he managed to bring out. 'Daddy said so.'

The situation was saved, for Miss Fothergill looked quite pleased. 'In that case perhaps you could stay a little longer.'

'Ought I to keep Alice waiting?' asked Eustace, with a nervous glance towards the door.

'Run and tell her it was a false alarm.'

Eustace lingered a moment in the hall to apologise to Alice for having given her trouble for nothing. The complaisance with which she accepted his explanations made him stay longer. When he returned to the drawing-room he found Miss Grimshaw there. She was standing with her back to him, talking to Miss Fothergill, and did not turn her head when he came in. There was a moment's silence while he threaded his way through the little tables and came to a halt between the two women. Miss Grimshaw ignored his outstretched hand. She was looking fixedly at Miss Fothergill who said:

'I tell you it's nothing, Helen. I've often been like this before.'

Her mittened hands made a fumbling movement as though to bury themselves in the lace and lilac of her long, loose sleeves. Her bosom rose and fell quickly and her head was pressed against the chair-back. Eustace stared at her, fascinated.

'I shall telephone for the doctor,' Miss Grimshaw said. 'Eustace, you had better run away now.'

Eustace looked from one to the other in doubt. Neither seemed conscious he was there, so lost were they in this new situation which seemed to shut him out. At last Miss Fothergill said, speaking less indistinctly than before:

'Let the boy stay, Helen. He can be with me while you telephone.'

Miss Grimshaw gave her a look which Eustace could not interpret, but he felt included in its resentment.

'Is it fair on the child, Janet?' she said as she turned to go.

How strange! Eustace reflected. He had never heard her call her that before. Why wasn't it fair on him? And did Miss Grimshaw really mind if it wasn't? In the past she had never seemed to take his part; but then why should she since Miss Fothergill always took it? He looked anxiously at the figure in the chair. She had her back to the fading light, and now that he was sitting down himself he could not see her clearly. The little fidgety movements which he knew so well and which her clothes and ornaments seemed to accentuate had ceased. A chill crept into his heart, as though his long friendship with Miss Fothergill had suddenly been annulled and he was alone with the stranger who had frightened him on the cliffs.

'Shall I get the cards again, Miss Fothergill?' he asked. 'Will you have time to play another hand?'

The sound of his voice emboldened him; the sound of hers, changed though it was, brought unspeakable relief.

'No, thank you, Eustace. I'm not sure that we should have time. You'll have to be getting home, won't you, and I——' she paused.

'You are at home,' put in Eustace gently.

'Yes, but I shall have to see this tiresome doctor—Dr Speedwell. I shouldn't say that, he's really a very nice man. He attended you, didn't he?'

Eustace said he had.

'He told me that he liked you very much,' Miss Fothergill went on. 'He said you had a lot in you, and it only needed bringing out. Don't forget that, Eustace, don't forget that.'

Eustace expanded under the compliment, but he couldn't help being surprised at the urgency in Miss Fothergill's voice.

'He only saw me in bed. He couldn't tell much from that, could he?'

'Oh yes, doctors can. He said,' Miss Fothergill continued, speaking a little breathlessly now, 'that you can't please everyone—nobody can—and that if you minded less about disappointing people you wouldn't disappoint them. Do you see what I mean?'

'You mean Hilda and Aunt Sarah and Daddy and Minney and——'

'And me too, if you like. We are all designing women. You mustn't let yourself be sucked in by us.'

'But didn't you say something like that once before?' said Eustace, a suspicion dawning on his mind.

'Perhaps I did . . . I forget . . . but Dr Speedwell said so too. And he said you were right to go on the paper-chase, it did you credit, even if you were ill afterwards. Remember that, Eustace, remember that.'

She stopped speaking and then said in what was meant to be a lighter tone, 'Can you remember anything nice he said about me?'

Eustace searched his mind desperately. Had Dr Speedwell ever mentioned Miss Fothergill, except in a reference to 'the old lady at Laburnum Lodge'? That wouldn't do; he wouldn't like to be known as 'the little boy at Cambo'. But anything else would be a story, a falsehood, a lie. Well, let it be.

'He said that you were a dear old lady and he was very fond of you.'

Miss Fothergill made an impatient movement.

'Oh, Eustace, I'm sure he didn't say that, you invented it. I'm not a dear old lady, and I never want to be called one.'

How swiftly retribution fell! Eustace was silent. When Miss Fothergill spoke again the tartness had gone out of her voice.

'Did he give you any suggestions as to how my character might be improved?'

That was easy.

'No.'

'He's a long time coming,' said Miss Fothergill, suddenly fretful, 'if he's so fond of me. And Helen's a long time at the telephone, too. Is everyone in the house dead? Your eyes are better than mine, Eustace. Is it really as dark as it seems to me? Can you see me? Am I here? Would you say I was really in the room?'

Eustace felt the tension of anxiety under her familiar bantering tone and was frightened.

'Yes, you're still there, Miss Fothergill,' he said as reassuringly as he could. 'It is rather dark, though. Should I——?'

'You might go to the window and see if you can see him

coming. No, no, that's silly . . . Turn on the light, could you? No, no, I don't want that either . . . Perhaps Helen was right. I oughtn't to have let you stay. It was selfish of me. But I was feeling better and there was something I wanted to say to you. I have said it. You do remember?'

'Yes, yes, Miss Fothergill.'

'Eustace!' she cried. The name was always difficult for her to say; the syllables got drowned and twisted by the physical infirmity that distressed her utterance. 'Eustace!' The sound was hardly more articulate than the surge of surf on the rocks.

'Yes, Miss Fothergill.'

'Eustace, will you hold my hand?'

Eustace approached her. For years Miss Fothergill had shaken hands with no one. It was obvious that she couldn't, and she had long since ceased to feel seriously embarrassed when a stranger offered to. She would refuse with a quick, petulant gesture. Indeed, the phrase, 'It was like shaking hands with Miss Fothergill', was commonly used in Anchorstone to describe a fruitless undertaking. To Eustace her hands had come to seem stylised, hardly more real than hands in a picture; he no longer thought of them as flesh and blood. To touch them now seemed an act of unbearable intimacy from which his whole being shrank—not so much in alarm, for his alarm had become too general to find new terrors in an ancient bugbear—as from an obscure feeling that he was breaking the rules, doing something that she herself, were she herself, would never allow. But he could not refuse her appeal, and seating himself on the woolwork stool which served as their card-table he felt for the mittened fingers and took them in his and wondered, for they were very cold. He turned to look into her face, stripped of the restraints she put on it, defenceless now, and as he did so he saw in the twilight the outline of two figures crossing the window. In another moment there were voices in the hall; the door opened, there was a click, and light sprang into the room.

'He was sitting there,' Dr Speedwell said afterwards, 'as

if he was taking her pulse. And he wouldn't move at first. Of course we got him away as quickly as we could. The telephone was out of order and Miss Grimshaw came to fetch me; otherwise I should have been there sooner. Poor little chap—always in trouble of one sort or another!'

CHAPTER XI

Drawing-room and Bath-room

'You may say what you like, Alfred'—Aunt Sarah's voice suggested there was something inherently wrong in saying what one liked—'but I don't think we ought to tell him.'

'Well, if we don't, you may be bound somebody soon will!' Mr Cherrington spoke on a note of excitement which he was evidently doing his best to damp down.

'I doubt if we even ought to accept it.'

'Why ever not, Sarah? And in any case it's not ours to accept or to refuse.'

He rose and stood with his back to the fireplace, taking his glass with him. The newly opened bottle with its attendant siphon stood on that nameless piece of furniture, neither sideboard nor dressing-table but with some of the qualities of each, which gave the drawing-room at Cambo its look of being both unready and unwilling for the uses of everyday life. These emblems of relaxation, together with the fire, surely a luxury in September, which crackled and spluttered as though angry at having been lit, were the only notes that offended against the room's habitual primness. But they were enough to change its aspect; it now assumed, with a very bad grace indeed, the air of giving a party. And this was the more odd because Mr Cherrington and his sister were both in black, and he when he remembered to, and she as of second nature, wore expressions of bereavement.

'Who would have thought the old lady had all that money?' mused Mr Cherrington. 'Eustace didn't tell us much about her, did he?'

'You saw yourself the lovely things she had, the day we went there to tea. Eustace used to talk about them, more than I liked sometimes. You couldn't expect a child of that age to know about money.'

'He will know now.'

Miss Cherrington took up the challenge.

'I don't think it wise that he should. It might distort his whole view of life. No one knows Eustace's good points better than I do, though I hope I don't spoil him; but he is easily led and if he knew he had all that money it would be very bad for him.'

'It isn't such a lot.'

'Isn't it? I call eighteen thousand pounds a great deal.'

'It will only be his when he comes of age, which won't be for ten years and more; and meanwhile the interest is mine, to spend at my discretion on his education.'

Miss Cherrington did not answer at once. She looked round the room, so clean and so uncomfortable, returning its unfriendly stare with another equally unfriendly; she looked at the unjustifiable fire, doggedly achieving combustion; she looked at the glass in her brother's hand. Then she said:

'There's another reason why we shouldn't accept Miss Fothergill's legacy. It might get us into extravagant ways too.'

Mr Cherrington walked across the room and refilled his glass.

'I don't know what you mean, Sarah, but I could do with a bit of extravagance myself, I can tell you.' He looked down at his sister, at the threads of grey contending with the brown, at the uprush of vertical lines that supported others as deeply scored across her brow, at the faded eyes fixed abstractedly on her tired-looking black shoes.

'I'm sure you could, Alfred,' she said, not at all unkindly. 'But think: there would be the income of this eighteen thousand pounds—over seven hundred a year, didn't you say?—much larger than your own, coming in, and you responsible for it to Eustace: what control would you have over him? And what would Hilda's position be, and Barbara's—penniless sisters of a well-to-do young man? I don't say they would feel jealous of him, or he . . . superior to them. I am sure they would all try not to. But nothing creates bad feeling so quickly as when one member of a family gets more than the others. It brings out the worst in everybody. And Miss Fothergill's relations are sure to feel aggrieved. You said yourself that some of them looked angry and disappointed when the will was read.'

'Miss Grimshaw certainly looked pretty sour,' said Mr Cherrington, chuckling reflectively.

'You could hardly expect her not to, could you, after all those years. And I dare say Miss Fothergill was a bit difficult sometimes.'

'I'm sure they fought like cats,' said Mr Cherrington, comfortably sipping.

Miss Cherrington frowned. 'We have no right to say that. People are only too ready to imagine disagreements between close friends. But supposing they didn't always get on, Miss Grimshaw may still have felt, and justly, that a lifetime's devotion deserved rewarding much more than the occasional visits of a little boy who couldn't do anything to help Miss Fothergill and must often have been in the way.'

'Don't forget she was paid for her devotion,' said Mr Cherrington. 'She lived at Miss Fothergill's expense, and in the end she got as much as Eustace did. There were heaps of other legacies too. She must have been worth nearly a hundred thousand.'

'I know, I know, but all the same I don't like the idea of it. What will everyone say? They'll say we put Eustace up to it and told him to work on Miss Fothergill's feelings, knowing she was old and lonely and perhaps not quite responsible after her stroke.'

Mr Cherrington took out a cigar and lit it carefully, if inexpertly, while his sister watched him as if he were a stranger violating the amenities of a non-smoking carriage.

'Well, it would be true in a way, wouldn't it? He didn't want to go—he slipped out on the paper-chase to avoid going—and you made him. I'm very glad you did, as it has turned out. But the boy's own instinct when he saw Miss Fothergill was to run as hard as he could in the opposite direction. He didn't want to make up to her.'

'Other people are not to know that. Of course I never meant Eustace to make a practice of going to see Miss Fothergill. I simply didn't want him to grow up with the idea that people are to be avoided just because they are old and ugly. You know how susceptible he is to pretty things. It sounds silly to say it when he's such a child, but he was half in love with Nancy Steptoe.'

'He's certainly got more out of Miss Fothergill than he was likely to get out of her.'

A look of distaste crossed Miss Cherrington's face.

'I don't like your way of putting things, Alfred. It's almost coarse. But there's something in what you say. The first time Eustace went to see Miss Fothergill he went from a sense of duty. Afterwards he went because he liked going. She made a fuss of him, she gave him an elaborate tea——'

'Well, his manners improved wonderfully under her tuition. He's quite a courtier now.'

'—and she taught him to play cards for money. I didn't like that, and I didn't like him going so often. Naturally Hilda minded it; though she never complained you could see she missed him. As you were saying, he went because he got something out of it. Not only a shilling or two—I didn't really object to that—but—oh, I don't know—a sense of luxury, a feeling that you have only to smile and speak nicely and everything will be made easy for you. Of course he wasn't aware of that; he just knew that tea and cakes were waiting for him at Laburnum Lodge whenever he chose to go: but my fear is, if we accept the money for him, that when he is older he may consciously look for a return for any little kindness that he does—and you wouldn't want him to grow up like that.'

'You mean that virtue should be its own reward?'

'I suppose I do.'

Mr Cherrington stretched himself.

'Well, I'm afraid you'll find that in this case the law takes a different view.'

To the sound of voices in the room above was added the thud of feet and other noises less easy to identify. Volleys of bath-water cascaded past the window, and the smell of cooking, never quite extinct at Cambo, poured through invisible openings and mingled with the perfume of Mr Cherrington's cigar. Supper couldn't be far off, supper under the gas-mantle that still needed changing, cold supper except for the vegetable which was now announcing itself as cabbage. Just time for another glass. It was his fourth, and it brought Mr Cherrington a degree of resolution that neither he nor his sister knew that he possessed. When they rose a few minutes later he had carried the day. Eustace was to have Miss Fothergill's legacy but, in deference to his aunt's wishes, he was not to be told of his inheritance or how it would affect his future.

Meanwhile, upstairs in the bathroom, another conversation was in progress. It was more than a year now since Eustace had been promoted to taking his bath alone. At first he viewed the privilege with dismay, it was fraught with so many dangers. The taps were of a kind that would turn interminably either way without appreciably affecting the flow of water. Even grown-up people, threatened with a scalding or a mortal chill, lost their heads, distrusted the evidence of their senses, and applied to the all-too-responsive taps a frantic system of trial and error. And there were many other things that might go wrong. Eustace no longer feared that he would be washed down the waste-pipe when the plug was pulled out, but he had once put his foot over the hole and the memory of the sudden venomous tug it gave still alarmed him. If his whole leg were sucked in he might be torn in two. The fear that the bath water might overflow, sink into the floor and dissolve it, and let him down into the drawing-room, the accident costing his father several hundred pounds, was too rational to scare Eustace much, though it sometimes occurred to him; but he had conceived another terror more congenial to his temperament. The whitish enamel of the bath was chipped in places, disclosing patches of a livid blue. These spots represented cities destined for inundation. Each had a name, but the name was changed according to Eustace's fancy. Sometimes a single submersion satisfied his lust for destruction, but certain cities seemed almost waterproof and could be washed out time after time without losing their virtue. Those he cared about least came lowest in the bath, and as the upper strata of sacrifice were reached so Eustace's ecstasy mounted. When at last, after much chilly manipulation of the taps, the water rose to Rome, his favourite victim, the spirit of the tidal wave possessed him utterly. But he rarely allowed himself this indulgence, for above Rome, not much above, an inch perhaps, there was another spot, the Death-Spot. If the water so much as licked the Death-Spot Eustace was doomed.

But tonight he was not to be alone. As a special privilege Minney was coming to tell him about the funeral. He had asked her about it the moment she got back, but she was busy and kept putting him off. 'You don't want to hear about funerals,' she said more than once. But Eustace did want to hear, and he obscurely resented the suggestion that he was too young to know about such things. Yet his nerves quailed before the ordeal. A mixed feeling of eagerness and dread possessed him which increased with every moment that Minney did not come.

He had lost count of the days between his last visit to Miss Fothergill and her death. They could not have been many, for he was told that she had never recovered consciousness, a phrase he did not fully understand, though it oppressed his spirits with its heavy importance, its air of finality, the insuperable barrier it placed between his imagination and Miss Fothergill. That warm region of thought, which for the past year she had furnished with objects delightful to contemplate and ideas that were exciting to follow, had seemed a gift for ever. Now she had died and taken it with her. The blinds were down, they said, at Laburnum Lodge, cheerful tradesmen no longer whistled their way to the back door, the postman had cut the house out of his rounds, all signs of life had stopped. Unused, the oak gate dropped still farther on its hinges, soon the catch would be rusted to the socket, and to get in one would have to climb over, but only bold errand boys would dare to do that. 'I shall never go that way again,' thought Eustace. 'I shall keep the other side, the lighthouse side, and the cliffs and the sands. And at least once a week I shall go to Old Anchorstone churchyard and put flowers on her grave.'

That grave was much in his thoughts. He had not seen it, for they had discouraged him from going to the funeral; they had not actually forbidden it, nothing seemed to have been forbidden him since Miss Fothergill's death. This added to his sense of strangeness, as if a familiar landmark, a warning to trespassers, for instance, had been suddenly taken down. She had not died, he was told, while he was with her; he must not worry over it, the hand he had held was not a dead person's hand. For a moment Eustace breathed more freely, though his sense of importance suffered: to have held the hand of a dead person was a unique distinction. No child of his age that she had ever known, Minney told him, had enjoyed such an experience, and Eustace, who already had a passion for records, felt disappointed, when he did not feel relieved, at having missed this one. He would have liked to boast of it a little, even if it was not quite a record, but they did not seem to want to hear him, and Hilda, whom he had obliged to listen, reminded him that he was crying when Alice brought him home.

But all the same she was impressed, he could see that, and she had been very kind to him this afternoon when the house had been emptied of its grown-up occupants and he and she had been left alone to look after Barbara, whose spirits were even higher than usual and who could not understand that this was no time for climbing about on chairs and bursting into peals of insensate laughter. Eustace thought she ought to have worn some sign of mourning, a black bow on her pinafore, perhaps, since her hair was too short to hold one; but this idea was not taken up. He himself had a black tie and a black band sewn on his sleeve. He looked forward to wearing them out of doors. Strangers would ask each other, 'Who is that little boy who seems to have suffered such a terrible loss?' and perhaps stop him and ask him too. And his friends—but then who were his friends? Not Nancy Steptoe, the belle of Anchorstone; painfully, conscientiously law-abiding now, he had not spoken to her since the day of the paper-chase. More than once, when he raised his hat to her, she had looked as though she would like to stop, her eyebrows lifted in a question, her mouth half smiled, but Eustace with averted head had passed on. And now she hardly recognised him, and her friends of whom she was the acknowledged queen, followed suit. Dick Staveley? But since Christmas Dick Staveley had made no sign. Lost in the vast recesses of Anchorstone Hall, moving beneath towering ceilings and among innumerable sofas, he carried on a glorious existence from which, even in imagination, Eustace felt himself shut out. If only Hilda had taken more kindly to his proposal to teach her horsemanship! There she was in her dark blue dress, the nearest thing to black her wardrobe afforded, her long legs making an ungainly V, her drooping head forming with her bent back the question mark that Minney so often deplored, when she might have been with Dick careering over the sands to the sound of thundering hoofs, while Eustace, standing on a rock or other safe eminence, acted as a kind of winning-post. 'Hilda wins by a head!'—but no. In vain to evoke this thrilling picture, in vain to imagine a life of action, of short-breathed emotions among radiant and care-free companions, quickly entered into and as quickly over. Disabled by the cruel reality of the paper-chase, that dream had fluttered with a broken wing; and then Miss Fothergill had almost exorcised it, Miss Fothergill who sweetened life by taking away its rough surfaces and harsh pressures, who collected in her drawing-room, where they could be enjoyed without effort, without competition and without risk, treasures that one side of Eustace's nature prized more dearly than the headier excitements of physical experience. Indeed, she had come to mean to him all those aspirations that overflowed the established affection and routine employments of his life at Cambo; she was the outside world to him and the friends he had in it; his pioneering eye looked no farther than Laburnum Lodge, the magnetic needle of his being fixed itself on Miss Fothergill.

Now, lying in the bath, waiting for Minney, he was aware not only of the pure pain her loss had caused but also of the threatening aspect of the outside world, fuming and coiling above its shattered foundations. And as often happened, his sense of general peril sharpened into a particular dread. 'Supposing I was the City of Rome,' he thought, 'and the tidal wave was really somebody else, perhaps Hilda, then it would kill me and without ever touching the Death-Spot at all.'

He scanned the sides of the bath. Rome was still high and dry; the inundation had only reached Odessa, which had been flooded out many times without giving Eustace any intimate feeling of power. Would it not be better, on this ominous evening, to be on the safe side, and let some of the water out? To do so would be to convict himself of cowardice; it was a course that, if persisted in, Eustace realised, might end in his not being able to have a bath at all; but surely when Fate seemed so active round him, it was allowable to make a small concession, to safeguard his peace of mind? He leaned forward to reach the chain, so intent on outwitting destiny that he did not hear the door open.

'Well!' exclaimed Minney, her businesslike tones heavily charged with apology. 'Am I so late? Have you finished? Were you just going to get out?'

Eustace recoiled from the chain into a supine posture, and to recover his self-possession began to pat the water with his hands.

'No,' he said mournfully, 'I was only going to let some of the water out, that's all.'

'Why, bless the boy,' said Minney, bustling forward, 'you haven't got half enough as it is. Do you want to be left with a high-water mark?' So saying she turned on both the taps; two boisterous undiscriminating torrents poured in, as though eager to wipe out all Eustace's landmarks. She was wearing a white apron over her black dress; it looked like a surplice. Through the steam he could see that her rather sparse honey-coloured hair was pulled back tighter and done more carefully than usual.

'I didn't have time to change,' she said. 'Barbara's been up to all sorts of tricks. She *is* a little monkey.'

Eustace felt too depressed to ask what Barbara had been doing; but he was interested in her state of mind, which already showed signs of independence.

'Did she say she was sorry?' he asked.

'No, you can't make her say she's sorry, you know that quite well. She just laughs, or she screams. Now, where are you dirtiest? Shall I do your face first, and get it over?'

Taking the flannel she leaned forward and screwing her face up bent on Eustace a look of ferocious scrutiny. He saw that her eyes were red.

'Why, you've been crying,' he said.

'Well, can't I cry sometimes?' Minney brushed away a tear as she spoke. 'You often do.'

A note of interrogation hung almost palpably between them.

'Did the funeral make you feel very sad?' asked Eustace.

'Oh well—it did a little, but not much; it was such a lovely day, for one thing. The sun shone all the time.'

Under Minney's vigorous ministrations Eustace was perforce silent. When she had finished wiping his eyes he said:

'I watched you all get into the carriage. Mr Craddock was in black too. And the horse was black. He's called Night-mare. Mr Craddock once told me so.'

'It's a she,' said Minney. 'And she can't help being in black you know. She hasn't anything else to wear. She would be in black for a wedding too.'

Eustace smiled wanly at this pleasantry.

'Did you walk all the way?'

'Oh no. Just up the hill through the town. When we got

to the high road, away from the houses, we began to trot. Now give me your left hand. What *have* you been doing? *You're* in black and no mistake.'

'Did you pass Anchorstone Hall?' asked Eustace.

'No, you ought to remember, you can only drive through the park on Thursdays. We went down the white road, as you used to call it, and one of those nasty motor things came by and smothered us in dust. The road follows the park wall round. Of course you can see the chimneys over the top of the trees—those tall chimneys, they're more like turrets, and you can see a bit of the house from the church door. Now give me your other hand. Oh! What a black-amoor!'

'Was Dick Staveley there?' asked Eustace, passively extending his right hand.

'Just as we drove up he was coming through that old-fashioned stone gateway that leads into the park. So pretty it is, all carved. And there's a pond in front of the church, do you remember that, with trees round one side and ducks swimming about? They sounded so cheerful, all quacking away.'

'Did you talk to Dick?' Eustace asked, trying to make Minney's picture fit in with his very hazy recollections of Old Anchorstone Church.

'Oh no, his mother and father were with him, you see, and a young lady who might have been his sister, and several more, quite a party they were. He bowed to us and took off his top hat. You don't talk to people going into church. We followed them in but they went right up in front, to a pew in the chancel.'

'And when did Miss Fothergill arrive? Or was she there already?'

Minney started.

'Why, what questions you ask. Now bend forward and I'll give your back a scrub. What a good thing you don't use it as much as your hands . . . No, she wasn't there then.'

'Was she in heaven?'

'Yes, I expect so. Only they had to bury her body, you

142

see, and that was outside the church door, in the coffin. They carried it in afterwards, down the aisle with the clergyman walking in front and the choir singing.'

'Was it dark in the church? Were you frightened?'

'Oh no. It's a very light church as churches go, no stained glass in the windows. I wasn't frightened. I've been to so many funerals. Besides, there was nothing to be frightened of . . . Now, let me have that foot. Why, I declare it's shivering. Are you cold? Shall I turn on some more hot water?'

'No, I'm not cold,' said Eustace. 'I was only thinking of her in the coffin. It must have been dark in there, mustn't it? And she couldn't move or get out, like I can here. She never could move very easily, of course. Perhaps it wouldn't be so bad for her. I always used to fetch little things for her, but she called for Miss Grimshaw when she wanted to get up. Was Miss Grimshaw there?'

'Yes, she was sitting in front with the relations, cousins I think they were.'

'I wish I'd been there,' said Eustace, 'I'm sure she wondered why I wasn't. I'm sure she'd rather have had me than Miss Grimshaw. If I had died she wouldn't have been well enough to go to my funeral,' he went on tearfully, 'but I was quite well enough to go to hers.'

'Now, now,' said Minney, scrubbing vigorously. 'Look at that brown spot. It doesn't come out whatever I do. It must be under the skin. We discussed all that. Little boys don't go to funerals. Miss Fothergill wouldn't have wished it. She said to me more than once, "I want him to enjoy himself." If it makes you cry to hear about it, what would you have been like if you'd been there? I've told you,' she added, 'it really wasn't so sad. She was an old lady, and ill, and she suffered a great deal, and I dare say she wasn't sorry to go.'

'Would it have been sadder if I'd died instead?' asked Eustace.

'Well, some people might think so, but I should say good riddance to bad rubbish. Anyhow you're not dead yet, not by any means. The other leg now, unless you've lost it!'

'What was the grave like?' asked Eustace. 'Was it a very deep hole like a well in the middle of the church? Could you see to the bottom?'

'She wasn't buried in the church,' Minney told him. 'She was buried outside in the churchyard, in the sunshine. There was a wind blowing, and the men had to hold on to their hats. Dick Staveley's came off, and he looked so funny running after it and trying to look dignified at the same time. Your Aunt Sarah looked very nice. I always say, the plainer the clothes she wears the better they suit her. And your Daddy looked such a gentleman. It's funny how a man always seems to look younger in a top hat. We'll have you wearing one, one of these days.'

'Should I look younger?' asked Eustace.

'You might, you look so old and ugly now.'

'I'm sure you looked very nice too,' said Eustace, momentarily hypnotised by Minney into seeing Miss Fothergill's interment as a kind of fashion parade.

'Oh, I don't care what I look like as long as I look neat. I do hate to look untidy. Especially,' added Minney incautiously, 'at a funeral. Stand up now,' she went on hastily, 'and I'll finish you off.'

Eustace obediently stood up. Minney had told him a great deal, but he felt that there was still something he wanted to ask her, some question which she had perhaps deliberately evaded. He did not know what it was, but as the ritual of the bath drew to an end the unspoken, un-formulated inquiry pressed at the back of his mind demanding utterance. He felt that if he failed to include it in his interrogation of Minney something would go terribly wrong; not only would this interview, which could never be repeated, be wasted, but the whole of his relationship with Miss Fothergill would be stultified and meaningless. A door would close on his memories of her to which he would never find the key.

It was some feeling that he wanted, a feeling that he

144

would have had if he had been present at the funeral, a feeling of which Minney, with her intuitive understanding of the paths of least resistance in his mind, was wilfully defrauding him. He felt sure she would supply the answer, release the sensation that his heart was groping for, if only he could surprise her into telling him. It must be something worthy of his friendship with Miss Fothergill, something that would recapture and retain for ever a fragment of the substance of his experience with her, since their original meeting near the Second Shelter. The minutes were passing and he would miss it, he would miss it.

'Was that all?' he asked lamely. 'Did you come away then?'

Minney felt, perhaps justifiably, that she had done very well. She had kept Eustace interested, as she could tell by the fact that he had stopped shivering, and by many other signs. She had made the funeral seem like an ordinary afternoon's outing, almost a picnic. She had soothed and calmed herself. If she was jealous of Eustace's affection for Miss Fothergill she was unconscious of being so, for she was a generous-minded woman; but she thought, as Miss Cherrington did, that it was looming too large in his life, and that it was an obstruction to the normal development of his nature.

In this perhaps she was right. The pressure, personal and moral, that Hilda had brought to bear on Eustace had deflected the current of his being. His spirit had been exhausted, not so much by his encounter with Miss Fothergill as by the act of rebellion with which he had tried to avoid it. The consequences of the paper-chase, that seeming judgement from Heaven, lay heavy on his health but still more heavily on his spirit, warning it off the paths of adventure it was just beginning to tread. Though disabled it was by no means broken; it had sought and found fulfilment in the charmed shelter of Laburnum Lodge. But at a sacrifice—if it be a sacrifice to escape from the muddy, turbulent main stream into an enchanted backwater. In an indoor atmosphere, prepared by affection and policed by money, youth's natural dislike of what is ugly and crippled and static had dropped away from Eustace. To find his most intimate satisfaction in giving satisfaction, to be pleased by pleasing, this was the lesson that Miss Fothergill had taught him. She did not mean to. She had tried not to. No woman, certainly no young woman, wishes a man she loves to be deficient in desire and indifferent to the call of experience. She is jealous of his emotional security even if it rests in her. That was why the female element in Cambo, directed by Hilda, had forced on Eustace the revolutionary step, the complete change of barometric pressure, that his commerce with Miss Fothergill involved. And that was why, when he began to thrive in the new climate, they instinctively felt he had vegetated enough. Minney, who was not the least fervent of his well-wishers, shared their view.

She heard his voice, more insistent now, repeating the question:

'Was that all, Minney? Did you go away after that?'

'Now let me see. Where was I? . . . Oh yes!' Minney thought she saw her way clear. 'Well, it wasn't quite over. You see, they had to bring the coffin out of church, and they carried it to the grave-side, and put it down with all the flowers, the wreaths and the crosses beside it——'

'Did you see my flowers?' Eustace asked.

Minney said she had. 'And then, of course, we all stood round without moving, the gentlemen bare-headed. Miss Cherrington and your father and I, we stood a little way back, because, of course, we weren't great friends of Miss Fothergill's, only acquaintances, through you really, and we didn't want to seem to push ourselves forward, since Miss Fothergill's friends and relations aren't anything to us, of course, and I doubt if we shall ever see or hear of them again. Now just slide down under the water, Eustace, and wash off all that soap, and then I'll give you a good rub with this hot towel here.'

Carefully, gingerly, unconsciously observing the economy of movement demanded by the peril of the Death-Spot,

Eustace allowed himself to be submerged; but his mind still cried out for the appeasement, the signal of dismissal, the final stab of intense feeling, without which the past year and all it meant to him would be like a victory without banners, a campaign without a history, a race without a prize.

'Tell me a little more,' he begged.

'There's nothing more to tell,' said Minney, relief brightening her voice. 'The clergyman went to the grave-side while the coffin was being let down, and said something over it.'

'What did he say?'

Minney hesitated. There was a passage in the Burial Service which she knew by heart: and it came at the exact moment that Eustace was asking about. She could not hear it without crying, and even the recollection of it pinched her throat and pricked the back of her eyes with tears. The emotion was her tribute to mortality everywhere, not especially to Miss Fothergill; but she didn't want to let Eustace see it, and she said:

'Oh, it's something they always say at funerals. They say it for everyone, you know, not just for Miss Fothergill. You wouldn't understand it if I told you.'

But while she was speaking an echo of the sentences made itself heard in her mind and altered the expression of her face. Eustace noticed the involuntary quivering of her lips and was immediately aware of an inner tingling, as though part of him that had gone to sleep was coming to life.

'Please tell me, Minney,' he said, 'it won't matter if I don't understand.'

His head pillowed on the dingy enamel he looked up at her, at her kind plain face which, under the stress of indecision, had become remote and impersonal and stern. 'Perhaps I can manage it,' she thought, and she opened her lips, but the tremor round her mouth and the ache in her throat warned her to stop. She drew a long breath and looked down at Eustace. His eyes were fixed on her in a look of entreaty, something shone in them that she had not seen

147

before and that at once kindled in her an answering flame and an overwhelming impulse to tell him what he wanted to know. She felt she owed it to him. Yet still she hesitated, by training, by second nature, unwilling to recognise his status as a human being, his right to suffer as grown-up people suffered. Yet why not? He would have to learn some time, why not now while there was still in sorrow the balm and healing which he unconsciously desired?

Minney's face assumed a solemn, set expression as though carved in wood, and in a voice unlike her own, but not unlike a clergyman's, she began to speak, looking across Eustace at an imaginary congregation beyond the bathroom wall.

' "I heard a voice from heaven saying unto me, Write, from henceforth blessed are the dead that die in the Lord . . ." '

Suddenly the wooden mask crumpled; her voice choked and she could not go on. Tears ran down her face and dropped with heavy splashes into the bath. Eustace gazed at her in bewilderment; he had never seen her or any grown-up person lose control before. Then, feeling in himself the effect that the words had had on her, and moved by the sight of her distress, he too began to cry. The sound of sobbing filled the room and mingled with the chuckling and gurgling of the hot-water tank. With a blind plunging movement Minney turned away and wiped her eyes on a corner of Eustace's towel. Meanwhile he, possessed by unrecognisable emotions and fearful of losing them, cried with unconscious cruelty:

'What else did he say, Minney? What else did he say?'

The habit of authority, which would have bidden her tell Eustace, 'Now, now, that's enough,' had forsaken Minney. She returned to the barrier of the bath, composed her face as well as she could, and forgetting where she had left off, began again:

' "I heard a voice from heaven saying unto me, Write, from henceforth blessed are the dead that die in the Lord; even so, saith the Spirit; for they rest from their labours." '

Eustace was transported by the beauty of the words. They glowed in his mind until, perhaps from some association with his present position, they turned into a golden sea, upon the sunshine-glinting ripples of which he and Miss Fothergill, reunited and at rest from their labours, floated for ever in the fellowship of the blessed. He had never felt so near to her as he did now. Perhaps he was no longer alive; perhaps what he once dreaded had come to pass, and he had been drowned in the bath without noticing it. If so, death was indeed a blessed thing, buoyant, warm, sunshiny, infinitely desirable.

Withdrawn in ecstatic contemplation, Eustace failed to see that on Minney the words of promise had had a very different effect. She was weeping more bitterly than before. In an effort to hide her emotion she had stooped down to pick up his dressing gown, which was lying on the floor. But her sobs betrayed her, and Eustace, hearing them and missing the much-loved face which had been the day-spring of his celestial imaginings, returned to reality with a painful jolt. Intent on comforting her he hastily pulled himself out of the bath, tidal waves of unexampled grandeur swept round it, and one slapping billow, not content with inundating Rome, climbed and climbed towards the Death-Spot . . .

So much he saw from the tail of his eye as he ran to Minney. 'No, no,' she said, forestalling with the bath-towel his proffered embrace. 'You mustn't kiss me. Look how wet you are. You're making a pool, and if you go on crying' (Eustace was now mingling his tears with hers) 'it'll grow into an ocean. There, there, I'll dry your eyes and you can dry mine.' Having rendered each other this service they smiled, and both were surprised, for it seemed as though they had been a long time without smiling. 'How tall you are,' said Minney. 'Why, you'll soon be right up to my shoulder. I should like to see you a little fatter though!' The clanging of a bell, rhythmical, irritable and insistent, interrupted her. 'You will be late for supper,' said Eustace, alarmed.

'Only a little,' said Minney. 'I can still hear them talking. Listen!'

The sound of two voices, each burrowing a separate track into the silence, came up from the room below.

'Do you think they're talking about the funeral?' asked Eustace.

'Oh, we're going to forget all about that; that's over and done with. Poor Miss Fothergill! Was there anything else you wanted to ask me?'

'Nothing else, Minney, thank you very much. Nothing else.'

CHAPTER XII

The West Window

THE succeeding days passed slowly for Eustace. He was aware of an emptiness in his life and he did not know how to fill it. Nothing beckoned from outside; social adventures he had none; since his illness any extra exertion, even the questionable pleasure of the dancing-class, had been ruled out. But rather to his surprise and Hilda's there had been several drives in the landau lately, drives which had taken the best part of the day and almost transformed Mr Craddock from an Olympian deity into a familiar friend. No longer did he insist on their joining him in the street by Boa Vista; he had mysteriously discovered that the rough, rutted track to Cambo was practicable after all, and now they had the satisfaction of seeing the carriage standing outside their door. In their excursions they had even gone as far as Spentlove-le-Dale, where the almshouses were, an expedition that needed two horses and had been undertaken by Mr Craddock only once before that year. On the way they passed a water-fall, foaming over a rock in a coppice with an effect of irresistible power and energy which delighted Eustace, and which in old days would have taken a high place among his mental mascots. But now his imagination seemed to have lost its symbolising faculty, and nothing that he saw took root and flowered in his mind. A kind of melancholy settled over it, an apathy of the spirit, a clear transparent dusk like twilight, in which everything seemed the same colour and had the same importance. It was as though the black band and the black tie had imparted their sombre hue to the very air around him.

Today they were bound for Frontisham, an unambitious goal, but it meant they would skirt the edge of the little moor where the heather and the bog-cotton and the sundew grew—a perilous place, almost a marsh, dotted with pools of dark or reddish water in which one might easily be engulfed. Eustace liked to imagine himself springing from tuft to tuft with the lightness of an ibex. And at the end of the journey was a sight he always looked forward to: the west window of Frontisham Church.

Mr Cherrington was wearing a new suit, an oatmeal-coloured tweed, and a pair of brown boots; he looked gay and dashing.

'Now you must pinch me,' he said to Eustace, who obeyed with docility but without enthusiasm. 'Harder than that,' he ordered, with the playfulness in his voice that Eustace loved and dreaded, for it might so quickly turn to irritation. 'You'll have to eat some more pudding.'

'Doesn't it hurt?' asked Eustace anxiously, his fingers embedded in his father's sleeve.

'Can't feel it,' said Mr Cherrington; 'it's just like the peck of a little bird. There, that's better. Now jump in and make yourself comfortable.'

Eustace looked round at the little group standing between the freshly painted white gate with 'Cambo' staring from it and the waiting landau. There was Hilda in her navy-blue dress and black stockings, a rusty sheen on both; Minney with Barbara in her arms; his aunt heavily veiled and hatted, her purplish skirt slightly stained with chalk dust where it swept the ground. Something in her bearing, for he could not see her face, implied dissent. Eustace hesitated.

'Oh, I forgot,' said Mr Cherrington jocularly, 'ladies first. Perhaps you'd like to ride on the box, Eustace.'

Eustace glanced at Hilda.

'Mr Craddock always lets her drive down Frontisham Hill.'

'And you don't want to?'

'Not specially.'

'Very well, then, do as you please.'

Seated between his father and his aunt, with Minney, and Barbara obviously waiting to do something unexpected, facing him, Eustace pondered. 'Do as you please.' The sentence sounded strangely in his mind: it made him feel unfamiliar to himself and filled his spirit with langour. His thoughts and impressions, which at this early stage of the drive usually followed a fixed course, began to lose their sequence. When, in obedience to time-honoured custom, they drove into the deep rut opposite Cliff House, a calculated mishap which made Hilda and even Miss Cherrington rock with laughter, the jolt and the lurch took Eustace completely by surprise: he even wondered what they were laughing at. Almost for the first time the imposing façade of The Priory, a superior boarding-house with grey-painted dormer window projecting from a steep slate roof crowned with a *chevaux-de-frise*, failed to impress him, and the knowledge that there were people rich enough to enjoy for months on end the luxuries of its unimaginable interior failed to comfort him with its promise of material security.

'Very well, then, do as you please.'

But wasn't the important thing to do what pleased other people? Shouldn't self-sacrifice be the rule of life? Why had his father asked him to get into the carriage before any of them? Was it just a slip of the tongue? He had tried to make it seem so, but Eustace didn't think it was. Since Miss Fothergill's death there had been several occasions, it seemed to Eustace now, when his wishes had been consulted in a quite unprecedented way, and especially by his father. That he had always been waited on and spoilt and protected from harm, he knew very well, but this was something different: it involved the element of deference. Minney showed it and even Miss Cherrington, though it sat uneasily on her. There was a change in their bearing towards him. In countless small ways they considered his wishes. Something of the kind had happened after his illness, he had been told not to tire himself, not to get excited, not to strain his eyes and so on: but he had always been told. There had been an increase of affection and an increase of authority. But now the voice of authority faltered; he was often asked, often given his choice, and sometimes he caught them looking at him in a speculative fashion, almost with detachment, as though he had been taken out of their hands and they were no longer responsible for him. What did it mean? Did it mean they loved him less? 'Whom the Lord loveth He chasteneth.' Eustace was well acquainted with this text. Might it not follow that when the Lord ceased to chasten He also ceased to love?

'Do as you please.'

For a moment Eustace contemplated an existence spent in pleasing himself. How would he set about it? He had been told by precept, and had learned from experience, that the things he did to please himself usually ended in making other people grieved and angry, and were therefore wrong. Was he to spend his life in continuous wrong-doing, and in making other people cross? There would be no pleasure in that. Indeed what pleasure was there, except in living up to people's good opinion of him?

But Hilda's attitude towards him had not altered. Her eye was still jealously watchful for any slip he might make. She still recognized his right to self-sacrifice. She had climbed on to the box without looking round the moment he surrendered his claim to it. True, she knew he was afraid to hold the reins going down Frontisham Hill, disliked seeing the horses' hindquarters contracted and crinkling as the weight of the landau bore down on them, was alarmed by the grating of the brake and the smell of burning; but still there was glory in it, and that glory Hilda had un-hesitatingly claimed for herself. She had taken the risk, and left to him . . . What exactly had she left to him? The satisfaction of doing what she wanted. This was what Eustace understood; this was what was right.

He looked round in a daze. They were trotting slowly up Pretoria Street. On the left was Mafeking Villa, as dingy as ever, the 'Apartments' notice still askew in the window, the front garden—a circular flower-bed planted with sea-shells, set in a square of granite chips—discreetly depressing; while a little way ahead, on the right, rose the shining white structure of the livery stable with its flag-pole and shrubs in tubs, as fascinating as the pier-head which, in extravagance of wanton ornament, it somewhat resembled.

Here Brown Bess would certainly want to turn in, as she always did, for it was her home; and Mr Craddock would say, 'Don't be in a hurry', 'All in good time', 'You haven't earned your dinner yet'—playful gibes which Eustace looked forward to and enjoyed hearing, callous as they were. But today he was in no mood to be disheartened by the one prospect or elated by the other. He remembered that when they reached the end of the street and turned into the dusty high road they would have to pass Laburnum Lodge.

He had not seen the house since her death, and he did not want to see it now. But how could he help seeing it? If he shut his eyes he would only see it more clearly in his mind. Mr Craddock drove inexorably on. Nothing could make him stop, nothing but a steam-roller or one of those motor-cars he hated so. For asking him to stop in mid-career without a good reason there might be a penalty, as there was in a train; several pounds added to the fare. No one had ever tried it, not even his father; who could tell what the consequences would be?

Do as you please.

'Daddy,' said Eustace, 'do you think we could go another way, not past Laburnum Lodge?'

The words were spoken. Minney's eyes opened in astonishment; Aunt Sarah's eyes were suddenly visible behind her veil; and Mr Craddock and Hilda, simultaneously turning inwards, craned their necks and gazed at him speechless. Eustace did not look at his father.

'Well,' said Mr Cherrington at last, 'if you want to go another way I suppose there's no objection. You don't mind turning round, Craddock, do you?'

Brown Bess had pulled up of her own accord, exactly opposite the livery stables.

'If Master Eustace wants me to, I'm sure I will,' said Craddock. 'Especially him being such a favourite with the late lamented lady.'

There was a pause. Brown Bess began to draw across the street towards the open doors of the livery stable, from beyond which came confused sounds of swishing and stamping and munching, doubtless inviting to her ears.

'Oh, I know what Eustace feels,' broke in Hilda, 'but he really will have to get used to seeing the house, won't he? It'll make us so late for tea, going all this way back through the town.'

'I think we ought to respect Eustace's wishes,' said Miss Cherrington decisively. 'He is the best judge of what he owes to the memory of Miss Fothergill.'

'Yes, we don't want to spoil his outing for a little thing like that, do we?' said his father, with a sidelong glance at Eustace, who sat silent, puzzled by his aunt's words and vaguely troubled by their impersonal tone. 'Eustace has to plough his own furrow like the rest of us, haven't you, Eustace?'

Eustace wriggled uncomfortably but didn't answer, absorbed in a vision of himself alone in an enormous field, holding the handles of a plough to which were attached two straining, sweating horses who kept looking round at him as much as to say, 'When do you want to start?'

'Don't you think Eustace might order us another pot of tea, Sarah? I think we might have another. And another plate of cakes too. A growing lad like him can't have too many cakes. They'll put some roses in his cheeks.'

Miss Cherrington raised her eyebrows slightly.

'I don't want any more tea,' said Hilda.

Barbara was understood to say she would like another cake.

'Well, perhaps Eustace would be kind enough to ring the bell,' said Miss Cherrington in an even voice, looking past him as she spoke. 'It's just by your elbow, Eustace.'

They were sitting in the garden of the Swan Hotel at Frontisham and they were all, except Barbara, a little conscious of their surroundings, for on previous expeditions they had had tea at the baker's, in a stuffy back room smelling of pastry and new bread.

Here they were under the shadow of the church. Vast and

spectacular, shutting out the sky, it rose sheer on its mound above them. From where Eustace sat the spire was almost invisible, hidden behind some trees. He regretted this, but the west window was in full view, touched here and there with fire by the declining sun; and it was the west window that really mattered.

'Tucked away in this little-known corner of Norfolk,' the guide-book said, 'is a treasure of the mediæval mason's art that lovers of architecture come miles to see: the west window of Frontisham Parish Church. Inferior in mere size to the west window of York Minster and to the east window of Carlisle Cathedral, the window at Frontisham easily surpasses them in beauty, vigour, and originality. It is unquestionably the finest example of flamboyant tracery in the kingdom; confronted with this masterpiece, criticism is silent.'

Eustace knew the passage by heart; he found it extremely moving and often said it over to himself. He did not share the guide-book's poor opinion of mere size: magnitude in any form appealed to him, and he wished that this kind of superiority, too, could have been claimed for Frontisham. But the book, which could not err, called the window the finest in the kingdom. That meant it was the best, the greatest, the grandest, the *ne plus ultra* of windows: the supreme window of the world. Eustace gazed at it in awe. It had entered for the architectural prize, and won; now it looked out upon the centuries, victorious, unchallenged, incomparable, a standard of absolute perfection to which all the homage due to merit naturally belonged.

It was not the window itself which fascinated him so much as the idea of its pre-eminence, just as it was not the guide-book's actual words (many of which he did not properly understand) that intoxicated him, so much as the tremendous, unqualified sense of eulogy they conveyed. He tried again, again not quite successfully, to see how the window differed from other church windows. But he could not see it through his own eyes, because he had so often visualised it through the eyes of the guide-book, nor could he describe it in his own words, because the author's eloquence came between him and his impressions. Feeling meant more to him than seeing, and the phrases of the panegyric, running like a tune in his mind, quickly started a train of feeling that impeded independent judgement.

Within the massive framework of the grey wall seven slender tapers of stone soared upwards. After that, it was as though the tapers had been lit and two people, standing one on either side, had blown the flames together. Curving, straining, interlocked, they flung themselves against the retaining arch in an ecstasy—or should we say an agony?—of petrifaction. But the builder had not been content with that. Higher still, in the gable above, was another window much smaller and with tracery much less involved, but similar in general effect. 'An echo,' the guidebook called it, 'an earthly echo of a symphony which was made in heaven.'

The word 'heaven', striking against his inner ear, released Eustace's visual eye from dwelling on the material structure of the mediæval mason's masterpiece. The design with all its intricacy faded from his sight, to be replaced, in his mind's eye, by the window's abstract qualities, its beauty, its vigour, its originality, its pre-eminence, its perfection. With these, and not for the first time, he now began to feel as one. Disengaging himself from the tea-table he floated upwards. Out shot his left arm, caught by some force and twisted this way and that; he could feel his fingers, treble-jointed and unnaturally long, scraping against the masonry of the arch as they groped for the positions that had been assigned to them. Almost simultaneously his other limbs followed suit; even his hair, now long like Hilda's, rose from his head and, swaying like seaweed, strove up to reach the keystone. Splayed, spread-eagled, crucified (but for fear of blasphemy he must only think the shadow of that word) into a semblance of the writhing stonework, he seemed to be experiencing the ecstasy—or was it the agony?—of petrifaction.

Meanwhile the interstices, the spaces where he was not, began to fill with stained glass. Pictures of saints and angels, red, blue, and yellow, pressed against and into him, bruising him, cutting him, spilling their colours over him. The pain was exquisite, but there was rapture in it too. Another twitch, a final wriggle, and Eustace felt no more; he was immobilised, turned to stone. High and lifted up, he looked down from the church wall, perfect, pre-eminent, beyond criticism, not to be asked questions or to answer them, not to be added to or taken away from, but simply to be admired and worshipped by hundreds of visitors, many of them foreigners from Rome and elsewhere, coming miles to see him . . . Eustace, Eustace of Frontisham, Saint Eustace . . .

Eustace . . . the word seemed to be all round him.

'Eustace! Eustace!' His father's voice was raised in pretended indignation. 'Stop day-dreaming! We want some more tea! You've forgotten to ring the bell!'

Coming to himself with a start, and avoiding the eyes of his family, Eustace glanced nervously left and right. Round about stood a few empty tables, on one of which a bold bird hopped perkily, looking for crumbs. He noticed with concern that the bird had been guilty of a misdemeanour more tangible than theft. Hoping to scare it away, he rang the bell more loudly than he meant to.

A maid appeared, with a slight flounce in criticism of the lateness of the hour.

'Did you ring, madam?'

For a second nobody spoke; they were all looking at Eustace.

'No, I did,' he said nervously, and then, as no one seemed inclined to help him out, 'Could we have another pot of tea and some more cakes?'

'Fancies?' said the waitress.

Another pause.

'Yes, fancies, please,' said Eustace.

'He fancies fancies,' said his father when the waitress had gone. 'Quite right, Eustace.'

'I'm not so sure,' said Miss Cherrington. 'I think their plain cake was better. What do you say, Minney?'

'I liked those sponge fingers we had,' said Minney, unwilling to be drawn.

'Shall I ask her to bring some of them instead?' put in Eustace, jumping up from the table.

'No, no, sit where you are,' said his father. 'Make your miserable life happy.'

Eustace sat down again, aware of cross-currents of feeling and not knowing which to join.

Conversation was desultory till the waitress returned, carrying a brown teapot in one hand and a plate of cakes, covered with pink and white icing, in the other. Eustace thanked her fervently.

'Now that we've asked for them we shall have to eat them,' said Hilda, looking across at Eustace. 'At least you'll have to. I don't think I need, but perhaps I'd better,' she said, thoughtfully helping herself to one from the dish.

'Nobody need eat one who doesn't want to,' said Mr Cherrington. 'What we don't eat we don't pay for. By the way, who's paying for this?'

'I will! I will!' or sounds equivalent to it suddenly burst from Barbara and everyone laughed.

'I think Minney ought to,' said Mr Cherrington, 'with some of that money she's collected for Dr Barnardo's Home.'

'I'm afraid I haven't brought it with me,' said Minney. 'I left the box at home because a little bird told me that someone was going to put something in it when they get back this evening.' She stopped, confused.

'I think that Eustace ought to pay,' said Hilda. 'At least he ought to pay for these extra cakes, because we got them for him.'

'But you've eaten two,' objected Eustace.

'Only so as not to look wasteful.'

'Anyhow,' persisted Eustace sorrowfully, 'I haven't got any money and I shan't have any till Saturday.'

'I'll lend you some if you promise to pay me back,' said Hilda.

'You wouldn't have enough,' said Eustace. 'A tea like this must cost a great deal.' He sighed.

'Cheer up, cheer up!' said his father, brushing away some crumbs which had lodged in the protective colouring of his waistcoat, and adjusting, not without self-complacency, the belt of his Norfolk jacket. 'We shan't go bankrupt this time, shall we, Sarah?'

Miss Cherrington carefully expunged all trace of expression from her features before she answered.

'One cannot be too careful about money, one's own or other people's.'

Her brother frowned, and his face suddenly looked lined and tired above his creaseless suit. 'Oh, why must I be a widower,' he thought, 'with three kids and a woman who nags at me?' For a moment another figure joined them at the table, invisible to all but him, there was no chair for her, so she had to stand; he could see her clearly enough in her pale, full dress, the big hat whose brim curled upwards at the back, the gentle eyes shining through her thin veil. He blinked to keep away the tears and when he looked again she had gone. 'Hilda!' he cried in sudden exasperation, 'do sit up straight. Some of your hair's in your tea, and some of it's in your plate. I should have thought they could have taught you how to sit at table by this time!'

Eustace listened in alarm and astonishment. His father's fits of ill-humour were almost always directed at him, and he could hardly believe that this one wasn't. How would Hilda take it? She had withdrawn her lovely locks from the table and pushed them back over her thin shoulders; a look of scorn mixed with suffering was establishing itself on her features; her long eyelids drooped over her violet eyes, but tears were stealing from under them. No one spoke.

'Well,' said Mr Cherrington uncomfortably, 'I suppose it's time we were going. Sorry, Hilda, unless it's Eustace I ought to say "sorry" to. He looks more upset than you do.'

'Eustace has no hair to speak of,' said Hilda in a far-away voice.

Mr Cherrington seemed baffled.

'I wasn't finding fault with your hair, only with where you put it. Now, what about paying? Shall we ask Eustace to foot the bill?'

'I haven't any money, Daddy,' said Eustace, aware of having said so before.

'Perhaps they'll let you have it on tick.'

'On tick?'

'It means you pay the next time you come.'

Eustace caught sight of his aunt's face; her expression was inscrutable.

'Oh I don't think they'd like that: you see, I might not come again.'

'Well, will you pay if I give you the money? You've got to learn some time.' Mr Cherrington felt in his pockets. 'Now be careful to get the right change.'

Eustace gazed in awe at the golden half-sovereign.

'Shall I pay for Mr Craddock's tea?'

'Yes.'

'And Brown Bess's?'

'Not if she's had a second helping.'

'And should I give anything to the waitress?'

'You might give her a kiss.'

'Alfred, Alfred,' said Miss Cherrington impatiently, 'you're filling the boy's head with nonsense. Give her sixpence, Eustace, that's as much as she'll expect.'

To Eustace, Frontisham Hill was a major event. It was the steepest hill in the district; the white road seemed to come foaming down like a waterfall. Many a horse had broken its knees on that dusty cataract. On its crest a notice warned cyclists to ride with caution; at its foot another, facing the opposite way, requested drivers to slacken their bearing-reins. Brown Bess did not wear a bearing-rein and carried her head at any angle she chose; but it was the Cherringtons' custom to walk up the hill to spare her all they could. Only Barbara rode, with Minney walking alongside to keep her from climbing out. The hill rose straight out of the town, so they had to scale it before making their dispositions for the homeward journey.

Eustace climbed on to the box, as was his due, and Mr Craddock tucked the familiar dusty green plaid rug round

him. Eustace noticed that he did this with unusual solicitude; it was yet another instance of the new attitude grown-
up people were adopting towards him, as if he must be
humoured, as if he might break, as if a barrier had arisen
between him and them, setting him apart, not to be taken
for granted like other children and fondly admonished, as
if he were seriously ill, as if——

'Well, Master Eustace,' said Mr Craddock, gently laying
his whip on Brown Bess's shabby collar, 'how have you
been getting on all this time?'

'Fairly well, Mr Craddock, thank you. How have you?'

'Just jogging along. Mustn't grumble, but it gets a bit
monotonous at times, you know.'

'I'm sure it must. But life is monotonous, isn't it?'

Mr Craddock smiled.

'Not for everyone it isn't, not by any means. There's
some I'd like to change places with, I don't mind telling
you.'

Eustace considered Mr Craddock's life; it seemed to
consist of taking people out for drives and in having his
dinner and tea at their expense. How desirable, how
enviable! Of course you must be fond of horses, but then
Mr Craddock was, or at any rate he was on good terms with
them.

'Who would you like to change places with?'

Mr Craddock appeared to ponder deeply. 'There's at
least one person not a hundred miles from here as I wouldn't
mind being in the shoes of, Master Eustace.'

'I don't know this part very well,' said Eustace, conscientiously scanning the horizon. 'Would it be whoever
that big house there belongs to?' indicating a square-faced
mansion on a hill, fringed by wellingtonias. 'He must be
very rich.'

'Someone nearer than that.'

Eustace stared at Mr Craddock's impassive profile. How
sly he was; he never gave anything away.

'Is it one of us?'

Mr Craddock's silence must be taken to mean assent.

But Eustace was still puzzled. He turned round and stole a glance at his family. Which of them could Mr Craddock possibly want to change places with? Eustace knew the effort that attended their lives; they maintained their places in existence with sorrow, toil and pain as the hymn said—all except Barbara, and Mr Craddock could not possibly want to be her. But his father was looking unusually carefree and even prosperous in his new suit with those fascinating leather buttons; he was wearing his holiday air and Minney had said he looked such a gentleman. No doubt Mr Craddock was thinking of him.

'But Daddy has to work, you know,' said Eustace. 'He catches the 8.32 train to business every morning except on Sundays, and he only has one half-holiday a week, on Thursday, like today. He's allowed to be away for things like funerals, of course. Then he has to work for us as well as for himself. I don't know if you have a family, Mr Craddock?'

With some emphasis Mr Craddock said he had.

'Then you know what an expense they are, always wanting new clothes and things, and being ill. I don't think you'd want to be in Daddy's shoes if you knew what his life was like.'

'It wasn't him I was thinking of,' said the driver.

More baffled than ever, Eustace took another stealthy peep at the party in the landau. He could only see the top of Minney's hat; the brown straw hat with a bunch of cherries in it that she always wore for these occasions. Of her three hats it was the one he liked best, and he felt a sudden longing to see her face underneath it. He loved her, and though he knew her too well to be consciously aware of her patience and sweetness, their well-tried perfume filled his mind as he thought of her. Mr Craddock could be bad-tempered when crossed; perhaps he envied Minney her serenity. But no, it was monotony he complained of, and how could his lot compare in monotony with hers?

Aunt Sarah had pushed back her veil and was watching the passing hedgerows with an eye that did not see them but that did see, Eustace could tell, a great deal that she would rather not have seen. Perhaps she too was wishing she was somebody else—not Mr Craddock, of course, for he belonged in her mind to the category of things that had not been properly washed, and Mr Craddock, though he respected her, was always a little crestfallen in her presence. Eustace did not believe that he wanted to change places with her, for what a spring-cleaning he would have to give himself !

There remained Hilda, Hilda whose prettiness Mr Craddock had once praised, declaring it superior to Nancy Steptoe's. She did look pretty now, Eustace could see that; her face lit up as she leaned forward to help Minney restrain Barbara from throwing herself out of the carriage. Prettiness caused you to be admired. Hilda had no wish to be admired, nor, Eustace thought, had Mr Craddock. But there might be advantages in prettiness that Eustace was too young to know about. Mr Craddock might care to be pretty; it would certainly be a change for him.

'Was it Hilda you meant ?' he asked.

Mr Craddock looked first amused and then rather serious.

'No, it wasn't Miss Hilda,' he answered, lowering his voice. 'She's a good girl, don't you forget that. I like Miss Hilda more than many of them, and she's as pretty as a picture, or she will be one day. But no, I shouldn't want to be in her shoes.'

'Why not ?' asked Eustace.

'She's going to have a rough deal, that's why,' said the driver, sinking his voice almost to a whisper.

Eustace did not know what a rough deal was; it sounded like something he ought to try to protect Hilda from. But to ask Mr Craddock at this juncture might be taken as a reflection on his use of English. Besides Eustace wanted to guess the answer to his riddle.

'Would you like to be Aunt Sarah, or Minney, or Barbara ?' he demanded all in a breath, just to make absolutely sure.

'No offence meant, but none of them,' said Mr Craddock.

'But there isn't anyone else!' exclaimed Eustace.

'If you say there isn't, there isn't,' said Mr Craddock, nor could all Eustace's persuasions induce him to advance another word. His sphinx-like profile gave no hint of what was passing through his mind. He seemed to be looking straight into the future. But after Eustace had sat for some time in the wounded silence that belongs to the hoaxed, he remarked in a solemn tone, and as one who opens up an entirely new subject: 'I hear we shall be losing you before long.'

'Losing me?' repeated Eustace.

'Yes, they say we shan't have you with us much longer. I shall be sorry, I don't mind telling you. There are several we could spare better than you, mentioning no names. They just clutter up the streets, asking to be run over. But there, it's always the way, the best go first, even when it's only a boy, begging your pardon, Master Eustace.'

'Do you mean I'm going away?'

'A long way away by all accounts. We've all noticed you haven't been looking any too grand lately—kind of pinched, if you know what I mean. Anchorstone's said to be a health resort but it doesn't suit everyone, not by any means. My sister's boy was a healthy-looking little chap when they came here to live; in fact, he looked a lot stronger than you do. But he hadn't been with us a twelvemonth when his liver began to grow into his lights, and the doctors couldn't save him. He was just about your age when he was taken. Nice little chap too.' Mr Craddock paused reflectively. 'Miss Fothergill would have missed you, wouldn't she? But she's gone too, poor old lady, though I expect it was about time.'

Eustace turned pale and his lips began to tremble.

'Do you mean that I'm going to——?'

'Craddock, Craddock,' cried a voice from below, 'excuse my breaking into your conversation, but will you go back the way we came? And, Eustace, do you mind changing places with Hilda, so that she can drive the last little bit?'

'I never said I wanted to drive,' remonstrated Hilda, 'and it isn't fair to Eustace.'

'You know you always like to,' said Mr Cherrington. 'Up you go!'

Still shaking, Eustace took Hilda's place between his father and Miss Cherrington; and for the rest of the journey he said not a word. His father took his silence for pique, and playfully tried to coax him out of it. Beset with terrors as he was, Eustace felt he would have preferred a scolding. The sounds of their arrival at Cambo must have reached Annie in the kitchen, for she appeared at the door before they had time to open it. Her face was stiff with urgency and importance.

'Oh, Mr Cherrington,' she said, 'while you were out a gentleman called. He was dressed in black and wearing a top-hat. He said he was staying at Laburnum Lodge, so I expect he brought a message from Miss Fothergill.'

'Come along, Eustace, bedtime now,' said Minney, and he heard no more.

'A gentleman in black with a message from Miss Fother-gill.' The phrase repeated itself again and again in Eustace's mind, until to his overheated fancy it began to have a monstrous significance. When Minney came to say good-night he determined to confide to her something of the fear that was oppressing him. Even to approach the subject by word of mouth was a torture, but he felt sure that the mere act of telling her would charm it away. He couldn't bring himself, however, to say exactly what the nature of the fear was, so he reported the substance of Mr Craddock's disturbing utterances on the box. 'He said I was going away,' said Eustace as lightly as he could, 'and that he wouldn't be seeing me any more. What did he mean by that?' But Minney, instead of making fun of him, seemed to get flustered and annoyed. 'What does he know?' she demanded almost truculently. 'He's only an old cabman. You shouldn't pay any attention to what he says, Master Eustace.' Master! Minney had never called him that before: it was another sign of the change that was taking the meaning out of all his relationships. 'But he seemed so certain about it, Minney,' he persisted. 'He even said he would be sorry to lose me.'

'There's others besides him that would be sorry,' retorted Minney. 'The cheek of it!' Eustace could hear tears contending with indignation in her voice, and his heart sank.

'But it wasn't true, was it, Minney?' he urged. 'I'm not going away, Minney, am I? I shall be here a long time yet, shan't I?' But Minney didn't answer him directly: she seemed to get more flurried and angry and unlike herself. 'Silly old fool, talking like that to a child! Don't you worry, Master Eustace. It'll all come right. Go to sleep now, you'll have forgotten about it in the morning!'

And with that assurance she left him. But he was not satisfied and for the first time in his life he did not believe her. She was in the secret: she knew that he was going away. Now he understood why they all made such a fuss of him and asked him if he wanted this and that, and let him pay for tea, and tried to make him feel important and called him 'Master'. It was because they knew, all of them except Hilda, that they were going to lose him. His thoughts kept snatching him back from the edge of sleep, and when he did drop off his dreams were haunted by a gentleman in black, bringing a message from Miss Fothergill; and the message, which was written on a piece of black-edged paper in a black bag he carried, said that Miss Fothergill was looking forward to meeting Eustace again very soon.

He awoke in the morning convinced that he was going to die.

CHAPTER XIII

Respice Finem

As Eustace tunnelled deeper into his obsession the acute terror passed and was replaced by a settled melancholy which did not interfere with the routine processes of his mind. He did his lessons, went for walks with Hilda and accompanied her on shopping expeditions with docility and punctuality; but they were the actions of a sleep-walker and had ceased to have the power of reality behind them. Like a servant under notice, he felt a sense of detachment from his present activities; their meaning, which postulated permanence, had gone out of them; and the centre of his life had moved to another plane of experience, a height as yet unfurnished with a landscape, from which he watched the Eustace of former days going through the motions of daily living. These activities were now utterly provisional; they no longer mattered—nothing mattered. This, for Eustace, whose whole outlook had been conditioned by the conviction that everything mattered, was the great change, the change which helped to make him almost unrecognisable to himself, the actual change, symbol of the change to come. And they all, except Hilda, seemed by their behaviour to accept the change as inevitable, just as he did. They looked at him differently and spoke to him differently, in prepared voices, he fancied, as though they had been in church. They fell in with his smallest whims, and even, as if disappointed that he had so few, invented for him small preferences and prejudices which, for fear of hurting their feelings, he did not like to disclaim.

Leading this posthumous existence Eustace felt lightened of all responsibility. Nothing mattered . . . But to those who are accustomed to listen for it, the voice of conscience is not easily silenced; it goes on mumbling even if it cannot find anything to say. Eustace was aware of the menacing monotone, as of some large noxious insect trying to find its way in through a closed window, but its angry buzz did not greatly disturb him. The voice was still inarticulate. But, as ever, there was a part of him which was in league with the enemy, a traitor who wanted to open the gates.

Eustace awoke one morning to find that the foe had forced an entrance, taken possession, formulated its charge and, unusually practical, told him what he must do to placate it. Eustace did not put up a fight. The demand, unlike so many of them, had reason behind it; he might really have thought of it for himself, without any prompting from his vigilant adviser. It was something that people in his circumstances always did. He felt under the pillow for the watch Miss Fothergill had given him. He could just make out the time—five minutes to seven. He stared at the watch a moment longer. He had treasured it so much that it seemed to have become a part of him, an extension of his personality. Now it gave him a look so impersonal as to be almost unfriendly —the kind of look on the face of someone else's watch. His eyes growing accustomed to the light he could see his hairbrushes on the dressing-table. The fact that they were handleless, a man's, had been a source of pride to him. Now they looked forlorn, unprized, reproachful. On the washing-stand lay the dark lump that was his sponge, and the white streak of his toothbrush.

Eustace pondered. It was not going to be easy.

'I don't think we'll do any lessons this morning,' said Miss Cherrington. 'Eustace is looking a bit tired. Why don't you both go down and play on the sands? It's only ten o'clock so you'll have all the morning for it. You won't get many more days like this.'

Armed with their spades they started off across the ragged stretch of chalky green that intervened between Cambo and the cliffs. On their left the sun shone brightly with a promise of more than September warmth. Its loving touch lay on everything they looked at, but Eustace walked in silence, dragging his spade. 'You won't get many more days like this.' Making for a gap in the broken fence they passed the threatening brown bulk of Mr Johnson's school. A hum of voices came from it, the boys were lining up for physical exercises in the playground. Almost for the first time Eustace felt a twinge of envy mingle with the mistrust in which he habitually held them. Soon, stretching away to the right, came the familiar vista, the First Shelter, the Second Shelter, the rise in the ground that hid all but the red roof of the Third Shelter, and then the mysterious round white summit of the lighthouse. Even at this distance you could see the sun striking the great rainbow-coloured lantern within, a sight that seldom failed to move Eustace. But it did not move him today.

They stopped from habit among the penny-in-the-slot machines at the head of the concrete staircase which zig-zagged its way majestically below, and looked down at the beach to see whether the rocks that formed the bastions of their pond had been appropriated by others. As they gazed their faces, even Eustace's, took on the intent forbidding look of a gamekeeper on the watch for poachers. No, the rocks were free—it was too early for marauders—and the beach was nearly deserted.

'A penny for your thoughts,' said Hilda.

Eustace started.

'If you give me the penny now, may I tell you my thoughts later on?'

Hilda considered.

'But you may be thinking something else then.'

'No, I shall still be thinking the same thing.'

'Very well, then.' Hilda produced a purse from the pocket half-way down her dress and gave him a penny. 'But why do you want it now?'

Eustace looked rather shamefaced.

'I wanted to see how strong I was.'

He advanced cautiously upon the Try-your-grip machine. Flanked on one side by a bold-faced gipsy offering to tell your fortune, and on the other by an apparatus for giving you an electric shock, the Try-your-grip machine responded to Eustace's diffident inspection with a secret, surly expression. Dark green and battered, it had a disreputable air as indeed had all its neighbours, and Eustace vaguely felt that he was in bad company.

'I shouldn't try if I were you,' said Hilda, coming up behind him.

'Why not?'

'Oh, you never know what they might do. Besides, it's wasting money.'

Eustace thought she was right, but he had gone too far to retreat with self-respect. He had issued a challenge and the machine, withdrawn and sullen as it was, must have heard: Destiny, which had its eye on Eustace, must have heard too. 'Moderate strength rings the bell; great strength returns the penny.' He pondered. After all, one never could be sure. Supposing the bell rang; supposing the penny were returned: wouldn't that prove something, wouldn't he feel different afterwards? He looked round. The green feathers of the tamarisk hedge were waving restlessly; he had liked them once but there was no comfort in them now, no comfort in the bow-windows, the beetling walls, the turrets and pinnacles of Palmerston Parade looking down on him: no comfort in the day.

He slipped the penny in the slot. The machine was cold and repellent to his touch; he screwed his face up and tried to give it a look as hostile as its own. Then he pressed his palm against the brass bar and curled his finger-tips, which would only just reach, round the inner handle, and pulled. The handle bit cruelly into his soft flesh; the indicator, vibrating wildly, travelled as far across the dial as the figure 10, and stopped, still flickering. Eustace saw that he must get it to 130 for the penny to be returned. Scarlet in the face he redoubled his efforts. The indicator began to lose ground. In desperation he was bringing up his left hand as a reinforcement when he heard Hilda's voice.

'That's against the rules! Your're cheating!'

Crestfallen and ashamed, Eustace relaxed his grip. The needle flashed back to zero and the machine, radiating malevolence from all its hard dull surfaces, with a contemptuous click gathered the penny into its secret maw. Breathing gustily Eustace stared back at it, like a boxer who has received a disabling blow but must not take his eyes off his enemy.

'I told you not to try,' said Hilda. 'You'll only strain yourself.' She added more kindly: 'Those machines are just there for show. I expect they're all rusted up inside, really.'

'Do you think Daddy could get the penny back?' asked Eustace.

'He couldn't have at your age. Now you must tell me what you were thinking of. I know you've forgotten.'

'I'll tell you when we get down on the beach,' said Eustace evasively.

They began the descent. September winds had blown the sand up to the topmost steps; they felt gritty to the tread. In the corners where the staircase turned, paper bags whirled and eddied; quite large pieces of orange-peel sprang to life, pirouetted and dropped down dead. Around, below, above, gulls wheeled and screamed, borne aloft on the airs that came racing from the sea. All this pother plucked at the nerves and whipped up the blood, but Eustace plodded stolidly in Hilda's wake, secretly examining his reddened palm and wondering how he would be able to hold the spade. If he was as weak as the machine said, he would soon have to stop digging anyhow.

'Let's make the pond larger this time,' said Hilda, when they reached the familiar scene of irrigation. 'We're earlier than we generally are, we may not get a chance like this again.'

'Much larger?' asked Eustace.

'Well, we could take in this rock here,' said Hilda, walking with long strides to a distant boulder. 'Then the wall would go like this'—and cutting with her spade a line through the sand she sketched an ambitious extension of their traditional ground plan. 'It will look wonderful from the cliff,' she added persuasively. 'Like a real lake.'

'Don't you think it's more than we can manage?' asked Eustace, still smarting from his defeat at the hands of the automatic machine.

'You can't tell till you try,' Hilda said, and immediately set to work on the retaining wall. Eustace walked slowly to his post at the far end of the pond. Their custom was to begin at opposite ends and meet in the middle, but Eustace seldom reached the half-way mark. Now that mark, thanks to Hilda's grandiose scheme, was at least two yards farther off than it used to be. Consciousness of this increased his bodily and mental languor. For him the pond had ceased to be a symbol. Of old, each time it rose from the sands and spread its silver surface to the sky it proclaimed that the Cherrington children had measured their strength against the universe, and won. They had imposed an order; they had left a mark; they had added a meaning to life. That was why the last moment, when the completion of the work was only distant by a few spadefuls, was so tense and exciting. In those moments the glory of living gathered itself into a wave and flowed over them. The experience was ecstatic and timeless, it opened a window upon eternity, and whilst it lasted, and again when they surveyed their handiwork from the cliff-top, they felt themselves to be immortal.

But what assurance of immortality could there be for Eustace now, when at any moment the clock would strike, the sounds in the house would cease, the call would come and he would pass through the open front door to find the chariot standing outside? Sometimes it was just the landau with Mr Craddock on the box, staring ahead; sometimes it was a hearse; sometimes it was a vehicle of indefinite design, edged with light much brighter than the day, and seeming scarcely to rest upon the ground. The vision never carried him beyond that point, but it brought with it an indescribable impression of finality, it was a black curtain stretched across every avenue of thought, absorbing whatever energies of mind and spirit he had left. Why go on digging? Why do anything? But no; even in this featureless chaos something remained to be done.

He straightened himself, and shook his head vigorously. 'What's the matter?' said Hilda. 'Is a fly bothering you?'

'No,' said Eustace, 'it was some thoughts I had.'

'Well, you won't get rid of them like that, and your hat will come off. Oh, and that reminds me! You promised to tell me what your thoughts were, and you haven't. I knew you'd forget.'

'No, I haven't forgotten,' said Eustace.

'Well, come on. I'm waiting.'

An overpowering reluctance, like a spasm in the throat, seized Eustace, almost robbing him of speech.

'Just give me a little longer.'

'Very well, then, I'll give you five minutes from now.' Digging her chin into her chest she looked at the watch which hung suspended there. 'That'll be five minutes past eleven.'

They worked on in silence, Eustace searching frantically for a formula for what he had to say and finding none. So acute was his sense of the passing minutes that he began to feel himself ticking like a clock. Twice he saw Hilda surreptitiously glancing at her watch.

'Time's up,' she said at last.

Eustace gazed at her blankly.

'Well?'

'Do you really want to know?' Eustace temporised, shuffling with his feet.

'I don't suppose it's anything important, but as I've paid for it I might as well have it.'

'It is important in a way, to me at any rate. But I don't think you'll like to hear what I'm going to say, any more than I shall like telling you. At least I hope you won't.'

Hilda frowned. 'What *is* all this about?'

The rapids were close at hand now and he could hear the roar of the cataract. He plunged.

'You see, I want to make my will.'

If Eustace had counted on making an effect, he ought to have been gratified. Hilda opened her eyes and stared at him. She opened her mouth, too, but no words came.

'You didn't know about me then? I didn't think you did.'

'Know what?' said Hilda at length.

'That I was going away.'

Hilda's heart turned over, but bewilderment was still uppermost in her mind.

'I thought they hadn't told you. It was so as not to worry you, I expect.'

'But who told *you*?' asked Hilda, making crosses in the sand with her spade.

'Mr Craddock told me first, the evening we drove back from Frontisham. He said I was going away and he would be sorry to lose me. And then I asked Minney, and she told me not to pay any attention to what Mr Craddock said because he was an old cabman. But she didn't say it wasn't true, and I could see she knew it was. You know how you can sometimes tell with grown-up people.'

Understandingly but unwillingly Hilda nodded.

'And then I asked Daddy.'

'What did he say?'

'He said something about not taking offences before you came to them, which I didn't quite understand, and not meeting trouble half-way. He was angry with Mr Craddock too, I could see that. He said he was a silly old gossip. He said it wouldn't be as bad as I thought, and that everyone had to go through it sooner or later, and I shouldn't mind much when the time came, and I wasn't to think about it, because that only made it worse.'

'They never said anything to me,' said Hilda.

'Well, I had to tell you because, you see, I wanted to give you my things before I go away.'

Hilda said nothing to this, but she sat down rather suddenly on a rock, with back bent and knees spread out, in the attitude Eustace knew so well.

'I've been thinking about it,' he went on with an effort, 'because, you see, unless I leave a will you might not get my things at all—they might go into Chancery. But I haven't many that would do for someone who isn't a boy' (Eustace was unwilling to call Hilda a girl, it would sound like a kind of taunt). 'My clothes wouldn't be any use, except my combinations, and they're too small. I should like you to have my handkerchiefs, though. They would be washed by that time, of course.'

'There's your red silk scarf,' said Hilda, with the stirring of self-interest that no beneficiary, however tender-hearted, can quite succeed in stifling.

'I was just coming to that. And my woolly gloves too. You've often worn them and they've stretched a bit. When you had the scarf on and the gloves, and one of my handkerchiefs, it would look almost as though I was still walking about.'

'No one could ever mistake me for you if that's what you mean,' said Hilda.

'It wasn't quite what I meant,' said Eustace, but a doubt crossed his mind as to what he really did mean, and he went on:

'My hairbrushes wouldn't be any good because they haven't got handles, and besides you have some. Perhaps Daddy could use them when his wear out. Then there's my sponge and toothbrush and flannel. Some poor boy might like them when they've been well dried.' Raised interrogatively, Eustace's voice trailed away when the suggestion met with no response.

'I doubt it,' said Hilda practically, 'but of course we could try.'

'There isn't much more,' said Eustace. 'I should like Minney to have the watch that Miss Fothergill gave me. Of course it's rather large for a lady, but it goes very well because I've never been allowed to take it out of my room, and hers doesn't; and you have yours, the one that belonged to Mother.'

'I've never seen a lady wear a watch that size,' said Hilda. 'But she could tuck it in her belt where it wouldn't show, though of course it would leave a bulge.'

A shadow passed over Eustace's face.

'Well, perhaps she could use it as a clock. Then I thought I'd give all my toys to Barbara, except Jumbo, who you take to bed. She uses them already, I know, so it wouldn't seem like a present, but she might like to know that they were hers by law.'

'I don't think she minds about that,' said Hilda. 'She takes anything she can get hold of.'

'Yes, she's different from us, isn't she?' said Eustace. 'She doesn't seem to care whether something is right or wrong. It will be a great handicap to her, won't it, in after life.'

'Not if she doesn't mind about it,' Hilda said.

'I've nearly done now, and then we can go on with the pond. I haven't anything to leave to Daddy and Aunt Sarah, so I thought I'd take two of those sheets of writing-paper from the drawing-room table, which we only use to thank for presents, and write 'Love from Eustace' on them. I think I should print the messages in different coloured inks, and then put them in envelopes addressed to Mr Cherrington and Miss Cherrington, and drop them in the letter-box when the time came, and they might think they had come by post, and it would be a surprise.'

'Yes,' said Hilda, 'that's a good idea.'

'And all the rest I should leave to you, Hilda. That is, my money in the money-box, and my books, and my guide-book, and my knife, and my pencils, and the ball of string, and the india-rubber rings, and the pink rosette that I wore at the election, and the picture postcard of Zena Dare, and the General View of Mt Pelée before the earthquake.'

'You won't want to be parted from that,' said Hilda. 'I should take that with you.'

'I don't think I should be allowed to,' said Eustace. 'You see . . .' marvelling at Hilda's obtuseness, he left the sentence unfinished. 'I won't leave the things lying about, I'll put them all in the drawer with the pencil-box—the one with marguerites on the lid—so you'll know where to find them.'

'I always know better than you do, really,' said Hilda.

Eustace let this pass.

'The only thing I'm not sure about is how to get my money out of the Post Office. There's quite a lot there, thirty-three pounds. Do you think if I went and asked for it they'd give it me? They ought to, because it belongs to me, but I don't think they would. Daddy once told me that banks use your money for themselves. I shall have to ask Daddy and I don't want to do that.'

'Why not?'

'Because I don't want to talk about it to anyone but you. And I only told you because I thought you didn't know what was going to happen. But I shall write everything down and put it in an envelope under your pillow, so that's where you'll find it when the time comes.'

'When will that be?' said Hilda.

'I don't quite know yet.'

Eustace picked up his spade and, returning to his unfinished portion of the wall, began to dig. He was a little disappointed with the matter-of-fact way in which Hilda, after the novelty was over, had discussed the items of his bequest; she might have been more demonstrative; but the relief of having told her was immense. All that remained to do now was of a practical nature and would make no call on his emotions. The question of the Post Office he tried to thrust out of his mind. After all, it was a grown-up's matter and grown-ups would know how to deal with it. He worked on, and only when his spade, instead of sinking into the moist sand, struck a stone and jarred him did he look up and notice that Hilda was not doing her piece, but was still sitting on the rock where he had left her. He stopped digging and walked across to her.

'What's the matter, Hilda?'

She lifted her face and he saw that it was full of pain. It kept twitching and crinkling in places where normally it was smooth and stationary. She tried to speak for a moment and then said:

'I don't see why you are giving all these things away, to me or to anyone else. You'll want them when you come back.'

So that was how it was. She hadn't understood after all. She didn't realise that he wasn't coming back, and how could he tell her, how could he deal her a second blow when the first had been so hurtful?

'I don't think I shall come back for a long time,' he said at length, hoping that this was not an implied falsehood.

'How long?' asked Hilda. 'A week, a month, a year?'

'It might be more than a year.'

Hilda stared at him through unshed tears.

'But where are you going to? Who's going to take care of you? You've never stayed away from home before and you know you can't look after yourself.'

'I don't know where I shall be,' said Eustace. Suddenly a picture of Anchorstone churchyard occurred to him, and of Miss Fothergill being laid in her grave that windy day. He had never before thought of his disappearance in terms of burial.

'Perhaps not very far from here,' he said.

'Oh, if you're not going far it won't matter so much,' said Hilda. 'Because we shall be able to drive over and see you and bring you things. But you must be somewhere, in someone's house, I mean. Everybody except a tramp lives in a house, and I shouldn't think you'd want to leave us just to become a tramp.'

'I don't want to leave you.'

'Well, who says you have to?'

'They all do, really.'

'But I don't understand—they can't turn you into the street—they're very fond of you. And who is there for you to stay with near here? It would have been different while Miss Fothergill was alive. You could have gone to her. But she's dead.'

Distress had made Hilda angry, as it so often did. Eustace's heart began to race; he couldn't bear the strain of all this talk at cross-purposes and must find some way of bringing it to an end.

'I missed her very much at first,' he began, 'but I don't miss her so much now. You see, she is with God. And perhaps you won't miss me very much when I go away.'

Hilda stared at him uncomprehending.

'Because it will be rather the same, you see.'

There was a long silence. Then Hilda said:

'Do you mean you are going to die?'

'Yes, I think so.'

Instantly a feeling of complete peace possessed him. His sense of his surroundings, never very strong except when they helped to intensify his thoughts, faded away; the long struggle with his fate, inside him and outside, seemed over. But Hilda's voice recalled him to actuality. She had risen from the rock and was standing over him, her face transformed with fury and pain.

'How can you say such a wicked thing? You don't know what you're talking about. You must be mad. I shall go straight home and tell them!'

Eustace rose too, and began to tremble. 'They'd only tell you the same as they told me.'

'It's nonsense. You're not ill, are you, I mean you're not specially ill? People don't die just because they say they're going to. You can't *think* yourself dead.' She glared at him accusingly. 'Don't you feel well?'

'I don't feel very well,' said Eustace, beginning to cry. 'But it isn't only that. I've had warnings and messages— you wouldn't understand. And I feel it here,' he made a vague gesture, his hand swept over his heart and rested on his forehead—'as though I hadn't long to stay. It isn't the same with me as it used to be, even here on the sands. Don't be angry with me, Hilda. You'll make me sorry I told you. I didn't want to.'

'But I *am* angry with you,' cried Hilda. 'How dare you talk like that? I see how it is—you *want* to go away—you *want* to leave us! You tried before, the time of the paper-chase, but you had to come back. You had to come back from Miss Fothergill too. You think you'll be with someone who loves you more than we do—that's why you talk about dying! But I won't allow it! I'll stop you! I'll see you don't slip away!' She looked wildly at Eustace and advanced a step towards him: he recoiled. 'I shan't leave you,' she whispered, still more excitedly and making passes at him with her spade. 'I shan't let them get by me, whoever they are, and I shan't let you. I shall always be there. I shan't let you walk along the cliff-edge alone, and I shall take away your knife, and your ball of string too, so that you can't do anything to yourself! You'd like to, wouldn't you? You'd like to get rid of us all!'

Eustace's eyes grew round with terror. Dimly the meaning of what Hilda had been saying began to detach itself from the violence of the words. The cliff's edge . . . the knife . . . the ball of string. He began to visualise them, and to realise what they stood for. The string was for his neck, the knife was for his throat, and the cliff's edge was for his whole body . . . Turning away from Hilda he began to stray and stumble towards the sea. The sun was in his eyes, dazzling him; it shone from the sky, from the foaming crests of the breakers, from the tiny water-furrows between the sand-ribs. Faintly the sound of hoof-beats caught his ears; sliding below his reasoning faculty, their rhythm started a vision in his mind. Clop-clop, clop-clop, on they came, and the chariot, too, came nearer, fringed with fire. But Hilda had flung herself at the horses' heads. In one hand she held the knife, with the other she was hanging to the reins. The near horse turned to bite her, and she fell; and the horses trampled on her and the wheels of the chariot passed over her.

Suddenly the air was full of voices, and Eustace heard his name called. He turned round and saw, not far away, a party of people mounted on horseback. No, they were not people, they were children, or two of them were, and he thought he recognised them, but his eyes were still too full of sun to see properly and his mind too troubled to take in what he saw. While he tried to adjust his faculties to this new situation, one of the riders drew away from the group and came towards him. The horse screwed and sidled and tossed its head, but she brought it to a stand within a few yards of him.

'We've come to congratulate you, Eustace,' Nancy Steptoe said.

Angels on Horseback

THE words were hardly out of her mouth when, as though at a pre-arranged signal, the other members of the party put their steeds in motion. To the accompaniment of much prancing, head-tossing and tail-swishing, they joined their spokesman, and after some manœuvring formed a rough semi-circle round Eustace.

'Congratulations, Eustace!' said Gerald Steptoe.

'Congratulations, Eustace!' said Dick Staveley.

'Congratulations!' after a second's hesitation said the lady on Dick's right.

Eustace stared at them in amazement.

'Aren't you going to speak to us, Eustace?' said Nancy, with a flash of her frosty eyes. 'Are you still angry? He isn't supposed to speak to us, you know,' she confided to the others, 'and now I expect he's too proud to as well.'

With the tail of his eye Eustace looked round for Hilda, but he could not see her.

'She's just behind you,' said Nancy, interpreting his glance. 'Good-morning, Hilda,' she called over his head. 'We were passing by, so we thought we'd stop to congratulate Eustace.'

'Good-morning, Nancy,' said Hilda shortly. 'It's very kind of you to congratulate Eustace, but I don't know what it's for and nor does he.'

'They don't know!'

'They haven't been told!'

'Well, really!'

Only the lady on Dick's right contributed nothing to the hubbub of incredulity and surprise. Erect and a little apart she sat, in a grey riding habit whose close fit made her seem to Eustace's eyes unbelievably slim and elegant. She wore her hair in a bun under her bowler hat. You could not expect her to speak, you could not expect a goddess to speak, her whole appearance spoke for her. But she raised her eyebrows slightly and made a movement with her shoulders, as if to imply that among ordinary mortals anything might happen.

High in the air above him, as it seemed to Eustace, the chime and jingle of voices went on. Now the little fountains of exclamation and interjection had died down, and they were discussing something, but the wind tore the words to pieces along with the wisps of foam from the horses' lips, and Eustace could not understand their drift. Soon the discussion became an argument, almost a wrangle: the figures seemed to stiffen on their saddles; arms jerked; heads turned abruptly. At last Dick appealed to the lady on his right.

'What do you think, Anne?'

She hesitated and looked down at Eustace with a greater appearance of interest than she had yet shown.

'I should tell him,' she said. 'I think it would be kinder.'

'You tell him, Dick,' said Nancy.

Dick Staveley braced himself, power and authority descended on him, and for the first time Eustace realised that he was once more in the presence of his hero.

'Here, come a bit nearer,' Dick commanded.

Eustace edged his way cautiously towards the towering rampart of tossing heads, shining eyes, and hoofs that pawed the sand.

Dick bent towards him.

'You've come into a fortune,' he said.

'A fortune?' repeated Eustace.

'You'll have to explain, Dick,' Anne said. 'He doesn't know what a fortune is.'

'Oh yes I do,' exclaimed Eustace; 'it's a great deal of money.'

'Quite right. Well, somebody's left you a great deal of money.'

'But who left it to me?'

'Can't you guess?'

Eustace shook his head.

'Just look at him,' said Dick. 'He doesn't know who left it to him, and he can't guess. He has such masses of friends waiting to die and leave him their money that he simply doesn't know who it is. We don't have friends like that, do we, Anne? Our friends never die and if they did they wouldn't leave us anything. I want to know how Eustace manages it. I expect he murders them.'

'But I haven't any friends,' cried Eustace.

'Well, one less now, of course. It was very suspicious, you know, the way she died. She was quite well in the morning. She called on her lawyer and said to him: 'Just get out some stamps and sealing-wax and red tape, and so on, because I'm going to change my will. I'm going to leave all my money to a young friend of mine, who is coming to tea with me this afternoon.' Well, you went and we know what happened. It did seem rather odd.'

'Miss Fothergill?' gasped Eustace. 'Do you mean Miss Fothergill?'

'You've got it,' Dick began to clap, and they all joined in, while Eustace, possessed by emotions so unrecognisable that he did not know whether they were painful or delicious, stared blankly at Dick's laughing face.

'You don't look very pleased,' said Dick at length.

'Oh, but I am,' said Eustace. 'I was just wondering what Hilda would think.' He turned to his sister as he spoke.

'Well, and what does Miss Cherrington think?' asked Dick, and as plainly as if it had been yesterday instead of a year ago Eustace remembered the coaxing voice in which Dick used to speak to Hilda.

'I think it's very nice for Eustace,' she said, speaking expressionlessly, as if mesmerised. 'I hope it won't make any difference to him—I mean,' she corrected herself. 'I hope it won't make him any different.'

'Oh, but it will!' Nancy's clear voice rang out in mockery and triumph. 'For one thing, he's going away to school.'

Going away, going away: so that was what going away meant: not what he thought it did.

As their dread meaning evaporated, the words seemed

to shrink and dwindle, from the capital letters of a capital sentence to the smallest of common type. Utterly insignificant, they now carried hardly any meaning at all, and the thing in Eustace that had been swelling like a tumour shrank and dwindled with them. But the word school still meant something; it conjured up a picture of the brown prison-house sidling up to Cambo like a big boy preparing to kick a small one.

'Not Mr Johnson's?' he said.

'Oh no,' said Nancy. 'Not a potty little school like that. Why, tradesmen's sons go there. No, a school in the South of England.'

Nancy's tone established for ever in Eustace's mind a conviction of the social superiority of the South over all parts of England, particularly East Anglia.

'St Ninian's at Broadstairs it's to be, I'm told,' said Gerald. 'Not half a bad place. Some very decent fellows go there, very decent. We played their second eleven at cricket this summer. We drove over from St Swithin's in a brake, and they gave us a jolly good feed. St Swithin's is in Cliftonville, you know. Of course, that's different from Margate. No trippers or anything of that sort.'

'Is it at all like Anchorstone?' Eustace asked. 'Are there any rocks?'

'I dare say there are, but you couldn't jump on them, you know. No one does. They wouldn't let you, and besides you wouldn't want to. It's a kids' game.'

Eustace felt as if the landscape of his life was streaming by him while he, perilously balanced on a small white stone in the midst of the flux, searched in vain for some landmark which would confirm his sense of the stability of existence.

'You'll like it at St Ninian's,' Dick Staveley said. 'It was my pri. too.'

Eustace looked puzzled.

'My private school, I mean. You don't stay there after you're fourteen. Then you go to a public school.'

'And then to the 'Varsity,' said Nancy.

'But when shall I begin to work?' asked Eustace. 'I mean, when shall I start to earn my living?'

'Oh, you won't ever have to do that, will he, Dick?' said Nancy. 'You'll be like Dick, you won't have to work, you'll be much too rich. You'll live at home and play golf, or shoot, or hunt, or something like that, and the rest of the time you'll spend abroad, at Homburg or Carlsbad or one of those places.'

The landscape was now flashing by at a speed that left Eustace no time to sort out his impressions. But Nancy's picture of a future exempt from toil and effort was one he never forgot.

'But will Daddy have to work?' he asked.

'Well, we really hadn't thought about that, had we? Yes, I expect so. The money doesn't belong to him. It's yours, or will be when you're twenty-one. I expect he'll come and spend his holidays with you if you ask him, and don't happen to be abroad.'

Eustace considered this. 'And Hilda——' he began. There was a pause, and no one spoke. Eustace looked at Hilda. Her cheeks were still damp with the tears she had shed a little while ago. Surely they ought to be dry now. Once or twice she looked round with an uneasy movement of her head, but her eyes, he could see, did not meet the eight pairs of eyes that looked down at her. She began to scrape the sand off her shoes with the edge of her spade.

'Miss Cherrington's face is her fortune,' said Dick Staveley, and Eustace thought he had never heard such a beautiful compliment. 'She'll find something to do while Eustace is away. We'll find something for her to do, won't we, Anne?' he said, turning to the lady on his right. 'I want you to meet Miss Cherrington. I've told you about her.' Very gently he took hold of Anne's bridle-rein and they moved a step or two nearer to Hilda. 'This is my sister Anne, and this is Miss Cherrington, whom everyone else calls Hilda. Two such charming girls. I'm sure you'll like each other.' He smiled with his eyes, and his sister bent her head and smiled too.

'Good old Hilda!' cried Nancy tolerantly.

'Well, not too good, I hope,' said Dick. 'But, you see, she's always had to look after Eustace. He's such a handful!' Dick Staveley smiled at Eustace, the smile of one man to another; his horse, with the white star on its forehead, tossed its head and had to be admonished by its rider. Infected by its restiveness the others, too, began to squirm and fidget and eye each other inquiringly, and it was some moments before order was restored.

Leaning on her spade, Hilda looked up unwillingly at Dick, and their eyes met for the first time.

'I shall have to look after Eustace when he comes back for the holidays,' she said. 'I dare say he'll need me more than ever.' She glanced at Eustace doubtfully. 'School may not be altogether good for him,' she added, almost hopefully.

'I don't suppose it will be,' said Dick lightly. 'You couldn't expect that, could you, Anne?'

'I don't think it's doing you very much good,' said his sister.

'Well, perhaps I was hopeless from the start. But it's never too late to mend, is it, Hilda?' he said. 'Now that you've made such a good job of Eustace, you must come and try your hand on me. Don't you think so, Anne?'

Anne gave Hilda a considering look.

'We should love to see you, of course,' she said. 'But you needn't pay any attention to him, he likes to tease.'

'But I want her to pay attention to me,' cried Dick, appealing to the company in general. 'You never did, Anne, you neglected me shamefully. You weren't a true sister to me. You're eighteen now, and what have you ever done for me? And Hilda's only—only how old?'

'She's nearly fourteen,' said Eustace, as Hilda did not speak.

'Nearly fourteen, that's only thirteen, and yet, thanks to the way she trained Eustace, he's now a rich man with thousands of pounds in the bank.'

'Fifty-eight thousand,' said Gerald Steptoe solemnly. 'Daddy told me.'

'But I didn't do it,' said Hilda. 'It wasn't my fault. I just told Eustace he must speak to Miss Fothergill, and not mind her being old and ugly. That was all I did.'

'But it was quite enough,' Dick Staveley said. 'Anne and I often used to pass Miss Fothergill when we were riding on the cliffs. And Anne could see that she was old and ugly just as well as Hilda could. But she never said, "Now, Dick, just get off a minute and be polite to poor Miss Fothergill".'

'You wouldn't, if I had,' said his sister.

'How do you know? I might, and then perhaps she would have left her money to me. It all came from having Hilda as a sister. Did Nancy ever tell you to speak to Miss Fothergill, Gerald?'

'Good Lord, no. We used to run a mile when we saw her.'

'There you are, you see. You sisters simply don't know your job. There was sixty-eight thousand pounds for the asking and neither of you would take the trouble to say, "Dick—or Gerald—I can spare you for a moment from my side, in fact I'm longing to see the back of you—just run over and talk to that ugly old lady. I know she's half paralysed, and whistles when she speaks, and her hands aren't very nice to look at, being rather like a lion's, but you'll find it well worth while".'

They all laughed, and the gay, happy sound was caught by the wind that played in their bright hair.

'But Hilda knows what's good for a chap, and that's why Eustace is going to spend the rest of his life in comfort, not sweating in banks, or offices, or chambers, but just lying about on deck-chairs and ringing the bell when he wants anything.'

'Just like Miss Fothergill,' said Nancy. 'We often saw Eustace going to Laburnum Lodge and Daddy laid a bet with Mother that she would leave him something. "Depend upon it, he doesn't go there for nothing," Daddy used to say. "That boy's got his head screwed on." '

'She always did give me tea,' said Eustace, 'but I never asked for it. I just happened to be there at the time.'

Nancy laughed.

'We aren't blaming you, Eustace. Now, tell me one thing: is it true she was really a witch?'

'A witch?'

'Well, everybody said so. They said she had a broomstick and flew out on it at night. I expect she kept it in the umbrella-stand in the hall.'

'I never saw it, Nancy,' said Eustace seriously.

'But she had a stick, hadn't she?'

'Yes, but for walking with.'

'Would you know a broomstick if you saw one?'

'I'm not sure that I should.'

'Well, I bet you she had one. And everyone said that she cast spells.'

'I don't think she did.'

'Well, didn't she cast one on you? Wasn't that partly why you were always going there?'

Eustace tried to see his friendship with Miss Fothergill in terms of a spell. It would explain a great deal, of course. But surely witches were wicked? Miss Fothergill represented the good; and in all his dealings with her he had had one aim, to increase the volume of good surrounding Eustace Cherrington and radiating from him over the whole world. It had been quite pleasant, of course, but then good things could be pleasant, once you had got over your initial distaste for them. They made you feel good, and a witch could never do that.

'Witches have familiars, you know,' Nancy went on. 'Do you know what a familiar is?'

Eustace shook his head.

'They're little boys generally, quite nice little boys to begin with. That's why the witch likes them. She has to look about very carefully to find the right kind: she might find one on the cliffs, of course. You see, most boys are so selfish, like Gerald: they wouldn't be any good to a witch, because she couldn't make them do what she wanted them to do.'

'What would she want them to do?'

'Oh, fetch and carry, you know, and run about after her,

and pick up her purse, and read aloud to her, and play cards with her, and forfeits, and give her kisses.'

'How did you know that?' cried Eustace, scarlet.

'A little bird told me. And all the time he thinks he is being very kind, but it's really the witch who is putting a spell on him. And then in the end, you see, she gets possession of his soul, and it becomes as thin as paper and she slips it under her pillow every night when she goes to bed. But of course he doesn't know anything about that. He imagines he still has his soul and it's the same size as usual. And then she dies and leaves him a fortune to show that she has paid for his soul and it really is hers. He never gets it back, poor little boy!'

Eustace stared at her fascinated. The wind had put a delicate flush upon her milky skin; a mischievous gleam was in her eyes; to the onset of the wind and the restless movements of the horse her slight figure yielded itself in a hundred attitudes of grace. Into Eustace's heart stole a sensation of exquisite sweetness; he remembered when he had last felt it—at the dancing class, on the afternoon when she rejected all his rivals and danced with him and for him. She had spoken of a spell—well, wasn't this one?

I believe *you're* a witch,' he said with a boldness that surprised him.

'I may be,' said Nancy, appearing to welcome this vile charge, 'but if I am it doesn't mean that I want to have anything to do with a familiar who has belonged to another witch. He would be secondhand, you see.'

She turned away pensively and looked across the head of her brother's horse at Dick.

'Don't listen to her, Eustace,' Dick said. 'She's been reading something in a book, you know, and she doesn't quite understand it—all that about familiars and souls, I mean. I'm sure your soul is as good as hers any day—I don't think she has one. Now Hilda'—his voice changed—'*she* has a soul, of course.'

Eustace, still with his eyes on Nancy's face, saw it harden slightly. 'What a pity there isn't a Mr Fothergill, eh,

Eustace ?' Dick went on, speaking to Eustace but looking at Hilda. 'Do you think if I got into a bath-chair, and made Gerald here push it along the cliffs, you could order Hilda to come and talk to me and have tea with me and—and all the rest of it ? Do you think you could ?'

'Well,' said Eustace, 'perhaps if you were really ill . . . But I don't think you ever would be.'

'No, I'm afraid not; too healthy. All the same I shall try it. One day you'll be out walking and you'll notice something crawling along in the distance and when you come up to it this is what you'll see'—and leaning forward on the horse he clenched his hands and curved his shoulders, as though his body had contracted to meet a sudden pain, and dropping his right eye and twisting up the corner of his mouth, he managed to force his face into a hideous resemblance to Miss Fothergill's.

Even Eustace laughed.

'You'd be like the wolf in Little Red Riding Hood,' he exclaimed.

'Yes, and Eustace would have to come and kill me. But he wouldn't, he'd be too lazy by that time. He'd just ring for another sherry and bitters and say, "Poor Hilda, I always knew she'd get into trouble!" '

'I shouldn't,' said Eustace indignantly. 'I should——' He stopped and looked helplessly at the towering horses, and at Dick who reminded him of the picture of a centaur.

'There, I knew it,' Dick Staveley cried triumphantly, 'he wouldn't do anything. He would allow his sister to be eaten and not bother to avenge her. That's what comes of having money. All the same, it's very nice to have it.' He looked at his watch. 'By Jove, it's half-past twelve. We must be getting along. Do we separate here, Nancy ?'

'I think we've just time to go back by Old Anchorstone with you,' said Nancy.

Dick caught his sister's eye.

'Excellent, as long as it doesn't make you late. But before we go let's give them both three cheers.' His face turned serious, his voice resonant with command. 'Three cheers for Hilda and Eustace, coupled with the name of Miss Janet Fothergill. Now all together. Hip-hip-hooray!'

'Hip-hip-hooray!'

'Hip-hip-hooray!'

Three times the sound rose and fell. Thin and light, it soon mingled with the greedy cries of the seagulls or was snatched out of earshot by the wind; but its quality was unique and unmistakable. Eustace had never heard cheering before but at once he recognised what it meant and his heart expanded and glowed. Four people all wishing him well, all cheering him to the skies!

It was a glorious moment. Noticing that Dick and Gerald had taken their caps off, he took off his hat too, and waved it with a proud and gallant air. Startled, the horses sidled and pranced, and seemed to bow to each other; they made a ripple of movement, upwards, downwards, sideways, and their riders moved sometimes in time with their rhythm, sometimes against it, as though they too had the freedom of the wind and sky. Laughing and self-conscious and a little sheepish, they turned to each other, and then, still with the same half-apologetic look, to Eustace and Hilda. 'Good-bye, good-bye, good luck!' their voices sang.

There was a convulsive stir among the horses; a swinging of heads, a dipping of hindquarters; in a moment sand flew up from thudding hoofs, and they were off. Still waving his hat, Eustace watched them out of sight.

CHAPTRE XV

One Heart or Two

'HE said it was half-past twelve,' said Hilda. 'We shan't have time to finish the pond now.'

'Yes, I mean no,' said Eustace.

'You don't know what you mean.'

Eustace gazed about him. In the foreground was a great untidy patch of sand, churned up by the horses' hoofs; it looked like a battlefield and gave him a curious thrill of pleasure. He drew a long breath and sighed and looked again. On his left was the sea, purposefully coming in; already its advance ripples were within a few yards of where they stood. Ahead lay long lines of breakers, sometimes four or five deep, riding in each other's tracks towards the shore. On his right was the cliff, rust-red below, with the white band of chalk above and, just visible, the crazy line of hedgerow clinging to its edge. Eustace turned round to look at the two promenades, stretching away with their burden of shops, swingboats, and shabby buildings dedicated vaguely to amusement; next came the pier striding out into the sea, and beyond it the smoke-stained sky above the railway station.

Yes, they were all there. But a fortnight ago, half an hour ago, they had not been. Eustace felt he was seeing them after a lifetime's separation. Experimentally, as it were, he drew another long breath. How gratefully, how comfortingly, his body responded! He knew it and it knew him; they were old, old friends and the partnership was not going to be broken.

'I feel so happy, Hilda,' he said. 'I don't think I ever felt so happy in all my life.'

'Why?' said Hilda. She had gone back to her rock and was sitting with her face half turned away from him. 'Is it because you've been given all that money?'

'Oh no,' said Eustace, 'I'd forgotten about that,' and

194

indeed, for the moment, he had. 'But aren't you glad too?' he went on. 'I mean, glad that I'm not going away.'

'But you are going away,' said Hilda. 'You're going away to school. I'm not glad about that, and I don't suppose you are. Or are you?' she added menacingly.

A shadow flitted across Eustace's face.

'Of course not. But that isn't the same as going right away.'

'I never believed you were going right away, as you call it.'

'You did!'

'I didn't!'

'You did!'

'I didn't!'

'Well, why were you so angry just now?'

'That was because I thought . . . Oh, I don't know what I thought . . . Then those people came and interrupted everything.'

'Weren't you pleased?' asked Eustace, his eye brightening at the sight of the patch of sand, the magnificent disorder of which had been created to do him honour.

'Yes, in a way, but they did rather spoil our morning.'

'Didn't you enjoy talking to them?'

'We didn't talk at all. They talked all the time.'

This was nearly true. Eustace tried again. 'Didn't you think Dick was nice?'

Hilda clasped her long thin hands together. 'He's always like that, isn't he?'

'Well, we haven't seen him often. Didn't you think it was funny what he said about riding in a bath-chair and pretending to be Miss Fothergill?'

'I don't think he ought to have made jokes about her.'

'Well, perhaps not. Shall you go and see him when I'm at school, like he asked you to?'

'I expect he'll be at school too. Anyhow I shan't have time. I shall have to help with Barbara, and the housework, and learn French and drawing so as to be a governess later on.'

'A governess?' cried Eustace. 'Whoever said you were going to be a governess?'

'Aunt Sarah told me months ago that I might have to be. I didn't tell you because I knew you wouldn't like it. Besides, I don't tell you everything.'

'I don't like it,' said Eustace. Primed as he was with happiness, invulnerable as it seemed to suffering, a pang shot through him. Hilda a governess! Of course she knew how to govern, he could testify to that. But without vanity he knew that when it came to governing he was an easy subject. Others might not be. Other children might be naughty and disobedient. At once he pictured Hilda's charges in a state of chronic insurrection. 'Sit still, Tommy, and do your sums as I told you.' 'I won't, Miss Cherrington.' 'Alice, how often have I told you not to draw pictures of me in your geography book?' No answer: Alice goes on drawing. 'Lady Evangeline,' (here Eustace's imagination took a sudden leap) 'May I ask you to remember the rule. I before E except after C?' 'You can ask me, Miss Cherrington, but I shan't pay any attention. After all, you're only a governess, and there are plenty more.' 'Butler,' said the Marchioness, 'ring the bell for Miss Cherrington. I'm afraid I shall have to dismiss her. You needn't order the trap. She can walk to the station.' Ring the bell, ring the bell! Why, that was what they said he, Eustace, would be doing. He would be ringing the bell for—what was it?—a something and bitters: and in another house, far away, beyond some mountains, perhaps, Hilda would be answering the bell, like a servant. A thought came to him.

'Do you think sixty-eight thousand pounds is a great deal of money?'

'They all talked as if it was,' replied Hilda in an indifferent tone.

'Gerald said it was only fifty-eight thousand.'

'Did he? There's not much difference, I shouldn't think.'

'I know that a thousand a year is a great deal of money,' Eustace persisted, feeling about in his mind for some way to interest Hilda in his financial prospects. 'I once heard

Daddy say of Mr Clements, "Oh, Clements is at the top of the tree. He's very well off. I shouldn't be surprised if he had nearly a thousand a year." '

'Mr Clements has been in the office much longer than Daddy. Besides, he's quite old. Most people get richer as they get older.'

'Aren't children ever rich, then?'

'Hardly ever. Besides, it wouldn't be good for them.'

'But I am,' said Eustace. 'They all said so. That's why they congratulated us and gave us three cheers.'

'It was you they were cheering,' said Hilda. 'They only cheered me because I happened to be with you. I haven't got any of the money, and I shouldn't want it either.'

'Oh, but wouldn't you?' cried Eustace. Fearful of his plan miscarrying, he put into his voice all the persuasiveness that he could muster. 'Think of the difference it would make. You wouldn't have to be a governess; you wouldn't have to do the housework, or any more than you wanted; you wouldn't have to bother about Barbara except to take her out sometimes for a drive or to the shops to buy toys for her.' Eustace paused and cast about for positive gratifications that might make money seem desirable to Hilda; he was handicapped because her whole attitude seemed to be stiff with rejection, and the only course that occurred to him was to credit her with a wish for luxuries which he would have wished for in her place.

'You could have all the clothes you wanted,' he began, 'and you could have a horse like Nancy has to go riding with Dick Staveley.'

'I have all the clothes I need, thank you,' said Hilda. 'And I don't want to go riding with Dick Staveley. I've told you that ever so often. And why she goes riding with him I don't know, because you can see he doesn't like her half as much as she likes him. I should have thought she would have more pride.'

'*Could* you see that?' asked Eustace, amazed at Hilda's insight.

'Of course you could if you had eyes,' said Hilda, 'and

weren't so silly about Nancy as you are. Anyhow, the horse isn't hers: it's one she hired from Craddock's—I know it, that bay mare with the white fetlock.'

Again Eustace was astonished by Hilda's powers of observation. But he was right in one thing: she had a passion for horses, although for some reason she took so much trouble to conceal it. And although her reception of his picture of her moneyed future was discouraging she had consented to argue about it, which was a hopeful sign.

'And then we could have a house together,' he urged. 'And servants to wait on us, and . . . and come when we rang the bell . . . and we could stay in bed for breakfast, and have deck-chairs in the garden and lemonade when it was hot.'

Eustace recollected that Hilda had a weakness for fizzy lemonade. 'And, of course, we should spend a good deal of the time abroad, at Homburg and Carlsbad . . . I don't quite know what we should do there, but it would be nice to be abroad, wouldn't it ? And we could go to other places. We might see Vesuvius in eruption or be in Lisbon when there was an earthquake.'

'I shouldn't want to do any of those things,' said Hilda. 'They sound rather silly to me.'

She spoke in her faraway voice and Eustace realized that he had awoken the mood of self-dramatisation in which, picturing herself as something other than she was, she might be accessible to his proposals for her welfare. But he had never learned to reckon with the austerity of her nature, its manifestations were a continual surprise to him. She seemed to do disagreeable jobs because she liked doing them, not because they were milestones on the steep but shining pathway of self-sacrifice. A future that would be dark for him might be bright for her. Acting on a sudden inspiration he said:

'And you could go to school too if you liked.'

Eustace saw that he had scored a hit. Hilda's head sank backwards, and her long eyelids drooped over her eyes. Speaking in her deepest voice, she said, 'What's the good of talking about it? Miss Fothergill didn't leave her money to me.'

'No,' said Eustace, 'but,' he added triumphantly, 'I can share it with you if you'll let me.'

'I won't.'

'You will.'

'I won't.'

'You will.'

'All right,' said Hilda. 'Anything to keep you quiet.'

Soon they were deep in money matters. How much would they have? How long would it last?

'It depends whether Gerald was right or Dick,' said Eustace. 'Gerald said fifty-eight thousand pounds and Dick said sixty-eight.'

'Perhaps they were both wrong,' said Hilda.

'Oh no, Dick couldn't be. He's got a lot of money himself. Nancy said so. Let's say sixty-eight thousand. Look, I'll write it on the sand with my spade.'

'It's vulgar to write things on the sand. Only common children do that.'

'Oh, it doesn't matter! Figures aren't the same as words. They couldn't be rude.'

The number 68,000 appeared in figures of imposing size.

'If we each had a thousand pounds a year, how many years would sixty-eight thousand last?'

'Divide by a thousand,' said Hilda.

'How do I do that?'

'You ought to know. Cut off three noughts.'

Eustace took his spade and unwillingly put a line through each of the last three figures, leaving the number 68 looking small, naked, and unimpressive.

'Sixty-eight years,' he said doubtfully. 'How old would you be then, Hilda?'

'Add fourteen.'

Eustace put 14 under 68 and drew a line.

'That makes eighty-two. And how old should I be?'

'Subtract four from eighty-two. You're nearly four years younger than me.'

'What a lot of figures I'm making,' said Eustace, his lips following the motions of his spade. 'That comes to seventy-eight. You would be eighty-two and I should be seventy-eight, or seventy-eight and a half. After that we shouldn't have any more money, should we?'

'We might be dead by then,' said Hilda.

'Oh no,' said Eustace, shocked. 'I don't suppose so. At least I shouldn't.' He broke off, not wanting to suggest that Hilda might die first. 'I mean,' he amended, 'people do live to be ninety. But perhaps we should have saved something. We needn't spend exactly a thousand pounds every year. You could save out of your thousand, and perhaps I could save out of mine.'

Hilda rose from her rock, brushed herself cursorily, and moved across to examine Eustace's figures.

'You haven't made those eights very well,' she said. 'You never could get them quite right. Now just make one for practice, and show me how you do it.'

Trying to hide his irritation, Eustace complied.

'You ought to go across first, instead of coming down. The rest of them seem to be all right.' With critical eyes she studied the figures, while Eustace, fearful of being detected in a mistake grew first red and then pale. Suddenly Hilda burst out laughing. She laughed and laughed, throwing herself backwards and forwards. At last she said: 'You'll have to do it all over again.'

'Oh, but why?' said Eustace. 'I did exactly as you told me.'

'I know,' said Hilda, still overcome by amusement. 'It was my fault really. I forgot you'd have to divide by two.'

'Divide what by two?' asked Eustace, now completely at sea. Mathematics had always been his weak subject, the only one, really, in which Hilda had the advantage over him. He felt flustered and disappointed. The calculation, which had been such fun, almost the only sum he had ever enjoyed doing, was ending, as so many sums did, in mortification and defeat.

'Now start again here,' said Hilda, inexorably leading

him to a clean patch of sand. 'Sixty-eight thousand, divided by a thousand, sixty-eight: that's right. Now you must divide sixty-eight by two to get the number of years.'

'But why?'

'Because there are two of us, silly.'

Still uncomprehending and indignant, Eustace did this piece of division in silence.

'Thirty-four,' said the sands.

'You see, the money will only last thirty-four years,' said Hilda kindly. 'How old shall I be then?'

A pause while the spade made its incisions.

'Forty-eight.'

'Let me look at the eight. Yes, that's better. And how old will you be?'

'I can do that in my head,' said Eustace peevishly. 'Forty-four.'

'You see what a difference there is?' said Hilda, still chuckling.

'Yes,' said Eustace. 'We might be alive a long time after that.'

'But of course if we only had five hundred a year each—would you like to work that out?'

'No, thank you,' said Eustace sulkily.

'Do you know what the answer is?'

'I think I can guess.'

'What is it?'

'I'll tell you later on.'

'I want you to tell me now. Or would you rather I told you?'

'No. Yes, tell me if you want to.'

'I should be eighty-two and you seventy-eight, of course!'

Eustace shrank into himself and looked malignantly at Hilda. It was to have been such a grand moment, this dividing of the treasure; at the prospect his whole nature had put out flags and blossoms; and how they were torn, how they were withered! All the glorious experience of giving reduced to the dimensions of an arithmetic lesson, and a lesson in which he had signally failed to shine. His eyes filled with tears. He looked away from Hilda at the scratched and scribbled sand. What use was a fortune if it failed one at the age of forty-four? This morning, to Eustace under sentence of death, forty-four seemed unattainably far away. Now it was only just round the corner: he would be there in no time—and then misery, penury, the workhouse. And the alternative? Five hundred a year till he was seventy-eight. But what was five hundred a year to someone who could have had a thousand? Would his father have called Mr Clements well off if a paltry five hundred a year was all Mr Clements had to boast of? There was no point, no sense in having five hundred a year: it would command nobody's respect. It was sheer beggary. One might as well be without it.

He glanced at the figures, only a moment since engraved with so much pride and excitement. They looked ill made, sprawling. No wonder Hilda had found fault with them. Divide by two, divide by two. Yes, there it was, the division, the simple piece of division, that had been so fatal to happiness. Supposing the sand was a slate, how easy it would be to wipe those figures off! And in a way it was a slate, for here was the sea crawling up to blot out what he had written. It was not too late to change his mind.

Hilda was a girl who didn't care much for money. When her brother Eustace wanted her to share his fortune with her, she made him do a lot of sums. She did not understand that that's not what money's for. It's for more important things like hunting and shooting and going abroad. You can do sums without having money, in fact if you have money you needn't do sums, you can pay someone else to do them. Eustace offered Hilda half his money, but all she did was to make him practise writing eights. So he said, 'I've changed my mind, I don't think I'll give you the money after all and you can be a governess as Aunt Sarah said.' And Hilda said, "Oh Eustace, I am so sorry I made you do the eights, after you had been so generous to me. Please, please let me have the money; I don't at all want to be a governess. I shall be terribly homesick and lonely, and they will all be very unkind to me, and say I am not teaching the children in the right way because I haven't been to school or got any degrees. Please, please, Eustace, remember how we were children together.' But Eustace said, 'I'm afraid it's no good, Hilda, you see I never change my mind twice.' Then Hilda said, 'Oh, but you've written it down, it's a promise and you can't break a promise.' But Eustace pointed to the sea and said, smiling, 'I'm afraid there won't be much left of my promise in a few minutes' time.' Then Hilda began to cry and said, 'Oh, how can you be so cruel?' but Eustace didn't listen because he had a heart of stone.

Strengthened and emboldened by this meditation, Eustace turned resolutely to Hilda who had taken up her spade and was negligently dashing off some very accurate eights.

'I suppose if only one person had the money, it would go on being a thousand a year till he was seventy-eight?'

'Yes,' said Hilda, without looking up. 'It would. I should keep it all if I were you. Don't bother about me. Let's pretend we were just doing a sum for fun.' She made another eight, more infuriatingly orthodox than the last.

This was not at all what Eustace had bargained for. His newly found firmness of purpose began to ooze out of him. Still, the pleasures of vindictiveness, once tasted, are not easily put aside.

'Should you mind being a governess very much?' he asked. It occurred to him that she genuinely might not mind.

'I dare say I shouldn't really,' said Hilda. 'It would depend what the children were like. They might not be so easy to manage as you are. Of course I'd rather go to school, but as you won't be here in any case, it doesn't matter much what I do.'

Eustace had to admit to himself that this was a handsome speech, and the more he thought about it the handsomer it seemed. Revenge died in his heart and was replaced by a glow of another kind. He looked at Hilda. Poised, doubtless, over another superlative eight, she stood with her back to him; on her worn blue dress where she had been sitting on the rock were seaweed and the stains of seaweed. The sight touched him as he was always touched when her habitual command over circumstances showed signs of breaking down. The taste of pride was sour in his mouth. He must make her a peace offer.

'Let me see if I can do an eight like one of yours,' he said placatingly.

Assuming her air of judgement Hilda watched him do it.

'Not at all bad,' she pronounced. 'You're improving.'

The stretch of sand on which they stood now bore the appearance of a gigantic ledger, but towards the middle there was still a space left, a vacant lot shaped like a shield, which challenged Eustace's feeling for symmetry and completeness. 'I'm going to draw something,' he announced. He moved over to the virgin patch and began to make a design on it. After a minute or two's work he drew back and studied the result, sucking his lower lip.

'What's that?' asked Hilda.

'You'll see in a moment.'

He returned to his sketch and added a few lines.

'I still don't see what it is,' said Hilda.

'It's meant to be a heart. A heart isn't very easy to draw.'

'And what's that sticking through it?'

'That's an arrow. Look, I'll put some more feathers on its tail.' Eustace got to work again and the tail was soon almost as long as the shaft and the head combined. 'Now I'll just make its point a little sharper.'

'I shouldn't touch it any more if I were you,' said Hilda, proffering the advice given to so many artists. 'You're making the lines too thick. A heart doesn't have all those rough edges.'

'It might be bleeding, from the arrow. I'll put in a few drops of blood falling from the tip and making a little pool.' Formed of small round particles rising to a peak in the middle, the pool of blood looked far from fluid.

'Those drops look more like money than blood,' said Hilda.

'They might be money as well as blood—blood-money,'

said Eustace, trying to defend his draughtsmanship. 'There is such a thing, isn't there?'

'Yes, it's what you pay for freedom if you're held in bondage,' Hilda told him.

Eustace turned this over in his mind. 'I don't think I want that. Blood looks better than money in a picture because it's a prettier colour. I never saw a picture with money in it.'

'You haven't seen all the pictures there are,' said Hilda. 'There might be one of the thirty pieces of silver.'

'No, because Judas kept them in a bag so they shouldn't be seen,' said Eustace glibly. This was one of those border-line remarks which he sometimes allowed himself when in a sanguine mood. The statement couldn't be disproved, so it wouldn't count as a lie even if he wasn't sure it was true.

'But have you ever seen a picture with blood in it?' asked Hilda.

'Oh yes,' said Eustace. 'Bible pictures are often bloody.' He felt there was something wrong with this as soon as he said it, and Hilda left him in no doubt.

'Daddy told you not to use that word,' she cautioned him. 'It's wicked and besides you might get taken up.'

'I meant blood-stained,' said Eustace hastily, and hoping the alternative had not jumped into his mind too late to avert the sin of blasphemy. Crime was much less heinous. 'Only here, in this picture,' he hurried on, as though by changing the subject he might conceal his slip from powers less vigilant than Hilda, 'I haven't made the drops run into each other properly. I'll put in some more. There, that's better. But wait, I haven't finished yet.'

He walked backwards and fixed on the diagram a scowl of terrifying ferocity. 'I think this is how I'll do it. Don't look for a minute. Shut your eyes.'

Obediently Hilda screwed her eyes up. A long time seemed to pass. At length she heard Eustace's voice say, 'You can look now.' This is what she saw:

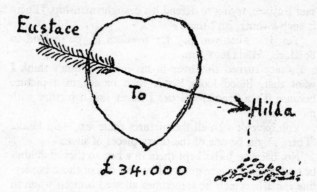

'You understand what it means, don't you?' asked Eustace anxiously.

'Yes, I suppose I do. Thank you, Eustace.'

'That's the right sign for pounds, isn't it, an L with a cross?'

'It ought to have two, but one does almost as well.'

Eustace felt pleased at being so nearly right.

'I had to make the arrow-head pointing at you,' he said, 'because, you see, it was going that way already, and I couldn't alter it. And of course it's bringing you the money. But it won't hurt you, at least I hope not, although I drew it at a venture. I don't think it will, do you? You see, it isn't touching you.'

'A sand-arrow couldn't hurt me, silly,' said Hilda. 'Besides, it's crooked. But I don't think Aunt Sarah would like us to write our names up anywhere. She's always been strict about that.'

Eustace looked troubled.

'I know what I'll do. I'll rub out all of our names except the capital letters.' He scrabbled on the sand with his foot. 'Now it just says E. to H.'

Thus edited, the diagram looked at once intimate and anonymous.

'Which of our hearts is it?' asked Hilda, after giving Eustace time to admire the beauty of his handiwork.

'Well, I meant it to belong to both of us,' said Eustace, 'I ought to have drawn two, perhaps, but I didn't quite know how to make them fit. If you like you can imagine another heart at the back of this one, exactly the same size. It would be there though you couldn't see it. Then the arrow would go through both and then of course they would be joined for ever. Unless you would rather think of us as just having one heart, as I meant before.'

'I think there had better be two,' said Hilda, 'because your heart is weaker than mine. I mean, you strained it once, didn't you?—and they might not beat quite together.'

'Very well,' said Eustace. 'I'll make a shadow here to show there's something behind.' He took up his spade.

'Now the heart looks as if it had grown a beard,' said Hilda, laughing. 'It's getting old, I'm afraid. How about the time? Oh, Eustace, it's one o'clock already. We must hurry. You won't be able to count the steps.' They set off towards the cliffs.

'Let's stay here just a minute,' panted Eustace as they reached the summit. 'I want to get my breath and I want to see what's happened while we were coming up.'

They paused, ignoring the stale challenge of the automatic machines, and clasped the railings with which the cliff, at this point, had been prudently fortified. How comforting, after all their tremors and uncertainties, was the feel of the concrete under their feet and the iron between their hands. They had to cling on, or the wind, shooting up the cliff with hollow thuds and mighty buffets, might have blown them over. Hilda's head overtopped the railings but Eustace still had to peer through. Putting on their watch-dog faces they scanned the rock-strewn shore. From here the waves looked disappointingly small, but every now and then the wind-whipped sea shivered darkly over its whole expanse. It was coming in with a vengeance; like many other creeping things it made more headway when one's back was turned.

'Look, Hilda,' cried Eustace, 'it's all covered up! All the bit that the horses kicked up has gone, and our hearts have gone too! You wouldn't know we had ever been there. It's just as though nothing had happened all the morning—the longest morning we ever spent on the sands!'

'There's still a bit of the pond left that we didn't finish,' said Hilda, 'and our footmarks coming away from it.'

'They'll soon be gone too,' said Eustace.

'Now don't stand staring any longer,' said Hilda. 'We ought to be home by now. Come on, let's run.'

They started off, and Eustace was soon left behind.

'Don't go quite so fast, please, Hilda,' he called after her. 'I can't keep up with you.'

He made the appeal for form's sake, not expecting her to heed it; but to his surprise he saw her slow down and then stop. When he came up with her she held out her hand and said a little self-consciously:

'Let's pretend we're having a three-legged race.'

Overjoyed, Eustace took her hand and they stood looking at each other inquiringly, as if they had just met for the first time, fellow-competitors measuring each other's strength.

'Who would it be against?' Eustace asked.

Hilda dropped his hand and thought a moment. She was never quick at choosing players to fill imaginary rôles.

'Well, the Steptoes perhaps. They always want taking down a peg. But anyone you like, really. The whole world.'

At the ring of this comprehensive challenge Eustace seemed to see cohorts of competitors swarming on the cliff and overflowing into the Square. Many of them, in flagrant disregard of the rules of the race, were mounted on horses.

'What will the prize be, if we win?' he asked.

'Of course we shall win,' said Hilda. 'Won't that be enough for you? You think too much about prizes. Prizes are only for games.'

'But isn't this a game?' said Eustace, who always dreaded the moment when practice ended and performance began.

'You can think so if you like,' said Hilda. 'I shall pretend it's real . . . Now where's my handkerchief?'

She brought it out of her pocket, fingered it for a moment,

then stuffed it hastily back, but not before Eustace had noticed how sodden and crumpled it was.

'I'm afraid mine's too small,' she said. 'Give me yours if you haven't lost it. You don't mind if it gets pulled about a bit, do you? It isn't one of your best.'

Protesting that he didn't mind, Eustace aligned his foot with Hilda's. Sinking on to one knee she passed the handkerchief round their ankles.

'Won't it come undone?' asked Eustace anxiously.

'Not if I tie it,' muttered Hilda. 'I know a knot that can't come undone, no matter how hard you pull.'

Straightening herself, she looked critically at Eustace's *Indomitable* hat and at the ridges and creases on its brim. A pinch here and there restored it to symmetry but could not make it seem the right kind of headdress for an athletic event.

'Now put your best foot forward,' she said.

'My best foot's joined to yours,' objected Eustace.

'Well, the other then. Ready? Steady?' Hilda hesitated, and then the light of battle flamed into her eye. 'Charge!'

They were off. Hilda had her right hand free. Grasped in the middle like a weapon at the trail, and swinging rhythmically as she ran, her iron spade seemed to be making jabs at the vitals of the future; while the wooden one that served Eustace as a symbol of Adam's destiny, dangling from his nerveless fingers, wove in the air a fantastic pattern of arcs and parabolas, and threatened momentarily to trip him up.

On they sped. Each lurch and stumble drew from Hilda a shrill peal of laughter in which Eustace somewhat uncertainly joined. 'Look, we're catching them up!' Hilda cried.

They crossed the chalk road in safety but a patch of rough ground lay ahead, mined with splinters and palings from the broken fence; and to Minney, watching from a window, it looked as if they were sure to come to grief before they arrived at the white gate of Cambo.

Commentary

COMMENTARY

This novel takes its title from the episode of a sea-anemone eating a shrimp which is occurring at the very moment that we begin to read. From the start we see the incident through the eyes of Eustace, the small boy who is gazing into the pool:

> His heart bled for the shrimp but on the other hand how could he bear to rob the anemone of its dinner?

Hilda, his sister, upon being called, has no such qualms; she feels that immediate action is called for and so she pulls the shrimp away from the anemone and thus destroys both of them. At once the incident has reflected for us an important difference between the characters of the two children. Eustace feels so involved in the situation imaginatively that he cannot bring himself to decide what must be done. Hilda shows no hesitation in climbing the rock, plunging her hand into the rockpool and doing what she can, even though her action turns out to be disastrous. As we read on and at a later stage look back to this opening episode, we begin to realise that it epitomises in several ways the relationship between Eustace and Hilda. Eustace has many 'shrimp-like' qualities—he is physically small and extremely vulnerable in every respect to the attitudes of other people. Hilda is potentially beautiful—more like the anemone than the shrimp, and like the anemone she is the predator while Eustace is the prey.

Eustace

Eustace is nine and a half when we first meet him. The fact that he is small for his age worries him. When he is sitting up on the box of the hired landau beside Mr Craddock the driver, they pass a spring of water stained rust-red with iron and Mr Craddock observes:

'If you was to drink that every day,' observed the driver, 'you'd soon be a big chap.'

'You don't think I'm very big now?'

'You'll grow a lot bigger yet,' said the driver diplomatically.

Eustace was relieved. He had been told that he was undersized. One of the tasks enjoined on him was to increase his stature.

Eustace is the only character in the book whose inner thoughts and feelings are described for us explicitly; those of the other characters, even Hilda, are usually conveyed to us as they would be in everyday life—by implication, through what they say and how they behave. But we can if we like identify ourselves with Eustace. His thoughts and fears and hopes and despairs are revealed to us in detail, and as he is a highly imaginative child the description of his dreams and fantasies is of immense importance. Like Leo in Mr Hartley's novel *The Go-Between* (who could in many ways be Eustace in adolescence) though outwardly weak and submissive he enjoys fantasies of Power and Destruction. In the opening episode for instance, when Eustace returns to Hilda who is sitting brooding on the rocks after his temporary desertion to Nancy, he 'conceived himself to be the Angel of Death' directing a volcanic flow of lava on its course of devastation:

Could Lisbon be destroyed a second time? It would be a pity to waste the energy of the eruption on what was already a ruin; but no doubt they had re-built it by now. Over it went, and in addition an enormous tidal wave swept up the Tagus, ravaging the interior. The inundation of Portugal stopped at Hilda's feet.

Similarly in his bath, the spots of 'livid blue' where the enamel has been chipped away 'represented cities destined for inundation' and above 'Rome, his favourite victim' there is the 'Death-Spot': 'If water so much as licked the Death-Spot Eustace was doomed.'

214

It would be misleading to give the impression that all Eustace's fantasies are morbid, although even the pleasant ones contain some element of suffering—as in the typically schoolboyish flights of fancy in which he is either being rescued by or is rescuing Dick Staveley from horrors worse than death. Often buildings like the water-tower and the lighthouse, or fragments of landscape, (a waterfall foaming over a rock on the way to Spentlove-le-Dale), thrill and excite him. The most memorable and detailed fantasy of this kind is his self-identification with the West window of Frontisham Parish Church:

> Disengaging himself from the tea-table he floated upwards. Out shot his left arm, caught by some force and twisted this way and that; he could feel his fingers treble-jointed and unnaturally long, scraping against the masonry of the arch as they groped for the positions that had been assigned to them.

Yet Mr Hartley is careful to point out, before this flight of Eustace's imagination is described for us, that 'It was not the window itself which fascinated him, so much as the idea of its pre-eminence . . . It had entered for the architectural prize and won'. It is this complexity, this mixture of normal schoolboy and hyper-sensitive child which prevents any impression of sentimentality from spoiling the author's presentation of Eustace.

It is not psychologically surprising to discover that Eustace, who seeks this outlet of fantasy for his sensations of suffering on the one hand and his destructive impulses on the other, is also continually constrained by a hyper-sensitive moral conscience. This has been carefully fostered and cultivated by his Aunt Sarah and even more arduously 'trained' by Hilda who puts Eustace through a kind of 'moral gymnastics course'—all for his own good naturally! Look for a moment at the opening page of the novel: Eustace draws back from the soggy edge of the pool because he *must not* get his feet wet. Hilda shouts to him that it is *his fault* that the bank of their pond has broken, and he is immediately aware of his conscience nudging him to leave the rockpool in order to help her to repair the breach: 'Ought he not perhaps to go to Hilda . . . ?'.

Each of these situations is trivial in itself but it is this continual awareness that he is 'obliged' to obey the dictates of his conscience that saps Eustace's energies and inhibits his spontaneity to a very marked degree. When he retreats to the nursery and to the undiscriminating praise of Miss Minney, his old nurse, after being reprimanded by his Aunt for failing to do his best in a Geography Test, 'He felt an exquisite sense of relief; the tongues of criticism that wagged around him all day at last were stilled'. Yet when later he reflects on his father's casual remark to him: 'Very well then, do as you please', he cannot imagine an existence spent in pleasing himself. 'How would he set about it? He had been told by precept, and had learned from experience that the things he did to please himself usually ended in making other people grieved and angry and were therefore wrong. Was he to spend his life in continuous wrong-doing, and in making other people cross? There would be no pleasure in that. Indeed what pleasure was there, except in living up to people's good opinion of him?'.

The trouble is that Eustace has so many fears—from his child's-eye view life seems to be one long obstacle race:

Not only must he learn to drive a horse, he must master so many different matters: ride a bicycle, play hockey, play the piano, talk French and hardest of all, earn his living and provide for his sisters and his Aunt Sarah and his father when he got too old for work . . . The future was to be a laborious business.

It is above all the thought that he must inevitably take over from his father as the 'man of the family' that oppresses Eustace and causes him to recoil from the future in his imagination.

We can only begin to enter into his world as he perceived

it, if we realise, as his father ironically failed to do, 'that the boy lived in his imagination and that the fancied horror of Miss Fothergill's, like the untested delights of Dick Staveley's society, were more real to him than any actual experience, as yet, could be'. Outwardly he may be subdued and submissive, but inwardly his life is full of crises. His dancing class every Tuesday afternoon is always a minor crisis, and because we are allowed to think and feel as if we were looking at the world through Eustace's own head, we are able to appreciate how for him the very idea of meeting Miss Fothergill at close quarters was a major crisis, too terrifying in the end to be faced at the prearranged time. Similarly, Eustace's growing conviction that he is about to die very shortly is entirely consistent not only with Craddock's ambiguous remarks but also with his own earlier preoccupation with Death and Destruction.

Hilda

Hilda on the other hand is notably unimaginative, and sometimes this is a great relief to Eustace. When he confesses his fears about Miss Fothergill's veiled face: 'supposing she hasn't got a head even, how could her neck end?', Hilda bursts out laughing and momentarily Eustace is comforted by the sound because it brings his fears within a smaller compass. Hilda sees herself primarily in the role of mother to Eustace. Their own mother died at the birth of Barbara, their young sister, and as a result Hilda sometimes appears to be considerably older than her thirteen and a half years. Even her Aunt Sarah admits that Hilda 'has an old head on young shoulders'. When Eustace slips for once from her grasp on the afternoon of the paper-chase she reproaches herself bitterly: 'It was all my fault. I could have saved him. I ought not to have let him out of my sight'.

She is a very forceful character, but unfortunately for Eustace all her energies are channelled into shaping his life for him. She is particularly enthusiastic about his moral development and as we have seen, she sets him exercises (such as speaking to Miss Fothergill) for his spiritual welfare. With all this puritanical fervour one might have expected Hilda to be a drab, plain-featured child. But not a bit of it. She has a 'heart-shaped beautiful face' and it is her physical beauty which immediately attracts Dick Staveley, heir of Anchorstone Hall and consequently Eustace's hero. He makes no headway, however, against Hilda's reserve; she shows no interest in any one of her own age outside the family circle, preferring rather to withdraw from the overtures of others—as we can see very clearly from her behaviour on the tobogganning expedition.

She is often intolerant towards other children, sometimes openly hostile; for instance, when she sees that Gerald Steptoe has deliberately ruined their pool she bursts out to Eustace that she would like to throw Gerald and his sister Nancy tied together over the cliff. Eustace is genuinely pained by this hostility, just as he is by Hilda's awkward and sullen behaviour in situations where she is deprived of her natural powers of leadership. At the dancing class he notices her 'in an attitude at once relaxed and awkward, as though defying her teachers to make a ballroom product of her. Twisted in its plait her dark lovely hair swung out at an ungainly angle; her face expressed boredom and disgust; she looked at her partner . . . as though she hated him'. We feel all the time with Hilda that because her self-chosen outlets for passionate feeling are so few, those she does allow herself run with particular depth and vigour. At the tobogganning picnic the eventual release of her pent-up feelings is so great that she actually screams her intentions at the grown-ups.

Her genuine love and affection for Eustace are demonstrated most clearly when he fails to return home after the paper-chase. Her face blotchy with crying, she is lying in bed full of self reproach for having failed in her responsibility towards Eustace ('she ought to have brought him up in such a way that he simply could not have gone off on his own like that'), but at the same time she is clutching his night-gown to herself for comfort. It is a gesture which is at the same time private, pathetic and moving—one of the few indications that Hilda gives of her own loneliness and vulnerability.

Eustace and Hilda

As the relationship between brother and sister is the chief theme of the book let us examine it a little more closely now that a picture of their individual characters is beginning to take shape. Although the book is written largely from Eustace's point of view so that we see all the characters and every important situation through his eyes, there are also several important points in the novel when the author unobtrusively introduces his own comments on the relationship. We are told for instance at the beginning of Chapter Three that 'The effort to qualify for his sister's approval was the ruling force in Eustace's interior life: he had to live up to her idea of him, to fulfil the ambitions she entertained on his behalf' and later in Chapter Seven the author again enlightens the reader's understanding of Eustace's attitude to Hilda:

> Almost for the first time in the history of their rela-
> tionship Eustace felt that Hilda was treating him badly.
> Angry with her he had often been. But that was mere
> rebelliousness and irritation, and he had never denied
> her right of domination. Lacking it he was as helpless as
> the ivy without its wall. Hilda's ascendency was the
> keystone in the arch that supported his existence.

We can see from both these remarks that Eustace has not only accepted a submissive role in relation to his sister; he has come to depend on it. And when he summons all his resources for his one act of rebellion—to be a 'hare' with Nancy in the paper-chase, the effort almost costs him his life.

On the other hand Mr Hartley makes it clear that Eustace is not always consciously cowed by Hilda's domination. Their relationship is considerably more complex than that.

When he wakes up on the day that Nurse Hapgood is to leave (she has been living in while he was seriously ill), he is pleased because her departure 'meant Hilda's return; that was why he felt so lighthearted'—and when he is secretly convinced that he is going to die, it is to Hilda that he plans to leave his most treasured possessions.

On her side too Hilda is deeply involved in her brother's feelings; she does not simply manipulate him like a puppet to serve her own emotional needs. If we glance back at the incident of the shrimp and the anemone for a moment, we shall see that Eustace uses Hilda's disastrous intervention deliberately to vent his anger on her for refusing to let him play with Nancy Steptoe:

> 'I want to play with Nancy,' he said at last, averting his eyes from his sister and looking small and spiteful. 'I don't want to play with you. I don't ever want to play with you again. I don't love you. You killed the shrimp and you killed the anemone . . . . and you're a murderer.' The words were awful to her. An overwhelming conviction came to her that he did not love her, and that she was a murderer. She hurried away, with great ugly sobs that sounded like whooping-cough.

Perhaps this sense that Eustace has deserted her for Nancy is partly why she insists so ruthlessly upon a demonstration of his love and loyalty to herself at the picnic with the Steptoes.

The Eustace and Hilda Trilogy

This is not the only book about Eustace and Hilda. It is followed by two more: *The Sixth Heaven* and *Eustace and Hilda*. Already however in this novel it is made plain that because Hilda has asserted so fiercely her right to make first claim on Eustace's allegiance she has inextricably involved her own welfare with his. This becomes increasingly clear in the two further novels which explore the continued relationship of brother and sister into adult life. In *The Sixth Heaven*, Hilda, much against her will, but to please her brother, agrees to accept Dick Staveley's invitation to a week-end house-party at Anchorstone Hall. This renewal of a brief childhood acquaintance has disastrous consequences which are described in the final volume of the trilogy. As so often in real life, there is a strong sense of tragic irony about the final outcome of events which initially caused much pleasure and satisfaction. One is reminded of the comment of Thomas Hardy, another writer with a keen sense of the tragically ironic: 'The vast difference between starting a train of events and directing into a particular groove a series already started is rarely apparent to the person confounded by the issue'.

When we look back at *The Shrimp and the Anemone* in the light of the two later works, one of the most striking features of this description of Eustace and Hilda as children is the way in which their fundamental attitudes both to themselves and to each other change so little as they grow older. Hilda never loses her urge to possess nor Eustace his desire above everything else to please. The parable of the shrimp and the anemone is played out in their lives with classic inevitability. Eustace's attempts to place Dick at the centre of Hilda's affections fail miserably and the measure of release, partial but not entire, which he enjoys in Venice (*Eustace and Hilda*) is brought to an end with his return to Anchorstone in order to place himself entirely at his sister's disposal. In striving to liberate her from the paralytic state into which she has withdrawn he overreaches his own strength, and on the night of her recovery he dies in his sleep. We must decide for ourselves whether Eustace has at last been totally consumed or finally liberated.

The Other Women in Eustace's Childhood

In a sense all the women in all three books appear to have something of the qualities of the sea-anemone. Outwardly beautiful, at heart they fully intend to possess the hapless males with whom they come in contact. Even Minney, who provides Eustace with the sense of comfortable security he so longs for as a child, bustles around him scrubbing behind his ears and making him sit up straight. No woman is ever content to let well alone . . . as Miss Fothergill says to Eustace just before she has her final stroke: 'We are all designing women. You mustn't let yourself get sucked in by us'.

We have already seen that Hilda wields by far the greatest influence over her brother. Also there are Miss Fothergill's own designs for Eustace, which take the shape of the large legacy which she bequeaths to him and which alters his life radically. In *The Sixth Heaven* we see Eustace first at Oxford enjoying the company of the 'well to do' set, and later at Anchorstone Hall, the Mecca of his childhood dreams. In *Eustace and Hilda* he is in Venice, mostly as the companion of Lady Nellie Staveley, the ageing beauty who is at once the most famous and infamous of the Staveley family.

To return to the women Eustace knew in the more restricted environment of his childhood. It is typical that his Aunt Sarah who has strictly puritanical views should mistrust Miss Fothergill's legacy and even attempt to persuade his father to refuse it. It is she more than anyone (except Hilda, whose views mirror her aunt's) who is responsible for Eustace's mistrust of any kind of pleasure, happiness or enjoyment for its own sake. Nancy Steptoe exerts exactly the opposite influence over Eustace, which is why his Aunt terminates their brief acquaintance with such finality—or at any rate attempts to do so, after the paper-chase. Prior to this, at the dancing class when Nancy persuades Eustace to accompany her on the chase, she selects him as her partner by telling all her other prospective partners that she has already promised to dance with Eustace. This is quite untrue of course and when Nancy casually admits the fact Eustace is shocked because 'he had been told that lying was one of the most deadly sins and he himself was morbidly truthful. Recognition of Nancy's fib struck him like a smack in the face. A halo of darkness surrounded her. His mind flying to fairy stories, classed her with the bad, with Cinderella's horrible sisters, even witches'.

This suggestion of witchcraft is brought up again by Nancy herself at their final meeting on the sands when she suggests that Miss Fothergill may have been a witch:

> Eustace stared at her fascinated. The wind had put a delicate blush upon her milky skin; a mischievous gleam was in her eyes; to the onset of the wind and the restless movements of the horse her slight figure yielded itself in a hundred attitudes of grace. Into Eustace's heart stole a sensation of exquisite sweetness; he remembered when he had last felt it—at the dancing class, on the afternoon when she rejected all his rivals and danced with him and for him. She had spoken of a spell—well wasn't this one? 'I believe *you're* a witch', he said with a boldness which surprised him.

Thus we have Hilda and Aunt Sarah ranged on one side of Eustace, both anxious to foster the workings of his conscience ('Eustace is better now at doing things he doesn't like', Hilda observes to her aunt), while on the other we have Nancy and Miss Fothergill who both fight, each in her own characteristic fashion, to release him from his moral burdens. As they are running along together in the paper-chase Eustace asks Nancy whether she thinks his family will be worried when they miss him. She replies: 'It doesn't matter if they are', and the author continues:

> This was a new idea to Eustace. He had always believed that for people to be worried on his account was, next to their being angry, the worst thing that could happen. Cautiously he introduced the new thought into his consciousness and found it took root.

Miss Fothergill is more directly concerned than Nancy (who is the most self-centred character in the novel) that Eustace should find some release from his fears and anxieties which seem constantly to hedge him about. Eustace confesses to her in a moment of confidence while they are playing piquet that he is sure that all his family are fond of him: 'But—I don't know how it is—if they see me really happy—for long together I mean—they don't seem to like it'. Almost with her dying breath she makes a courageous effort to pass on to Eustace Dr Speedwell's views on his over-conscientious approach to life: 'He said', Miss Fothergill continued, speaking a little breathlessly now, 'that you can't please everybody—nobody can—and that if you minded less about disappointing people you wouldn't disappoint them'.

Plot

The plot is basically simple. All the major events of the novel are important because they loom large in Eustace's life. They take place over the late summer months of two consecutive years and although some of them might have seemed trivial to an outsider, each situation is dwelt upon with extreme sensitivity to detail (especially to those details of emotional response in which Mr Hartley excels) because each situation calls for total involvement from the main character. There is the opening incident at the rockpool which can't have lasted for more than ten minutes or so, but it affects Eustace's imagination so deeply that the scene recurs to him years later at the moment of his death. Then there is the picnic on the Downs which involves Eustace in an exhausting demonstration of his loyalty to Hilda. Later Nancy bewitches him at the dancing class and inspires him to make his almost fatal act of rebellion. After his recovery, the long dreaded visit to Miss Fothergill in fact opens up new vistas for Eustace, and although we only see his first visit and his last they make his growing appreciation for that 'sense of luxury', which his Aunt mistrusts, very clear. Every situation in fact serves to illustrate some aspect of Eustace's character; there is no scene in which he is not the focus of attention.

Events which are to have a far-reaching influence on his

life arise out of apparent trivialities just as they do in our own lives. If Eustace had never brought himself to speak to Miss Fothergill on that first occasion on the cliffs, she would never have invited him to tea—and he would never have had the incentive to escape on the paper-chase with Nancy. As a result of the chase, his heart, already weak, is weakened further, and the knowledge that he must not exert himself too much overshadows the rest of his life. While he is ill Miss Fothergill continues to show an interest in him so that he does after all find himself walking up the gravel pathway to Laburnum Lodge once he has recovered from his bronchitis; the friendship which he forms almost immediately with Miss Fothergill is to result after her death in her generous legacy to him. This (as well as his heart condition) is to be the factor which is to alter fundamentally the entire pattern of his life. We can see the links in the chain very clearly when we look back after reading the whole trilogy, but the author's skill ensures that they are barely perceptible in the flow of present events.

The novel ends as it began, with another morning on the sands which for Eustace moves from crisis to crisis. First he nerves himself to confess his fears of imminent death to his sister, then there is their joint confrontation with the group on horseback, the Staveleys and the Steptoes, who seem to be from another world as they tower over Eustace's head. Once they have left there takes place the final pact between brother and sister which reflects and illuminates all that we have learnt in the novel of their relationship with each other, and finally we have their last climb up the concrete steps to the cliff top followed by the three-legged race home— Eustace's 'best foot' tied to Hilda's by a knot which she says 'can't come undone, no matter how hard you pull'. The whole of this last morning is so full of apparently small episodes 'layered' at different levels of implication, that rather more must be said about Mr Hartley's use of symbols.

Symbolism in the Novel
Elsewhere Mr Hartley refers to the symbols in one of his

later novels *The Go-Between* as 'an integral part of the story intended to deepen its meaning' and this remark would certainly be applicable to *The Shrimp and the Anemone*, where at times the ambiguities of meaning give the novel the kind of depth one normally associates with poetry. The episode from which the book takes its title is an excellent if obvious example, even though Mr Hartley writes in the essay to which I have just referred that he was not fully aware of the symbolic relevance of the shrimp and the anemone until after he had completed the novel. There are many examples of this kind of pointer from an explicit incident or detail to an implicit pattern which is rooted not in the outside world of sights and sounds and happenings, but in the inner world of personalities. There is for instance Hilda's iron spade and Eustace's wooden one. The author makes no direct connection between the spades and the children but somehow the iron spade seems to reflect Hilda's decisive personality while the wooden one which requires the more plodding effort is in this respect a symbol of her brother's character.

Several incidents are explored in much greater symbolic detail than the passing reference to the two spades. There is the diagram of the heart which Eustace draws on the sands, shot through with an arrow from which drop gouts of blood—to Hilda these look more like money, 'blood-money' as Eustace says. The episode is a prophetic forecast of their future relationship yet it is arrived at naturally through an incident which is quite credible as a piece of childish behaviour.

Another interesting example of the same kind is that of the pond-making. It is an excellent instance of a pastime which looked at from one angle is a perfectly normal activity to expect from children on a beach. But like the water which is the pond's essential element, it has unexpected depths which reveal truths and insights about the two children in a subtle and indirect way. For Hilda the pond is one outlet for the single-minded concentration and vigour of her character:

There was no doubt that it was Hilda who kept the spirit of pond-making alive. Her fiery nature informed the whole business and made it exciting and dangerous . . . Desultory amateurish pond-making was practised by many of the Anchorstone children . . . Often, so little did they understand of the pond-making spirit, they would wantonly break down their own wall for the pleasure of watching the water go cascading out. And if a passer-by mischievously trod on the bank they saw their work go to ruin without a sigh. But woe betide the stranger who, by accident or design, tampered with Hilda's rampart.

This excerpt reveals so much implicitly about Hilda's own character—the way in which her energies have been repressed and dammed up by her strict upbringing,—and her total involvement in whatever she happens to be doing, even when it is only an activity as transient as pond-making.

For Eustace, his changing attitude to the pond indicates a development and a change of perspective in his own character as he grows older and is subjected to a wider range of people and experiences. It was primarily Dick Staveley's reference to 'those beastly rocks' which shattered Eustace's childish allegiance to the pond. At any rate on their last visit to the beach we read: 'For him the pool had ceased to be a symbol. Of old, each time it rose from the sands and spread its silver surface to the sky it proclaimed that the Cherrington children had measured their strength against the universe, and won. They had imposed an order; they had left a mark; they had added a meaning to life'. Perhaps in a deeper sense of which Eustace would naturally be unaware but which the above passage suggests, the pool was a symbol at this point in the trilogy (it becomes an increasingly complex symbol as they grow older) of their innocence as children, as yet uncorrupted by the adult world. At any rate, when Eustace returns to Anchorstone at the end of the trilogy, he never re-visits the scene of their pond-making although he remembers it vividly and intends to do so. His final return to this particular beach is only in a dream, at the moment of his death.

Background

The intense drama of the inner world of Eustace's feelings and thoughts is played out against the background of leisurely Edwardian times. The family are living in the opening decade of the twentieth century in a small house called Cambo which has pretensions to gentility but which doesn't quite make the grade. The road which leads to the house is not made up and Mr Craddock refuses to drive his landau up to their door—until the news of Eustace's legacy becomes general knowledge. The parlour has plush covered armchairs, lace curtains and a black marble clock, but Mr Cherrington is distastefully conscious of the smell of cooking which pervades the house at meal-times. The garden, like the house, is small but at least it is one step up from living in 'the dingy side street in Ousemouth . . . at such close quarters round and above his father's office'. Eustace's father is a chartered accountant, but money has clearly been hard to come by until Eustace receives his legacy from Miss Fothergill with its £700 a year interest. Indeed, when Miss Fothergill first meets Eustace in his 'darned blue jersey' her immediate assumption is that he must be looking for some way of earning a little extra money when he offers to push her bath-chair.

To glance for a moment at the clothing of the period: it may seem strange that Eustace wears a hat even on the beach, until we remember that the fashion in the early 1900's was to cover up the body rather than to expose it. For driving, the ladies are heavily veiled and Miss Cherrington's purplish skirt is 'slightly stained with chalk dust where it swept the ground'. For the outing to Frontisham, Hilda (still regarded as a child) wears a navy blue dress and black stockings.

Anchorstone itself (' "Anxton" was the fashionable pronunciation') reposes in an atmosphere of quiet gentility.

There is Palmerston Parade for instance, 'that majestic line of lodging houses whose beetling height and stately pinnacles always moved Eustace to awe'. When he returns to Anchorstone as a young man, he is saddened to see that the lighthouse 'whose great rainbow-coloured lantern seldom failed to move him as a child' has been transformed into a teahouse: 'The building had been dismantled and decapitated, and the headless trunk, stark as the base of an abandoned windmill, had been painted a hideous maroon'. It makes Eustace realise, even while he is accepting the change, that some of the magic with which the place had been invested for him as a child has irretrievably withdrawn. Looked at from a broader angle, the old gentility to which the town like their own little house still clung at the turn of the century, has changed with the times. When Eustace returns, the First World War is a thing of the past, and the newfound freedom of his younger sister's generation can be registered in such small changes as the 'decolleté and informal costumes disclosing patches of red flesh' which passed Eustace's Aunt Sarah 'on their way down to the beach'. But in the first novel life is still leisured; motor-cars, which Minney refers to as 'those nasty motor things' are still an intrusion sufficiently rare to be worth a special comment. Eustace's own pastimes as a small boy are more or less summed up when he says naively to Miss Fothergill at their first meeting: 'I can't think of anything I'd rather do except perhaps make a pond or paddle, or go on the pier, or ride on a toboggan . . . '. Significantly the one pastime he omits froms his list is his weekly visit to the local dancing class which he attends in a spirit of trepidation rather than pleasure.

There is also the natural background to the children's lives which is unchanging in a way that clothes and people and pastimes are not. The lighthouse may have been demolished when Eustace comes back to Anchorstone in the twenties, but Frontisham Hill is still as steep as ever, the cliffs are still there 'rust-red below with the white band of chalk above', and below the cliffs the sands and the sea with its long line of breakers and its incessant pattern of withdrawal and advance.

The Topography of the Novel

From the topographical details which Mr Hartley includes in his novel it is possible to place the exact whereabouts of Anchorstone, Anchorstone Hall, the Downs, Ousemouth and Frontisham. To take Anchorstone first of all: the description of the cliffs which has just been mentioned in the previous section: 'rust-red below with the white band of chalk above' corresponds very closely to the description in the *County Books* series (Norfolk) of Hunstanton: 'The fame of Hunstanton as a pleasure resort lies in its sands. We reach first Old Hunstanton where the family of Le Strange has lived since the Dark Ages . . . In this parish the Breckland Chalk crops up in a double range of hills called 'the Downs' and at the edge of the sands it forms a cliff sixty feet high; this however is New Hunstanton. It is a most interesting cliff geologically, showing carstone at the bottom, brown shading up to yellow, then a bank of red chalk and on top of pure white chalk'.

The Downs receive a more detailed geological description in Nikolaus Pevsner's *The Buildings of England* series (N.W. and S. Norfolk): 'The foundation of Norfolk is the Chalk, but comparatively little of the countryside resembles the familiar S.E. English downland. Nevertheless the general line and character of the Chilterns and the Cambridgeshire Gog and Magog Hills stretches northwards through W. Norfolk from Thetford to Castle Acre, Massingham Heath and Ringstead Downs to the sea at Holme. Unlike the true Downs, these East Anglian Heights rarely rise above a couple of hundred feet and in Breckland they are covered with a thin skin of sand and gravel'. Perhaps this is why tobogganning was evidently a summer as well as a winter pastime.

We further learn from Pevsner's Guide that Hunstanton has a Lighthouse built in 1830 and 'Water Towers built in 1897 and very prominent'.

The description of Hunstanton Hall in *The Buildings of England*, 'a moated mansion, partly of about 1500, partly Jacobean, partly Victorian,' corresponds very closely to the detailed architectural description of Anchorstone Hall which occurs in *The Sixth Heaven*.

Ousemouth, where Eustace's father had his office, is in fact King's Lynn, which stands at the mouth of the Ouse where it flows into the Wash. Frontisham must be Snettisham—it even echoes the sound of the place. This is how Nikolaus Pevsner describes the church of St Mary at Snettisham: 'Perhaps the most exciting Decorated parish church in Norfolk; . . . the crowning conceit of the church is the West front, with its fabulous six-light window'. Pevsner does not eulogise about the window as fulsomely as the writer of the guide book which Eustace possessed, but his enthusiasm for the West window is clearly evident from this excerpt. In Mr Hartley's own words: 'It is a wonderful flamboyant window, like the West Window of York Minster, and the East Window of Carlisle Cathedral'.

Here is a simple sketch map to indicate the relative positions of Hunstanton, King's Lynn and Snettisham to each other—or for the purposes of the novel, Anchorstone, Ousemouth and Frontisham:

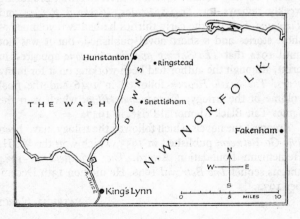

A Note on the Author

L. P. Hartley was born on the 30th December, 1895—almost exactly the same period as Eustace in *The Shrimp and the Anemone* (Eustace tells an Oxford friend of his in *The Sixth Heaven* that he left Anchorstone in 1907 when he was eleven years old). Mr Hartley's father was a solicitor and he spent most of his childhood in Peterborough, although he knows the area of N.W. Norfolk which provides the setting for *The Shrimp and the Anemone* very well from holidays spent at Hunstanton as a child.

Like Eustace, Mr Hartley was sent to a 'prep' school at a later age than was usual and he also shared Eustace's delicate health. Mr Hartley writes: 'I spent most of my army life at Colchester and Walton-on-the-Naze, defending the East Coast from possible invasion! I was discharged in August 1918 by a Medical Board presided over by Sir Frederick Travers, a surgeon who had removed King Edward VIII's appendix. He said to me "My poor boy, you have done your utmost for your King and Country".'

At this point Eustace's career once more reflects that of the author, as they both won scholarships which took them to Oxford. Upon leaving Oxford, however, their paths diverged. Eustace only dabbled with writing, but Mr Hartley rapidly became a serious literary critic, producing weekly reviews for *The Spectator*, *Weekend Review* and *Time and Tide*. In the early thirties he had two volumes of short stories and a short novel published, but it was not until 1944 that *The Shrimp and the Anemone* appeared in print, although the author had been working on it for many years. *The Sixth Heaven* followed in 1946 and the final volume of the trilogy, *Eustace and Hilda*, which won the James Tait Black Memorial Prize, in 1947.

Amongst the novels which followed the trilogy, have been *The Go-Between*, published in 1953, which won the W. H. Heinemann Foundation Award, *The Brickfield* in 1964 and its sequel *The Betrayal* 1966. He died on 13th December 1972.

PATRICIA D'ARCY

Notes

NOTES

The notes in this edition are designed for students overseas as well as for those in the U.K.

5 *anemone:* Sea anemones are sedentary and usually solitary marine animals whose flower-like appearance is striking: the radial arrangement of the usually colourful tentacles around the disc which bears the mouth at its centre is reminiscent of the petals of a flower. Most anemones adhere tenaciously by their bases to hard substrates such as rocks. They seldom move although a slow creeping is possible. Anemones possess stinging nematocysts on their tentacles which make it possible for them to capture other animals. As far as the author can remember there

Sea-anemone species Actiniaria

are no *coloured* sea-anemones in Hunstanton, only whitish ones. He is doubtful about the 'plumose' anemone being there, but says that Eustace liked the name, and may have read about it in Charles Kingsley's *Glaucus, or the Wonders of the Shore.*

8 *Hilda's ruthless recognition of an evil principle at the back of the anemone affair:* Hilda accepts that the anemone is a predatory plant which must eat its prey in order to survive.

9 *Diddums-wazzums:* Baby talk, meant to take you down a peg or two.

12 *Batey:* Originally 'bate' in Middle English: to contend with blows or arguments, hence: liable to get into a temper.

15 *Accordion-pleated skirt:* Pleated like the folds of a piano-accordion.

16 *the cone of Cotopaxi:* Cotopaxi is a mountain in the Andes of Ecuador in S. America, probably the world's highest volcano. It has a long history of violent eruption

and the country about its base has many times been
devastated by earthquakes or buried in pumice and
ash blown out of the crater. It has a beautifully symmet-
rical cone.

16 *Lisbon:* The capital and chief port of Portugal, it stands
on the right bank of the Tagus. Because it is built on
rocks of a tertiary formation Lisbon has always been
subject to earthquakes. In November 1755 it suffered its
severest shock—a great part of the town was destroyed
and about 40,000 people were killed. The tremor was
felt throughout Europe.

► *Tagus:* The second largest river of the Iberian peninsula.
The river divides below Salvaterra into two arms which
enclose a deltaic formation. Both branches terminate in
a broad tidal lake immediately above Lisbon.

17 *ten Vestal Virgins*: Eustace's classical allusion is doubly
incorrect. The city should have been Rome and not
Athens and there were only six spotless virgins whose
job it was to tend the sacred fire which Aeneas brought
from Troy and which it was subsequently the duty of the
State to preserve in a sanctuary in the Forum at Rome.
Eustace's history was more emotional than accurate!

22 *tamarisks:* Graceful evergreen shrubs with slender
feathery branches. They grow well in sandy soil and are
a common feature at the sea-side, especially in the South
of England.

► *Palmerston Parade:* Palmerston was the prime minister of
England in the 1850's and 60's. His name immediately
suggests, in this context, the solid Victorian architecture
of the period.

► *Bath-chair:* A hooded wheelchair of a kind originally
used at Bath.

► *Eustace's contumacy*: Eustace's perverse and obstinate
resistance of authority.

24 *as though the magnetic north had suddenly repudiated the
needle:* this is referring of course to the magnetic needle
of a compass: 'an instrument for determining the
magnetic meridian'. 'When a magnet is suspended

freely, one of its poles (hence called the north pole) points approximately north, and the other (the south pole) approximately south'. [Encyclopaedia Britannica].

Hilda believed her dominion was founded upon grace: The language here is theological. Hilda felt that there was no need for her to give any reasons for her governing position over Eustace.

26 *Ousemouth:* see p. 231.

► *The Downs:* cf. p. 230.

29 *She died when your sister Barbara was born:* Later Eustace tells Miss Fothergill: 'Mother died when Barbara was born. It was a great pity because only Hilda really remembers her'. Now if Eustace is nine and a half this would suggest that Barbara is at least four or five, but she is always referred to as 'Baby' and in Chapter Two she is apparently asleep in her pram outside the house in the middle of the morning. We asked the author about this apparent anachronism and he explained that unintentionally there has been a confusion about Barbara's age because his own younger sister was eight years younger than he and consequently he thought of Barbara as being eight years younger than her brother. It is clear that had this been the case, Eustace would have been able to remember his mother quite clearly.

Other famous authors have been known to make similar mistakes (in *Wuthering Heights* for instance Emily Brontë talks of wallflowers blooming in September). It is of far greater importance in this instance to notice that for artistic purposes it is essential that Barbara should be too young to impinge upon Eustace's relationship with Hilda, and in the two later novels it is equally important that Barbara should belong to a younger age group than her brother and sister—she is emancipated both from the ties that bind them to each other and from the stringent moral code to which they both succumbed. 'Truth' in the novel is not necessarily a matter of fact.

31 *Preparatory School:* A school for boys from the age of seven or so to thirteen, the age for Common Entrance examinations into the Public Schools; it is for this examination that these schools prepare their pupils. Almost all are private schools outside the State system of education. Nowadays they are commonly referred to as 'prep' schools but Dick Staveley later refers to his as a 'pri'—the popular term at Harrow in Edwardian times.

► *in crocodile form:* In a long line, 'two by two'.

► *Landau:* A four-wheeled carriage, with a top in two parts, so that it may be closed or entirely thrown open. It is named after Landau, the German town where these carriages were first made.

33 *Water-tower:* A tower containing tanks in which water is stored so that it may be delivered at sufficient pressure for distribution to an area.

34 *Iron-spring:* A spring of water which, because it runs through ground where there is iron ore, is stained brown with the rust which the action of the water on the ore has produced by a process of oxidisation.

36 *They're near, if you ask me:* The driver means that in his opinion the Steptoes are 'close' with their money, to use a similar metaphor. I.e. 'mean' or 'stingy'.

► *Savoir-faire:* 'know how' (lit. from the French 'to know [how] to do').

38 *toboggans:* wooden sledges, sometimes with low runners, used for coasting down slopes (usually of snow or ice but in this case of turf-clad chalk). It is clear from the text that the driver of the toboggan sat upright with his feet on a cross bar, holding in his hand a piece of rope attached to the front of the toboggan to help him to guide it on its course.

► *mollycoddle:* someone who coddles (spoils) himself, or is spoilt; an effeminate man.

41 *funk:* schoolboy slang for coward.

43 *seventh heaven of delight*: An expression which means 'supremely happy'. Some medieval mystics (The Cabbalists) maintained that there are seven heavens,

238

each rising in happiness above the other, the seventh being the abode of God and all the angels. Lady Nellie uses the phrase 'the sixth heaven' to Eustace (and significantly it is also the title of the second volume of the trilogy) after he has watched Hilda flying off in an aeroplane with Dick Staveley. A little later he asks her why she used the phrase and she replies: 'I expect you always keep one heaven in reserve'. And in fact it is only when he is on the point of death that Eustace dreams of 'the souls of the righteous . . . in the hand of God'—though once before in his childhood (*The Shrimp and the Anemone* Chapter Nine) he has a vision of the 'seventh heaven': 'a golden sea upon the sunshine-glinting ripples of which he and Miss Fothergill, reunited and at rest from their labours, floated for ever in the fellowship of the blessed'.

51 *Washing-stand:* A wooden stand which held a large bowl in a specially shaped frame, underneath which was a platform for the pail into which the dirty water was poured, or for the large jug (ewer) which contained the clean water.

► *Oxidised copper:* Copper which has turned green (as church spires often do) as a result of continuous exposure to the air—hence the oxidisation.

52 *Shelters:* Seaside structures to enable people to sit sheltered by a roof but with no outside walls to obstruct their view of the sea, the cliffs or the promenade; the bench seats are usually fixed round a central square and all face outwards.

53 *Sick and in prison and I visited you:* Hilda is thinking of Matthew Ch. 25 v. 36: 'I was sick and ye visited me: I was in prison and ye came unto me'.

55 *A whited sepulchre:* Matthew Ch. 23 v. 27: In Biblical language the phrase is used to mean 'hypocrite'.

56 *Impresario:* The manager of an operatic or concert company.

► *Prima-donna:* Lit. Italian for 'First lady' i.e. the first or principal female singer in an opera.

56 *Her voice bubbled a little:* As a result of her stroke Miss Fothergill's mouth was badly drawn up at one side; the passage of air through her lips and the flow of saliva was therefore unnaturally constricted. A doctor recently told the author that, as a result of the stroke, Miss Fothergill's mouth would in fact have turned the *other* way.

➤ *Muff:* A cylindrical covering, often of fur, into which both hands are thrust usually to keep them warm—but in Miss Fothergill's case to hide her misshapen fingers.

58 *St Christopher:* Described in legend as 'a saint who lived on the bank of a river in order to ferry people across. One day Christopher was carrying a child across when the waters rose alarmingly and Christopher's burden seemed as heavy as the weight of the whole world. On reaching the opposite bank the Child revealed himself as Jesus Christ'. ['Saints and their emblems' in *English Churches*—Milburn.]. Miss Fothergill's reference is an ironical one of course, the link being the difficulty that Eustace is encountering in his self-chosen task.

61 *The cavalcade:* The little 'procession' of Eustace and Miss Fothergill followed by Hilda and Miss Grimshaw.

➤ *Why do all donkeys have a cross on their backs?:* Hilda is referring to the dark marking on a donkey's hide along the spine and across the shoulders. Miss Fothergill quotes a popular superstition which attributes this marking to the occasion when Jesus rode on an ass for His triumphal entry into Jerusalem a few days before His crucifixion.

63 *She has hands like a lion:* A popular rumour has it that Miss Fothergill has claws instead of hands which is why she keeps them hidden in her muff. Cf. Nancy's vivid and malicious description to the terrified Eustace in Chapter Six: ' Well, they're not really hands at all but steel claws and they curve inwards like this, see! . . . And once they get hold of anything they can't leave go, because you see they're made like that. You'd have to have an operation to get loose'.

65 *Eustace prevailed on her to sacrifice her prerogative:*
Eustace persuaded Hilda to forgo the claim which she
had to an extra hour downstairs in the evening before
she came to bed.

➤ *It was sufficiently swept and garnished to let in . . . other
devils worse than the first:* A reference to the story Jesus
told about the man who, when one devil was cast out
from him found that seven more came to live in the
untenanted space. (Luke Ch. 11 vv. 24-26).

➤ *Neurasthenic:* Neurasthenia is 'a state of excessive
fatiguability, or lack of vigour, both bodily and mental,
often accompanied by hypochondria and sometimes by
phobias'. [Penguin Dictionary of Psychology].

66 *Eustace's obsession:* An obsession is 'a persistent or
recurrent idea, usually strongly tinged with emotion'.
[Penguin Dictionary of Psychology] (cf. also Ch. 13,
p. 169).

68 *Phenomena:* In this context the sense is: All these objects
which were immediately present to Eustace's per-
ception . . .

➤ *Frisson:* Shiver of anticipation whether of fear or
pleasure.

71 *Grace Darling:* Daughter of James Darling, keeper of the
Outer-Farm lighthouse, off the coast of Northumberland,
who with her father in 1838 gallantly put out in a fishing
boat in a heavy sea and rescued several passengers of the
wrecked steamer 'Forfarshire'.

➤ *The belle of the ball:* The most beautiful woman (girl)
present.

73 *Hare and Hounds:* Another name for a paper-chase—the
child (or children) chosen to be 'hare' carries a bag of
paper (cf. Chapter Seven, pp. 85 and 88) so that he
can lay a trail for the other children, the 'hounds', to
follow. The aim is for the hare or hares to complete the
chosen course before the hounds catch up with them.

79 *The Prodigal Son:* Cf. Luke, Ch. 15.

➤ *The keystone in the arch:* The stone at the summit of an
arch which locks the whole together.

80 *He had cried 'Wolf' so often* . . . : The allusion is to the well known fable of the shepherd lad who so often cried 'Wolf' merely to make fun of the neighbours, that when at last the wolf came no one would believe him.

83 *China tea like hay with no comfort in it:* Minney clearly likes 'a good strong cup of tea'. China tea is drunk chiefly for its fragrance; it is very pale in colour as compared to Indian tea and is not mixed with milk or sugar.

84 *Johnny Head-in-Air:* From 'Struwwellpeter' by Heinrich Hoffman. The poem begins:

'Look at little Johnny there
Little Johnny Head-in-Air . . . '

► *The Town-crier:* A man employed by the town council to proclaim public announcements in the streets; the crier would preface his announcement with the cry 'Oyez! oyez!' (Hear ye!). Some councils still employ a town-crier for special occasions though his function nowadays is entirely ceremonial.

85 *Appliqué:* Lit. 'applied'. The paper swallow had been stitched onto the linen bag.

86 *The Babeş in the Wood:* Eustace is referring to a popular fairy story about two small children who lost themselves in a wood and were covered with leaves and bracken by the birds and the animals as they slept—cf. p. 88 when Eustace looks at the paper which he and Nancy have just emptied out of their bags.

88 *Eustace you are a cake:* Period slang suggesting softness and weakness.

► *Bath Bun:* A large fruit bun with a sugared top.

90 *The Tragic Muse:* In Greek mythology there were nine sister goddesses, the offspring of Zeus and Mnemosyne (Memory), called the Muses. Melpomene was the name of the Muse of Tragedy.

► *Gas mantle:* The white dome-shaped covering over the gas-jet which provided light in the days before electricity.

91 *Bobby:* A slang nickname for a policeman, after Sir Robert Peel who first instituted the police-force as we know it by introducing the 1828 Police Act.

94 *The bronchitis kettle:* A kettle with a specially perforated spout. The constant escape of steam (cf. p. 103) kept the air moist to reduce as much as possible any dryness which would irritate the throat and set off one of those 'paroxysms' of coughing which is described on p. 96. Sometimes herbs such as Friar's Balsam were placed in the boiling water and inhaled by the patient.

95 *Spittoon:* An object rather like a very large ash-tray into which Eustace could spit phlegm—one of his bronchial symptoms.

99 *With a gesture of infinite grace:* This describes Dick as he is seen through Eustace's eyes. To Eustace Dick is a hero, so any movement that he made would be 'infinitely graceful'.

► *An old family retainer:* Dick is using 'retainer' here in the sense of 'a dependent or follower of some person of rank or position'; he is being half teasing but because Eustace is not familiar with the word the joke falls flat.

101 *Palfrey:* A literary word for 'horse'—it immediately suggests the medieval world of Chivalry and Romance and thus reflects Eustace's idealisation of Dick.

102 *Harrow:* One of the better known English Public Schools.

105 *In season and out of season:* i.e. All the time, whether the moment was appropriate or not.

Fait accompli: A deed which cannot be retracted.

107 *Queen Alexandra:* The wife of King Edward VII.

110 *Hilda made Eustace stop and speak to her . . . . :* It is made very clear in this chapter that it is Hilda and Aunt Sarah who force Eustace to choose Miss Fothergill, 'the half-paralysed old lady' as a companion rather than Nancy. Just as he is beginning to show some initiative of his own it is stamped on firmly and unhesitatingly by his family and although Eustace's visits to Miss Fothergill become a source of pleasure to him, at the same time they ennervate his impulses of adventure and self-assertion.

243

110 *All the anxiety and expense we've had from his illness . . . :*
Eustace was living of course before the days of the
National Health Service—Cf. Mr Cherrington's remark
on p. 113: 'What with the doctor and the nurse and
having to take a room for Hilda outside, we've used up
our money . . . '.

111 *His father listened so attentively that he even began to
draw aside the veil from the less extravagant of the
Staveley-Anchorstone Hall fantasies:* This picture of
Eustace beginning to come out of his shell, only to be
completely misunderstood and subsequently squashed
by his father is one of the most pathetic and moving in
the novel.

➤ *The ruling forces of his inner life:* The forces of Eustace's
imagination.

112 *Eustace's apologia:* Eustace's defence of his behaviour.

➤ *'Nearly half past nine' sobbed Eustace:* The Editor's
own three year old son recently informed her: 'I used to
be a little boy years ago'. Upon being asked how long
ago, he replied 'At six o'clock I was a tiny boy'. Under
considerable emotional stress Eustace reverts to this
infant's method of expressing a concept of time.

113 *Cock-a-hoop:* The origin of the phrase is obscure; it
means 'in a state of elation'.

114 *Minney, Minney, I want you!:* Having reduced his son
yet again to a state of complete dependence, it is appropriate that Mr Cherrington ends his interview with
Eustace by calling for his old Nurse.

117 *Fumed oak:* Oak darkened by ammonia fumes.

118 *In that moment Eustace lost his terror of Miss Fothergill, and
only once did it return:* See p. 128: 'A chill crept into his
heart, as though his long friendship with Miss Fothergill
had suddenly been annulled and he was alone with the
stranger who had frightened him on the cliffs'.

➤ *Physical ugliness ceased to repel him and conversely
physical beauty lost some of its appeal:* If we continue to
bear in mind Nancy's comment (p. 74) 'I suppose you
know she's a witch', then Miss Fothergill certainly gains

244

a victory here in any symbolic contest that we might imagine taking place between herself and Nancy. The dark laurel bushes (poisonous) and the maid who 'hides' Eustace's hat and coat could also be subtle suggestions of Miss Fothergill's sorcery, but whether they are or not he stops being afraid of her.

119 *His eyes . . . pleased with the bright, soft colours, the glint of silver and china, the clusters of small objects:* This marks the moment of Eustace's entry into a cultured world which his legacy is later to enable him to enjoy more extensively.

120 *Piquet:* Under the name of 'Sant' or 'Cent' Piquet was played in England as long ago as the 1550's. It took the French name (Piquet) about a hundred years later after the marriage of Charles I to Henrietta Maria of France.

► *Dealing the cards in alternate twos and threes:* Each of the two players receives twelve cards, so the deal would be: 2/3/2/3/2. *Hoyle-up-to-date, The Official Rules of Card Games* states that 'the cards are dealt two at a time'—perhaps this was Miss Grimshaw's method of dealing!

► *A point of seven:* 'Point' is 'the greatest number of cards in any suit; this scores for point as many cards as are held. As between two holdings of the same length, the one with the greater pip total scores. If the players tie in point, neither scores'. Eustace must have had seven cards of the same suit, but he was forced to discard one in order to keep his four kings (the non-dealer has, according to the rules, to discard at least one card before declaring how many points he has in his hand).

► *I had to keep my four kings:* Four kings comprise a 'quatorze' i.e. four cards of the same rank higher than nine. A quatorze scores 14, whereas a 'trio' only scores 3—hence Eustace's: 'four kings, fourteen, three aces, seventeen, three knaves, twenty'.

► *Foolish fellow ! You must count up the pips now:* It is not clear how Miss Fothergill knew that Eustace originally had 'a point of seven' but she evidently has a point of six herself and so she and Eustace must both count up the pip totals of their runs of six to see which is to be scored. Miss Fothergill's total must come to more than 56 as she makes the correct picquet reply 'no good', i.e. I have a better total than that.

121 *A rod in pickle:* A scolding or punishment in store. Birch rods used to be laid in brine to keep the twigs pliable.

► *And I've got a carte major too:* A 'carte major' is a sequence of four to the ace, which takes precedence over any other 'cartes', though neutralised by a 'carte major' in the opponent's hand.

► *Here's your discard. I haven't looked at it:* As the 'non-dealer' Eustace has only discarded one card and therefore only taken one card from the 'stock'. Technically if he leaves any of the first five cards in the stock, he is allowed to look at them if he wishes to do so, without showing them to the dealer.

► *Partie:* Each 'game' comprises six deals. The player with the highest cumulative score at the end of the game wins the difference of the totals plus 100 for 'game' —hence: ' "I sixpence a hundred and you . . . " "A kiss". Eustace finished the sentence for her'.

122 *They don't but—:* Eustace was going to say 'but Miss Grimshaw does'. (Cf. p. 123). Miss Fothergill guesses what he left unsaid.

125 *Miss Fothergill seemed to make a calculation. Suddenly her face grew extremely sad . . . :* We can only guess what the calculation was and why it made Miss Fothergill look sad but as they have just been talking about the problem of Eustace's schooling, she is probably calculating how much longer there is before it will be too late for him to go to a good school. He is ten and a half, which means that there is really very little time to waste if he is to attend a 'Prep school' prior to entering a Public school at the age of thirteen. Miss Fothergill must know that Miss Cherrington—and Mr Cherrington

—would never accept money from her while she is alive, and so perhaps it is the thought of either living and depriving Eustace of his education, or facing the thought of her own death which would make Eustace's schooling possible, that saddens Miss Fothergill.

125 *You'll take two shillings this time?:* Eustace could have won four 'parties' to score more than 400 points, or he could have 'rubiconed' his opponent, thus adding her score to his plus 100.

128 *He said you had a lot in you . . . :* Miss Fothergill's efforts here, even in the face of her approaching loss of consciousness, to give Eustace some incentive to assert his individuality—contradict to some extent at any rate the earlier suggestions that Miss Fothergill is to be an evil influence in Eustace's life (cf. the references to her as a witch which Peter Bien emphasises strongly in his book: *L. P. Hartley*). That she turns out to be a bad influence inadvertently is typical of the irony which runs through the whole story.

130 *The sound was hardly more articulate than the surge of surf on the rocks:* Note the sea imagery as death makes another advance towards Miss Fothergill. It is to be used later at the moment of Eustace's own death in *Eustace and Hilda*—the last book of the trilogy, and is also present in his vision of himself and Miss Fothergill in heaven (Chapter Eleven, p. 149).

132 *The newly-opened bottle:* Mr Cherrington is drinking whisky to celebrate the news of Eustace's legacy which he and his sister have just heard about at the reading of the will after Miss Fothergill's funeral. The newly lit fire is another sign of unusual indulgence.

133 *The unjustifiable fire, doggedly achieving combustion:* The touches of humour in this scene are especially welcome after the sombre tones of the previous one at Miss Fothergill's house.

134 *What will everyone say? They'll say we put Eustace up to it and told him to work on Miss Fothergill's feelings . . . :* This is just what Dick Staveley does say, half teasingly

but half not, when he is talking to Eustace and Hilda on the sands—see Chapter Fourteen, p. 189.

134 *A cigar:* Mr Cherrington's third luxury.

137 *That warm region of thought, which for the past year she had furnished with objects delightful to contemplate and ideas that were exciting to follow, had seemed a gift for ever. Now she had died and taken it with her:* In fact, through Miss Fothergill's legacy Eustace is able to receive an education which finally carries him to Oxford and to the cultural privileges which it had to offer to intelligent and wealthy young men. (But cf. pp. 139 and 145-6 where the author comments in greater detail on the effect that Miss Fothergill had upon Eustace's later development).

138 *For a moment Eustace breathed more freely, though his sense of importance suffered: to have held the hand of a dead person was a unique distinction:* An excellent example of Mr Hartley's ability to perceive a child's thoughts and feelings realistically. Cf., p. 138 also: 'He himself had a black tie . . . terrible loss'.

140 *The magnetic needle of his being:* see note for p. 24.

➤ *Why bless the boy . . . :* Minney in her black and white clothes which 'look like a surplice' seems intent on some ceremony of purification as she turns on both taps to their fullest extent and begins her 'vigorous ministrations'.

144 *She was buried outside in the churchyard, in the sunshine:* Minney is trying her best not to make Death sound gloomy and foreboding and ironically she succeeds most when she stops trying and cries bitterly as she quotes the words from the funeral service, because Eustace's vision (p. 149) of the golden sea with its sunshine-glinting ripples makes death appear 'indeed a blessed thing, buoyant, warm, sunshiny, infinitely desirable'.

148 *Unwilling to recognise his status:* To Minney, Eustace is always a small child. Even when he returns to Anchorstone in his 20's, she treats him just like a small boy again. This scene is the only occasion on which she forsakes her role as nurse.

148 *'I heard a voice from Heaven . . .':* See: The Revelation of
   St John the Divine, Ch. 14.

149 *He hastily pulled himself out of the bath . . . :* In his haste
   to help Minney, Eustace jeopardises his own life—in
   fantasy—by sending the water swishing up the sides of
   the bath towards the Death-Spot. At the end of the
   trilogy, in his desire to help Hilda he again risks his life,
   but in reality on that occasion and in his dream at the
   moment of his death 'the water was bitterly cold'.

151 *Rather to his surprise and Hilda's . . . :* Neither of the
   children know of the new affluence for which Miss
   Fothergill's legacy is responsible.

► *Spentlove-le-Dale where the almshouses were:* There is a
   foundation at Castle Rising—about twelve miles from
   Hunstanton—'for twelve women of the neighbourhood'
   'called Trinity Hospital or Bede House. It was founded
   by Henry Howard, Earl of Northampton, in 1614 and
   the almswomen, who are presided over by a 'governess'
   live under rules which prescribe the wearing of red
   cloaks with the badge of the Howards, and high peaked
   hats. Castle Rising is famous chiefly for the great
   mound, probably British, which is the remains of the
   castle, but Trinity Hospital is described in the *County
   Books* Series as being 'more pleasing to the eye'.

► *It was as though the black band and the black tie had
   imparted their sombre hue to the very air around him:*
   Before the day is over, Eustace becomes convinced that
   very shortly he is going to die himself.

► *Frontisham:* see p. 231.

152 *Now you must pinch me:* Mr Cherrington may be trying
   to make a joke out of his new 'pepper and salt mixture'
   suit.

153 *Chevaux-de-frise:* Fr. lit. 'horses of Friesland' because
   first employed there in the Dutch War of Independence. It is a large joist with six sides, traversed with
   iron-pointed spikes above six feet long, and crossing
   one another. Originally it was used to check cavalry
   charges and stop breaches.

154 *Pretoria Street ... Mafeking Villa:* Both these names
are taken from South African localities which became
famous during the Boer War (1899-1902).

156 *I think we ought to respect Eustace's wishes:* Even Miss
Cherrington is influenced by the fact that Eustace has
been left a large amount of money; only Hilda, as
ignorant of the money as Eustace is, acts true to her
character.

► *Eustace has to plough his own furrow:* Eustace has to
make his own way in life.

157 *Frontisham Parish Church:* see p. 231.

► *Flamboyant tracery:* In architecture, the last phase of the
Gothic in France, characterised by the dominance in
tracery of the line of double curvature known as the
'ogee curve', which generates the flame-like forms which
give the name 'flamboyant' to the style.

► *Ne plus ultra:* (Latin) Nothing further, i.e. perfection.

► *... it was not the guide-book's actual words ... that
intoxicated him, so much as the tremendous, unqualified
sense of eulogy they conveyed:* Cf. Eustace's similar
intoxication with the words which Minney quotes for
him from the Book of Revelations (p. 148).

158 *Splayed, spread-eagled, crucified:* Cf. the tobogganning
picnic: 'As Eustace climbed the slippery hillside
tugging at the rope of the toboggan with determined
jerks, he suddenly thought of the Crucifixion and
identified himself with the main figure. The image
seemed blasphemous so he tried to put it out of his
mind'. In this passage too, 'for fear of blasphemy he
must only think of the shadow of that word'—but the
phrase 'high and lifted up' a little later in his fantasy
reminds us yet again of the figure of Christ.

159 *Fancies:* Cf. p. 160: 'A plate of cakes covered with
pink and white icing ... '.

160 *Dr Barnardo's Home:* An orphanage; there are now over
one hundred Dr Barnardo's Homes in the British Isles.

► *Norfolk jacket:* This term has been used since 1866 to
describe a loosely fitting jacket with a waist belt.

162 *On tick:* 'On tick' or 'to go on tick' means to owe for what one buys. In the 17th century 'ticket' was the ordinary term for the written acknowledgment of a debt, and one living on credit was said to be living 'on ticket' or 'tick'.

► *Dusty cataract:* The author is combining here the metaphorical image of the waterfall with the literal image of the steep white road.

► *Bearing rein:* A short fixed rein which passes from the bit to the saddle and keeps the horse's head up and its neck arched.

163 *Wellingtonias:* Large fir trees.

166 *I hear we shall be losing you before long:* All Mr Craddock's remarks from this point in his conversation with Eustace are couched in ambiguous terms. His reference to his 'sister's boy' who died, obscures the literal gist of his conversation more than his earlier comments by themselves might have done.

167 *His father took his silence for pique:* i.e. because he has had to descend from the box of the landau.

169 *Respice Finem:* (Latin) Look to the end. The sense of this saying is that we must live our lives in an awareness of death.

► *A height as yet unfurnished with a landscape:* i.e. life after death.

170 *Eustace awoke one morning to find that the foe had forced an entrance . . . :* Eustace's conscience has been nagging him about the proper disposition of his possessions once he has gone; he wakes up with the realisation that he must make a will (Cf. p. 175).

171 *The great rainbow-coloured lantern:* A reference to the prisms out of which the reflectors of a lighthouse lantern are constructed.

172 *Maw:* The stomach or cavity of the stomach—originally an Old English word, it is used frequently in medieval Romances and consequently conjures up a picture of bloodthirsty monsters eager to devour unsuspecting victims.

251

174 *The chariot:* Cf. the Negro spiritual:
'Swing low, sweet chariot
Coming for to carry me home . . . '

181 *She had risen from the rock and was standing over him,
her face transformed with fury and pain:* Hilda's immediate reaction is characteristically egotistical—she
cannot face the thought of living without Eustace
altogether. She even accuses him of trying to escape:
'You tried before, the time of the paper-chase but you
had to come back'.

183 *The lady on Dick's right:* We meet Dick's sister Anne at
greater length in *The Sixth Heaven* when Eustace and
Hilda spend a weekend at Anchorstone Hall.

186 *The thing in Eustace that had been swelling like a tumour:*
His growing conviction that he was about to die.

187 *Carlsbad:* Carlsbad (now called Karlovy Vary) is a
celebrated spa in Czechoslovakia. Before World War I it
was a gathering place for the wealthy invalids of Europe.

► *Her eyes, he could see, did not meet the four pairs of eyes
that looked down at her:* For once Hilda is at a loss and
shows it. Even Nancy can afford to say tolerantly
'Good old Hilda' because her enemy is so clearly
worsted.

188 *Fifty-eight thousand pounds:* Rumour, typically, has
exaggerated the actual amount wildly—and within
seconds it has become 'sixty-eight thousand pounds'!
The actual sum was eighteen thousand pounds—see
p. 133.

190 *Familiars:* A 'familiar spirit' was believed to be a demon
or evil spirit supposed to come whenever his master or
mistress called him. The familiar spirits of witches were
believed to reside in some constant companion such as a
cat or a toad.

192 *Excellent, so long as it doesn't make you late:* It is clear
throughout this episode that Nancy likes Dick more than
he likes her (cf. Hilda's remark p. 197).

194 *'I feel so happy, Hilda', he said. 'I don't think I ever felt so
happy in all my life':* Eustace's initial response to the news

he has just heard is one of intense relief that the threat of death has been lifted from him. His second reaction is still not directly connected with the legacy but is one of pleasure that he and Hilda have been included in the magic circle of the Staveleys and the Steptoes.

199 *'All right'*, said Hilda. *'Anything to keep you quiet'*: Hilda's grudging acceptance reveals her uncomfortable sense of vulnerability. For once Eustace is in a superior position and it is consequently difficult for Hilda to act as though she were pleased when her true feelings are quite the reverse! Her carping attitude is maintained while Eustace struggles with the business of the sums on the sand because it is essential for Hilda to regain her sense of superiority even at the expense of spoiling Eustace's act of generosity.

204 *Blood money . . .'it's what you pay for freedom if you're*
–5 *held in bondage,' Hilda told him*: In adult life, having already divided his legacy with Hilda, Eustace makes out increasingly large cheques to his sister in order to salve his conscience for staying away from her.

206 *Eustace's heart diagram:* Symbolically, Eustace is ready to pay his blood money to Hilda immediately.

207 *'I think there had better be two,' said Hilda, 'because your heart is weaker than mine'*: Hilda is certainly not willing to consider herself as indistinguishable from Eustace—devouring him is quite another matter!

▶ *Every now and then the wind-whipped sea shivered darkly over its whole expanse:* The sea is such a persistent symbol throughout the trilogy that any reference to it is important. In this instance, coming as it does immediately after the pact between brother and sister, it appears ominous and foreboding; it makes us feel that trouble lies ahead.

208 *'Let's pretend we're having a three-legged race':* The obstacle race of Eustace's life is set in motion again by Hilda when she ties his best foot to hers with a knot 'that can't come undone, no matter how hard you pull'. It is highly significant that in the closing words of the

novel, Minney takes a very pessimistic view about the outcome of the race: 'it looked as if they were sure to come to grief before they arrived at the white gate of Cambo'.